SERIOUSLY, SITARA?

Nishat Fatima is editor, *Harper's Bazaar*, and has written for *Conde Nast Traveller* and *Mint*, amongst others. When she's not rushing to meet deadlines or at the beck and call of a spoilt feline, she likes to travel, bake, do crosswords and sudoku and sleep.

Seriously, Sitara?

Nishat Fatima

hachette
INDIA

First published in 2013 by Hachette India
(Registered name: Hachette Book Publishing India Pvt. Ltd)
An Hachette UK company
www.hachetteindia.com

SRD

ISBN 978-93-5009-352-8

Hachette Book Publishing India Pvt. Ltd
4th/5th Floors, Corporate Centre,
Sector 44, Gurgaon 122003, India

Typeset in Requiem Text 10.5 /13
by Saanavi Graphics, Noida

Printed and bound in India by
Manipal Technologies Limited, Manipal

FSC
www.fsc.org
MIX
Paper from responsible sources
FSC™ C104740

Shiv rose to the bait beautifully. 'You should' – the gleam in Nasser's eyes registered – 'be ashamed of trying to wind up your best friend.'

'How can I resist? You're so easy. And you still need to get rid of the facial growth.' After thirty fuzz-free years, Shiv had suspiciously become an aficionado overnight. 'Or you can tell me why you are growing it.'

'I'm a man. What other reason do you need?'

Shiv was definitely holding out on something. He had shuffled his feet, a sure sign that a person was lying according to today's informed opinion in the highest-selling national daily. Plus there were Nasser's own suspicions.

'Admit it,' Shiv continued. 'You have hair envy. That's what happens when you spend your life waxing your chest.'

'My waxed chest is the recipient of hundreds of women who fling themselves at it. I don't need to be envious of your hair.' Nasser skirted an overdressed arrangement of sofas and started towards the bank of elevators.

Shiv strolled alongside. 'You're going against your biological imperative. That's why you're reacting so strongly to my magnificence.'

'And not because you look like a particularly slimy drug dealer?'

'No drug dealer looks slimy anymore. They look like cool dudes. People whose style statements we need to follow. Especially you.' Shiv gave Nasser's outfit a disdainful glance. Shiv had been trying – and failing – to get him to upgrade the jeans-and-T-shirt combo he'd lived in all his adult life.

'To quote somebody, I'm a man. And a big enough star not to need to make style statements.'

'Dude! That's so not metrosexual of you. Don't let any woman hear you. You'll lose your fan following.'

Nasser gave him an incredulous look. 'Are you accusing my fans of being interested in my feminist leanings? What do you think my waxed chest is for?'

'You poor thing,' Shiv commiserated, but his gaze was unexpectedly searching. 'Did I hear an undertone of unhappiness at being objectified? Do you want people to look beyond your chest? Does that mean you're going to keep it under wraps from now on?'

'Yeah, I've decided I'll only leave the top three buttons open in my next movie. Tantalize them with glimpses of it. I could even grow some hair.'

Shiv considered the statement before replying. 'That's actually quite disgusting, you know. In fact, this entire conversation smacks of a certain lack of intellectualism.'

'Not at all. I think the changing definition of masculinity and masculine appeal in the twenty-first century is a very intellectual discussion. It's something everybody should be talking about.'

An uneasy silence fell between them. 'Or we could talk about your prankster,' Nasser said.

There was a relieved sigh from Shiv. 'Good choice.'

'Good choice? How come? Didn't he unscrew all the handles to the cutlery drawers at your Sunday brunch? People clamouring for knives and forks all around and your sous-chefs became washing staff?'

Shiv shuddered at the memory. Then he pulled himself together. 'Yeah, but the good thing is that he's going department by department. I'm betting it's Housekeeping next. Your mom thinks Reservations.'

'It's Reservations then.' Nasser came to a halt in front of the lifts and nodded at Suresh to call the elevator.

Shiv threw up his hands. '*Dude*! Can't you call the lift yourself?'

Sitara glared at the road ahead. The sliver of sea shining on the horizon through the taxi's dusty windshield was blinding and the approaching edifice of Bandra's most star-friendly hotel just a dark smudge. The day matched her mood – steaming.

Good and mood weren't words that would be strung together to refer to Sitara Gopalasundaram for a while. Not after last night's fiasco. Actually, all of yesterday sucked big time. Between her jerk of a boss and Mr Ineligible from the previous evening, it had been a day from hell. And here she was, on a manic taxi ride to an assignment that was most likely the beginning of the end. She wasn't sure the end of what yet, but she was guessing things like happiness and peace at work.

All because of her editor. Debashish Bose was a man with a singular mission: to make life as difficult as possible for those who worked under him. Sometimes he picked them off one by one; sometimes, it was more genocidal. Sitara had a feeling yesterday's meeting was a lead-in to the latter but for the moment, all she could say with any certainty was that he had her, the most-often ignored arts person, in his sights.

Debashish's particular genius lay in turning colleagues into enemies, because one person's good fortune was always at another's expense. He had a sixth sense when it came to picking the points that really hurt. And he had certainly picked her off yesterday.

The memory of his smile rose in her memory, and Sitara shuddered. The smile was a sight to behold – two perfect rows of shiny white teeth that had been some orthodontist's down payment for a new car; probably a Merc. It wasn't a familiar sight, usually flashed only at people higher up in the food chain or pretty interns (and they were all pretty, even the men). The only time the team got to see his pearly whites was when he was delivering bad news. And they had been the first thing she'd seen when she'd answered his summons.

Dread had immediately settled in her gut. It had taken resolve to not make an excuse of illness and flee.

'HQ's very impressed with your features,' her editor, extremely ordinaire, had fired his opening salvo.

'Uh.' Sitara had played it safe.

'Yes. A couple of editions want to syndicate your last month's art story.'

'Oh.' She had continued in the same vein.

'HQ thinks your style is exactly what *Homme's* writing should be about.'

'Uh huh.'

'Please, enough. Your response is overwhelming.' Debashish had a nice line in sarcasm. He got enough practice. The smile had completely disappeared by now, and the shadow of a line had appeared on his brow, signalling his displeasure. Last month, it would have been a deep frown. But then he'd walked into the art department to check pages and had been treated to a zoomed-in version of his deeply furrowed brow being airbrushed on Photoshop. His shock and horror, mimicked by one gifted member of the design team, had been the entertainment mainstay of the office for weeks. Not twenty minutes later, his assistant Canice Mascerenhas had furtively asked the grooming writer for the phone number of a dermatologist renowned for her Botox expertise.

Sitara wondered whether Debashish knew Martin had given his design team instructions to have that image at the ready if Debashish were ever in the vicinity. She had muttered something she hoped could be interpreted as enthusiastic and watched him banish the annoyance as he leaned forward at his desk and steepled his fingers, his patented unfathomable look in place. It was an expression he knew looked good on his already attractive face. Interns practically drooled when he used it on them, which he did fairly often.

How could anybody be such a git? A superior, interfering, womanizing, lazy-assed, incompetent, psycho git at that. And what trick of fate had seen fit to hand him looks, smarm and the ability to string sentences together acceptably so he'd landed the rather prestigious position as editor of the Indian edition of international men's magazine *Homme*?

'There is a feeling that we are limiting your talent...' he had continued, '...that we should give you room to expand. Spread your wings. Do bigger, more important stories.'

'A cover story on art?' This was...exciting. She'd never have thought it of him.

'No, no. We are talking about bigger things here.'

'Bigger than a cover story?'

'No. The cover story!'

Sitara ran a hand through her curls. 'Okay. I'm totally confused. What are you saying?'

'They want *you* to do the cover story,' he enunciated slowly.

'So when I said cover story...'

'*Art* is not a cover story,' Debashish said coldly. '*Art* does not sell magazines. You should know that by now.'

Sitara wondered whether having his Hermès paperweight make forceful contact with his face would alter Debashish's worldview a little.

'We're talking Bollywood.' Debashish smiled. 'You're going to interview Nasser Khan.'

It was diabolic. In one corner of her brain, Sitara even appreciated his deviousness. With one stroke he had put her in territory she hated, made her unpopular with half the team, awarded himself the advantage in his ongoing war with Mukul *and* hit Mukul where it hurt most. 'But...' Sitara had been beyond concealing her shock.

'Yes?' Debashish looked like he'd lapped up a bowlful of cream.

'But Mukul...' Sitara groped for the words – will kill me for entering his territory, for taking his interview, for doing the cover story, for getting Nasser Khan – and settled rather weakly on – 'He's spent so much time setting it up.'

That much was true. Nasser Khan, the biggest Khan on the block after the original triumvirate, had turned media-shy. It was at about the same time as the break-up of a long and public engagement with actress Richa Bali and it had been a hard slog to get him to agree to the interview. As features director, Mukul Sinha had pulled every string he had. And had only gloated about it, oh, a million times.

'Yes. But he has set it up for the magazine,' Debashish said grandly. 'And as long as the magazine gets the interview, it doesn't matter who does it. We are a team. This magazine is not about personal glory.'

Who did he think he was kidding? Mukul demanded 'With Inputs From' when he got anybody in the office so much as a quote. And he got them the quotes in the first place because he refused to part with the contact numbers of any of his precious stars.

And this was the man from whom Debashish was snatching the one interview everybody in the media would kill for. The interview in which Nasser Khan was going to break eighteen months of silence.

Mukul would tandoor her. After chopping her into tiny pieces, of course. With a blunt knife.

Sitara shuddered, and then realized it hadn't only been at the memory. Her taxi driver had taken her 'Drive Fast' edict to heart and was speeding in a manner that could soon require her to find a brown bag.

She could have done with a brown bag last evening, too, when the 'oh-so-eligible' suitor her aunt had set her up with had asked her what her favourite bits about sex were, suggested 'oral' before she could utter a word, and looked at her expectantly.

How could she have just gone back into the living room without a word? Sitara still couldn't forgive herself for not unleashing her inner Lorena Bobbitt and cutting him down to size. Instead she'd meekly gone and sat down next to her aunt. What a wuss she was turning out to be!

And then she'd had to listen to his mother.

'...trying to marry her off for years, no? And she lives alone here in Mumbai.' The woman might as well have said in this city of sin. She had made no attempt to hide her disapproval of Sitara all evening. 'Wears sleeveless, no doubt. How old is she? Thirty? It doesn't show on her face. Yet. But she's getting on...'

Her aunt, Kamala Chithi, had placed a restraining hand on her arm.

'We are the same age, Amma,' the sleazoid had followed her in. 'And I think it's great that she's already so Westernized. She'll fit in perfectly in the US.'

Sitara could have laughed as the gloom became doom on his mother's face. She had almost told her that it would be a cold day in hell before she married her son. Almost.

The sleazoid was talking again. 'And I would love to take this further. I hope I will be able to meet Sitara again.'

'N–'

'*Of course,*' Kamala Chithi's voice drowned hers. 'I will talk about this with her parents and we will stay in touch.'

'I d–' Sitara began again and found herself the focus of her aunt's gimlet stare, honed over years of practice.

'We will do this through the proper channels,' her aunt had continued. Proper channels! She would–

Sitara was jolted out of her brooding when the taxi driver came to a screeching halt in front of the hotel. *In front of the hotel!* Blast and damn! She had reached the hotel! Without reading a single interview. Oh no, oh no, oh no.

What was she going to ask him? Her cousin Kadam's panting fandom – his chest! his gaze! his smile! – pretty much summed up all she knew about the actor. That and the fact that his father had been a cinematographer sometime in the 60s or 70s.

Which, on second thoughts, was more than enough, Sitara decided, as she walked into the lobby of Bollywood's favourite hotel.

The smell of jasmine assaulted her senses at the same moment that her gaze registered the tonnes of gilt and the reproduction French vibe of the place. Oh god! Sitara hurriedly jabbed at the lift buttons. She didn't need anything further to make her sick. Her interview was going to be enough.

'What did you say about the *halwe ke puris*?' Nasser's outrage was writ large as he turned to Shiv.

'Your mom got me some.'

'She didn't make enough to give you some,' Nasser said darkly. 'Those were all supposed to be for me. I'm supposed to take them with me to Italy. Did she–'

'Please don't say these things out loud. Nobody will believe you're a well-travelled superstar if you carry food with you every time you go abroad. Next you'll be packing pickle and MTR meals to take with you.'

Nasser felt his eyes shift before he could stop them. He focused his gaze back as squarely as he could on his friend. Maybe Shiv had missed the earlier telltale movement. No such luck.

'Oh my god, you were!' And Shiv was off and running about his favourite subject. Also his work. As F&B manager he had strong opinions about food and, unfortunately for Nasser, he voiced them freely.

'It's people like you who give India a bad name. Can't you lose a bet like a man? I've picked a cooking course in Tuscany, not Japan or China. You can survive four paltry weeks without Indian food. Packaged food! My god.' He stopped to take a breath. 'Just immerse yourself in the cuisine, embrace the flavours. *Ready-to-eat meals*? Honestly? Next you'll be searching out Indian restaurants in Tuscany.'

Since he had done exactly that last night, and had the printout in his suitcase, Nasser struggled not to hunch his shoulders. Why should he apologize for his tastes anyway? He tried to stare Shiv down, and he hated that there was a hint of apology in his voice. 'You've never been away for long schedules. You don't know of the yearning for masala...'

Shiv flung an arm out dramatically. 'Masala. This is too much. I am putting my foot down. No friend of mine will sully the land of parmesan with pickle. Ready-made meals in the land of slow cooking! Can you imagine how badly this would reflect on me?'

Nasser looked at his friend for a moment. 'Uh. I know a really good counsellor – I think you should see her about your megalomaniac issues.'

Shiv opened his mouth to retort, and froze. Nasser turned around to see what the matter was and found himself in a *Matrix* moment; only it wasn't bullets making their way towards him in slow motion, it was the contents of a can of cola.

His senses were extra sharp, and they registered every small detail: the collective gasp, the stunned expressions, the cell phones that were being turned in his direction to capture the moment, the soft sounds of footsteps walking away from him, the steady drip down his face.

Then everything went into fast-forward; unlike Keanu Reeves, however, he wasn't kicking butt – if anything, his was the butt that had just been kicked. Nasser stared blankly for a moment at the retreating figure of his former fiancée before he regained his senses and thought of damage control.

The first step was to stop standing in front of the open-mouthed crowd while dripping cola. He pivoted and punched the button for the lift, earning himself a disappointed look from the hapless Suresh. He almost flung himself in, well onto the side, pushing the buttons to close the doors immediately.

A few drops delicately spattered off his eyelashes.

Nasser wiped his face and tried to make sense of what had just happened. Had he missed the bulletin about Richa going around hotel lobbies throwing things in people's faces? And surely it was too much to believe that his former fiancée had lost her temper a year and a half after they had broken up.

After you dumped her, an inner voice corrected him.

His manager Anjali Rane opened the door before Suresh could ring the bell. Nasser had a feeling she'd spent a fair amount of the evening wrenching that door open at random intervals, hoping to find him on the other side. His suspicion was confirmed by the look of surprise on her face. An aggrieved look replaced it in the blink of an eye.

'Why haven't you answered...?' She got a good look at his face – his dripping face, to be precise – and the cloud of grim that nimbused around him. 'Wha...?'

He had finally managed to render Anjali speechless.

'Get some clothes sent up from the car, will you? Immediately,' He strode past her into the suite.

'But what *happened*? Why haven't you answered a single phone call? Do you know how long this reporter has been waiting?' Anjali had recovered.

Nasser didn't bother to answer as he walked away in the opposite direction towards the bedroom.

Anjali followed him. 'What is wrong with you?' her voice climbing with each word.

Nasser faced her in the bedroom's doorway. 'Besides darling Richa who has just thrown some drink in my face in front of half of Mumbai and a moron director who can't make up his mind about how he'd like two simple shots, nothing much. Now, can I get my clothes? Ask Suresh to leave them on the bed.'

'But, wait...' Anjali began urgently.

The door shut in her face. She heard the lock click in place.

Three and a half hours ago Sitara had been upset because she was late and hadn't done her research. Her relief at learning that her subject was running late – even if the notification had emerged from the inferiority-inducing vision half her size in linen pants and a nautical striped T-shirt, aka Nasser's manager Anjali Rane – had been overwhelming. She had been asked to wait in his room and told that he'd be up shortly.

Two hours ago, when she'd finished reading all his interviews, writing her questions *and* listing them out alphabetically, she'd started to get a little angry.

An hour ago she'd been furious.

But in the last hour, the anger had slowly been replaced by the certainty that she was going to die of boredom. So she'd done what any sane woman would do in the circumstances – she'd retired to the loo to play with some make-up.

She should have stuck to death by boredom.

Sitara stared glumly at her reflection in the bathroom mirror. Green was just not her colour. Especially when it appeared in a big fat smear down the front of her T-shirt. She must be the only woman whose eye-shadow stick would fall on her person. Hundreds – no, millions – would drop theirs straight onto the floor.

It wasn't that Sitara was clumsy. Accident prone was more accurate. Things happened to her. Around her. Things that were usually embarrassing. For her, and for those around her.

She looked at herself again. Smear was an imprecise understatement. She now had a diffused, wet patch of green from where she had used water to try and get it out. Unsuccessfully.

Okay, she couldn't stand around dismayed. Action was required. Sitara whipped off her shirt and washed out the offending part with soap and water till the green had disappeared.

A door shut outside. A phone rang. Somebody answered. Somebody male. Eff, eff, and eff. He had arrived.

A thought made Sitara drop the shirt in the sink and lunge to the door to check that it was locked. It was. Thank god.

How was she going to dry her top now? There was no disguising the sound of the hair dryer. And what would her explanation be? 'My head was so close to exploding from the three-hour wait that I decided to dunk it in water to cool it down?' Almost true though.

She would have to wait for him to leave the room.

His phone was ringing again. He seriously contemplated not answering, but he'd been too well trained about what was polite and what wasn't. By the very person at the other end of the line.

'Amma, I'm a little busy right now...'

'I told you right away there was something off about that woman.' There was a wealth of satisfaction in Ayesha Khan's voice. Jungle drums. Shiv must have called her immediately.

'No, actually, you didn't,' Nasser corrected testily. 'I didn't even know you didn't like her till you threw a party to celebrate the break-up. This, after we'd been together three years, one of them engaged.' It was still a bit of a sore subject. 'And to be precise, I didn't know till my best friend told me halfway through the party that it was an exercise in relief on your part.'

'You really have to learn to let the past go,' his mother admonished. 'Learn from it – by letting your father and me choose your bride – but let it go.'

'Did you want something?' Nasser interrupted rudely. The need to get out of his shirt and into the shower was overwhelming. He toed off his sneakers.

His mother ignored his question. 'I've told you so many times. I thought you were just having a fling, so I was polite to her. Then you announced that you'd asked her to marry you – without asking for our opinion, I might add – and I would have felt like a clichéd *saas* if I told you I didn't like her.'

'That is so lame, Amma.' He knew it was true, but it was still lame. His mother had been well-drilled in *tehzeeb* in her pre-married life in Lucknow – which made her perfect for the hospitality industry – and he had known for years that what she thought of as mere politeness was often considered warm, loving friendliness by others. He'd never considered that it could be used on him. 'Yeah, you're right. It's old news. I'd better go shower now. I'll call later.'

'Wait!' his mother's voice rang out urgently.

Nasser sighed. His mother didn't easily let go of the conversation when Richa was the subject.

'Did you get a look at what that witch threw at you?'

'What?' Nasser was thrown himself.

'Just tell me,' Ayesha said.

He had a picture of the can swinging towards him before the contents splashed over his head and face and dripped down his chest.

'Diet Pepsi, I think.'

'Diet Pepsi. I knew it.' his mother repeated loudly. She sounded oddly jubilant. A curse filtered through from the background.

'Why did you want to know?' Nasser felt suspicion bite him in the butt.

'Oh nothing, nothing,' his mother's voice was fakely hearty. 'I just made a stray remark to someone that it must have been some diet drink. You know how she was always afraid of gaining an ounce if she ever drank the real thing.'

'What is all that noise around you?' he asked dangerously. He had an idea but didn't want it to be true. Over the years his mother had regaled them all at the dinner table with stories about what she and her colleagues often did to pass the time on boring afternoons. 'Amma, did you start a pool? Were you betting on what drink was thrown on me?' There was a slim hope that his mother would deny this categorically, but Nasser wouldn't place any bets on it.

'Sorry, you broke up a bit then,' his mother said. 'What did you just say?' Nasser could hear stifled laughter behind her. 'Hello. Hello. What did you say? Hello. I can't hear you *beta*. I'll call you later.' The phone went dead in his ear.

His mother had hung up on him! What was the world coming to when you couldn't even trust your own mother? Women, Nasser thought explosively. What was wrong with them?

His phone began ringing again. He switched it off and chucked it on the bed. He flung his T-shirt on the floor. His thoughts turned again to Richa – why had she done it? If he knew her at all – and after three years of being with her he could claim a little knowledge – she definitely had a scheme up her sleeve.

Richa was one of life's planners. When she wanted something, she always had a plan to get it. And she wanted things quite often. It had driven her mad that he would just wait for directors to approach him – she always knew which director and actor she wanted to work with, and always had a plan in motion that would lead to them approaching her and offering her a role she wanted. Her success rate was 99 per cent – the one percent was when he had called off their engagement.

Was publicity what Richa wanted now? Nasser started to unbutton his jeans when he registered a muffled sound. It seemed to be coming from the bathroom. Was it the...hairdryer?

He was still talking.

Sitara had wrung out the water and flapped her T-shirt about, tried it on to see how bad it was – her ratty bra was clearly visible – taken it off again and was flapping it about, and Nasser Khan was still talking.

And they accuse women of never getting off the phone, Sitara thought bitterly. Where were the strong silent types when you needed them?

On the other hand, he probably wouldn't hear anything over the sound of his own beloved voice.

Galvanized into motion at the insight, she turned the hair dryer on. It took her a moment to realize that the reason it sounded so loud was because everything was silent outside.

Uh *oh*.

Sitara strained to hear his exit.

The doorknob turned.

Sitara stared at it paralysed.

The doorknob turned again. Harder.

A squeak emerged from Sitara.

'Is anybody there?' a voice asked finally.

She would have to reply. 'Uh, yes. I am.'

'Oh, *you* are. Fascinating. And who are you?'

Okay, she might have left herself wide open to that, but there was no need to be so sarcastic. 'Sitara,' she began before she caught herself. Her name would make no sense. 'I'm here to interview you.'

'I see. And will you emerge from the bathroom at some point soon to do that?'

Red spots danced in front of her eyes. After making her wait three hours he was giving her attitude, wanting to know whether she would emerge *soon*? She hoped his bladder burst.

'Yes,' she said shortly, keeping a tight rein on her temper.

She switched the hair dryer on full blast. Let him think what he wanted.

A knocking on the door interrupted her. Sitara considered ignoring it. But she'd be interviewing him soon... She switched off the dryer reluctantly. 'Yes?'

'Your hairstyle won't affect the interview, you know. And I already have plans for tonight. So, if you are done?'

Nobody had accused Sitara of being slow on the uptake. She almost flung the door open to tell him what he could do with himself and his plans for tonight. Only the thought of putting her bra on display stopped her.

'I'm drying my shirt,' she informed him, outraged. Not waiting for his reply, she switched on the dryer again. Moments later, wearing a dry non-green spotted shirt, she wrenched the door open.

And stopped short. Lounging in the hallway leading to the bathroom was Nasser Khan. Shirtless. Was this some Bollywood interview etiquette she knew nothing about?

Not that she couldn't admit it was a nice chest. And maybe raising her gaze facewards took a little longer than she'd thought. But once up there, she had no trouble switching on the glare.

He was staring at her chest.

The lout. Slimy snake. Worm.

'It's dried very well,' he said blandly, meeting her gaze.

Sitara gave him a withering look – nobody would believe her if she said it had been justifiable homicide.

That had got her, Nasser thought with satisfaction. How dumb did she think he was? He'd noticed the eye make-up right away. Though why she'd bothered to dry her curls, he couldn't think. They looked like something you'd end up with if you plugged your finger directly into a socket.

Drying her shirt, indeed! He didn't think anybody had tried that to snag his interest before. Did she imagine it would have him wondering about what lay beneath, and things would immediately follow from there?

He must ask her whether she'd had any success with that line before.

Maybe if she annoyed him any more he would.

Like, maybe, right now. If she twiddled around with the doorknob instead of leaving.

'You have to turn the knob clockwise,' Nasser prompted. 'To your right,' he enunciated slowly.

There was the sound of a sharply drawn breath. Then a very controlled voice said, 'I know. I'm not an id--' Another deep breath. 'It's stuck.'

'Cue *Hum Tum Ek Kamre Mein Bandh Ho* as the soundtrack?' he asked negligently.

She moved quickly when she wanted to, Nasser noted, as curls spun around. Ah, the 'if-looks-could-kill' routine.

Since he remained undead, Nasser didn't move an inch. 'Try harder, babe. Maybe this one opens in the opposite direction?' he suggested. 'Anyway, when you get the door open, tell the man to lay my clothes out on the bed, will you? I'll just go have my shower.' He picked up his phone, walked into the bathroom and shut the door softly.

2

Her star was stuck in his bedroom with a reporter. Or he would be, as soon as he emerged from his shower. At which point, it would be his semi-clad talent and one badly clad reporter.

Anjali looked at the offending door and wondered whether she should call housekeeping and get them to fix this problem. That's what she'd told that fat, badly dressed woman – really, *jeans*! Who wore them anymore? – she was going to do.

But after the scene downstairs, she hadn't been eager to risk any more notoriety for Nasser. Two incidents with two different women – not that she was upset about Richa; her first reaction had been to cheer – the press would live off that for months.

If only he was your normal star, not this neo-Garbo publicity recluse, Anjali thought bitterly. And while she could have got away with all-publicity-is-good-publicity this one time, and made his producer and director very happy in the bargain, she couldn't risk it. Because her star was taking things to the next level – he was going to drop off the face of the earth for two months. If things blew up in her face, which was a good possibility in matters that involved Richa Bali, she would have to deal with it on her own.

A peripheral movement had her directing a killing glance at the man next to her.

Suresh fell back, though his hand spasmed unconsciously and his gaze was fixed longingly on the expanse of wood. He had taken it very personally that he couldn't open the door. When he'd first realized what had happened, he had spent five solid minutes shoving his shoulder against the door and twisting the door knob, undeterred by his lack of success. He'd been like a man at the slot machines hoping to hit the jackpot with the next crank of the handle.

Anjali had nearly brained him with her phone. She'd had to visualize cool blue seas before she'd been able to get him to step away with no harm to his person.

Now she had to wait till her star emerged from his shower – what sort of a man went in for a shower when he was locked in?

Anjali went back to practising her breathing.

'Still here?'

Sitara didn't turn around. She was sitting in a chair from where she couldn't see the bathroom door. She'd positioned it carefully, after all. 'Your manager's getting Housekeeping,' she said coldly.

'Housekeeping? Don't you think...' He stopped mid-sentence. There was something there...

An edge of white terrycloth intruded on Sitara's field of vision. It took an effort of will to watch the progress of the bathrobe-clad figure across the room without pondering the immediate, uncontrollable question – was he wearing anything *under* it? She was grimly satisfied when he grasped the doorknob and it turned all the way. Without making any difference to their stuck-in-the-room status.

Welcome to my world, Sitara thought.

'We *are* stuck.' He sounded surprised.

He was obviously unused to things not going his way, even doorknobs. Must be a huge change from having the world scamper around trying to do his bidding or smooth things out for him. Sitara could picture the hotel staff in uproar at this disaster.

Unconsciously, Sitara sneered.

'What did–' Her expression blitzed all thought from his mind. God, what a sneer! He tried to commit it to memory – he was going to have to use it in his next movie. You weren't handed gifts like this every day.

Sitara arranged her face and tone along neutral lines; she wasn't sure she was entirely successful. 'What?'

'What did Anjali say?' Nasser said automatically, his mind still occupied with that sneer.

'Just that she was getting Housekeeping.'

'Who don't seem to be here yet. Service standards at the hotel are falling. Unless–' He switched on his phone, and called Anjali. 'Did you call Housekeeping?'

What the...? Sitara shot out of her chair. *Housekeeping hadn't been called?* His next words stopped her in her tracks.

'What am I wearing? What sort of question is that? A bathrobe. What does that have to do with us being locked in? I don't care if the press hears about it... Anyway, this is the one hotel where they won't hear about it. I don't care about the next two months – what am I doing?' he muttered, and cut the call. He dialled another number.

'Shiv. You just won a lot of money. Housekeeping was next.'

'Huh? What?'

Nasser could almost hear the penny drop.

'Oh. And you know this because?' Shiv asked cautiously.

'I'm locked in. In the suite's bedroom.' Nasser paused, then decided the best thing to do was let him know the full extent of the damage. 'The lady who's here to interview me is also in here. And I'm in a bathrobe.'

There was silence at the other end. 'Interesting. Did you say interview?' Shiv imbued the last word with a wealth of insinuation.

'Just get somebody here,' Nasser snapped.

'Absolutely. Is this bathrobe fetish a new development?'

Nasser jabbed at the screen to disconnect the call.

His phone started ringing almost immediately. Anjali. He supposed he should answer that. He looked at Sitara and considered reassuring her, but he really didn't feel like talking to another crazy woman today. He struggled with his better instincts, but was able to overcome them. She could figure out the situation – it would keep her amused till the rescue team arrive. He walked away to the other side of the suite to answer the call.

By the time Operation Unlock Door was done, with as much cloak and daggerness as the hotel could –

once the carpenter had the door unlocked, he'd been whisked away before opening it, probably confirming the compromising position of the star within – there was only one overriding thought in Sitara's mind.

Food.

She was starving.

Sure she was going to make the interview absolute hell for that sorry excuse of living matter who hadn't got off the phone till the door was open, but she couldn't muster up enough killer instinct on an empty, rumbling stomach.

She'd been just about ready to give in and call room service when the rescue squad had finally done its job.

Her first act as a free person had been to place her order. Her humongous order. Now she stood over the phone wondering whether she had impressed upon them the need for speed. Maybe she should call back and tell them again.

A phone rang. Her own, she realized, lunging for her bag.

'Is the interview done?' Debashish sounded strange. Stranger than usual, she corrected herself.

'It hasn't even started,' Sitara began.

Debashish cut her off before she could launch into her story. 'Excellent. We couldn't have asked for anything better.'

Sitara's stomach rumbled.

'Now listen carefully. Don't say anything. Don't show any emotion. Don't let anybody in the room know that you have received this information. Then you can take them by surprise.'

It didn't sound like her boss. Sitara brought the phone in front of her and stared blankly at the screen for a moment. The screen said Debashish, so the call was definitely from his phone. But when had her editor started moonlighting as James Bond? She tucked the phone back at her ear, trying to arrange her face along expressionless lines.

'I'll make this short,' he continued. 'A friend of mine just told me that Richa Bali dumped a can of cola on Nasser's head in the lobby of the hotel. I'll feed you all the information I can find out and you can attack him with it when the time is right.'

It took Sitara a few long moments to realize that she was listening to the dial tone, and a few longer moments to make some sense of what he had said. So Nasser's ex, Richa Bali, had chucked cola in his face. Sitara dropped into the sofa, savouring the image that came to mind. It also explained a lot of things including the shirtlessness and the shower. But it *so* didn't cancel out the rudeness.

The actress ought to have done it long ago; it might have improved her fiancé before he became this self-satisfied arrogant jerk. Sitara had been willing to give him the benefit of doubt despite having read his interviews – could that man talk! – but the past half hour had convinced her she was being too nice.

The fact that he'd acted in four of the biggest blockbusters ever, and a sprinkling of super hits, didn't make a whit of difference.

Her stomach rumbled loudly and Sitara looked around. Had the super-thin manager heard that? Anjali was on the phone, looking unhappy. Sitara's eyes were drawn back to the room phone. Why was it taking so long to send up her food? Should she call again?

She heard a door open and a vastly different Nasser Khan emerged.

For a start, he was clothed.

Much too nattily for an interview, thought Sitara, taking in his suit. She didn't have to be Sherlock or even Robert Downey Jr. to deduce that he was on his way elsewhere.

Sitara watched him engage in a low-voiced conversation with Anjali and was treated to her first view of the manager not on the cell phone. She wondered how long it would take for the withdrawal symptoms to hit. Were they conferring about his close encounter with the cola? Sitara tried to listen, but they had perfected the art of low-voiced conversation and it took only a moment to admit defeat.

Anyway she had more important things to contend with. Namely, the struggle not to march up to the actor, yank him to the sofa and start shooting questions at him. She really, really hoped that he wasn't going to postpone the interview. Scratch that. Let him try to postpone it – any excuse would work to kick him in the shins. And other places. A look at her watch confirmed that it was now four hours since the scheduled time for the interview.

Four hours.

Grievous bodily harm. That's what would follow if he dared cancel this interview or postpone it further.

'Owww!'

For a wild moment Sitara thought she had managed telekinesis and transmitted the violence through her mind as she watched the actor rub his middle. It took a while to figure out that Anjali had carried out her wishes.

'You're fired,' Nasser said, heatedly rubbing his middle where his manager had just poked him hard.

His manager remained unmoved. 'Don't try to be smart.'

He'd tried for some humour when she had asked him what she was supposed to tell the media. 'Tell them it was Diet Pepsi that Richa threw at me.'

Anjali hadn't appreciated it. It had, however, restored his sense of humour. He'd launched into the realms of probability theory. Whether it was luck that Richa had been holding a can of cola when she came face to face with him, or whether she had been lying in wait for him after secretly finding out his schedule. He'd been in the middle of how Richa had settled on Diet Pepsi as her weapon of choice, because she couldn't bear to touch any drink that wasn't zero-calorie, and didn't think of water because it was so infra-dig – when Anjali had stopped him mid-sentence with a strong poke.

She was breathing deeply. 'I've been waiting for four hours. You haven't answered your phone once. My wedding is in just over a month. My fiancé is still five kg overweight and he's sacked his trainer. His clothes won't fit him for the wedding. He's not listening to me. I am not in a good mood. Don't annoy me. Don't be smart. Just give me something so that we can move on to the rest of your evening.'

Sheesh. Brides-to-be had no sense of humour. Especially brides-to-be who were former girlfriends.

Besides, once you'd written poetry for a girl and recorded a tape full of mushy love songs for Valentine's Day, you could never quite regain the upper hand. Even though he'd been fifteen at the time and hadn't reconnected with her for nearly a decade, the employer–employee relationship had remained unachievable. Especially when this ex-girlfriend knew exactly how to make money.

'I will fire you one day and make it stick,' Nasser told her.

Anjali continued to look at him expectantly.

Nasser gave up. 'Does poor Harsh know what he's getting into by marrying you?'

Anjali's hand twitched and Nasser took a few hasty steps back. 'I assume you haven't found out anything from her entourage? Then tell them to ask Richa. Anything else is going to make me look like an idiot. Or you could tell them that I am rethinking my cola endorsements,' Nasser tacked on, knowing his flippant reply would annoy her. He kept a safe distance from the finger, though. 'Even better, you could cut a deal with Pepsi. Tell them that the official line of my statement will be "The only thing we can confirm at this point is that it was Diet Pepsi that made the big impact." We could even spin it out into a campaign in the future.'

Anjali looked at him thoughtfully. She nodded a few times.

He didn't like it.

'Hmm, that's...possible,' she said finally. 'That's quite smart actually. The first sensible thing you've said in all this time. I could plant it...I know somebody who handles the account... Let me figure out whether it will help your image or not.'

Nasser looked at her in disbelief. He had long given up expecting her to have a sense of humour, but even he was impressed at how low she could fall.

Anjali pulled herself back to the present. 'Till I hear from Pepsi, I'll draft a statement about it...'

'Which mostly says "No comment." I want to see it before it goes out,' Nasser said definitely. 'And I'm not taking any calls from the media about this. You can handle them.'

'Why bother with a statement? The public expects only a "no comment" from you these days anyway.'

Nasser ignored the sour note in her voice. This was well-worn territory and he wasn't going to rehash that argument again. 'Yes Anjali, I know I don't understand the ground rules of this movie star business if I imagine I can get privacy.' Eighteen months of familiarity with this argument had led to extreme indifference. 'You'll just have to work around it.'

'You aren't here anyway from tomorrow to clarify anything,' the sour note deepened. There would soon come a time when they would have to deal with all this dissatisfaction, but Nasser was happy to postpone the inevitable for a bit.

'At least it's good timing on Richa's part – it will be great publicity for your movie.'

Sometimes his manager was downright scary, Nasser thought. Thankfully she didn't seem to expect a reply, because he really didn't think he could have said anything polite.

'What about that interview now?' Anjali said.

'What about it?'

'You have that awards thing and then the party and you're flying out early morning. And you *have* to give this interview. You promised the magazine. She's been waiting for you for hours.'

'So what? It's the job of a film journalist to wait. That's what sets them apart anyway – their patience and perseverance. Not to mention their ability to sit around for hours while stars work and eat and entertain friends and ignore them.'

Anjali instinctively looked over her shoulder to make sure he hadn't been overheard.

'Yeah that's fine. But she's not a film journalist. She's from *Homme*. And this is a big interview. So do you want me to cancel anything?'

'No. I'm going for all of them. I've promised I would.'

'You're going to be asked a lot of questions about this cola thing. I don't know if she–' Anjali jerked her head toward the journalist '–knows about it, but it's very likely. And we haven't decided what you will say. It could become difficult.'

'I'll say "no comment". Call up those organizers and tell them I'm not giving sound bites. Now can I please get this show on the road? I have to go home and pack for the trip.'

'You mean tell your mother what you want to take with you,' Anjali said nastily.

'I do my own packing,' Nasser said forbiddingly.

'That's not what Aunty told me when I spoke to her today.'

Nasser gave her a steely look meant to remind her that she worked for him.

Anjali replied with one that told him not to kid himself. Thankfully, she moved onto other things. 'Don't look like you're enjoying yourself too much,' she conceded. 'It will make you seem heartless. And people might question whether this was a publicity stunt.'

Nasser felt a pain in his jaw and realized that he was gritting his teeth.

'Tell the journalist she can interview me in the car,' Nasser replied evenly. 'She can talk to me en route to the awards.' He turned to the hovering Suresh and listened to the messages the man had taken. He caught a fulminating look on the journalist's face when Anjali broke the news about the change in venue. Not pleased, was she, he smirked inwardly. She would just have to lug it. He smiled pleasantly at her.

If he had to suffer through an interview, it was only fair that his interviewer suffer a bit, too. Or a lot.

The reality of the mind-numbing boredom of interviews had come back to him sharply this week. Being nice to journalists, repeating the same thing a dozen times, answering asinine questions, fending off personal ones, pretending indifference, lying through his teeth when he was particularly bored or annoyed, but in the end just answering the same questions again and again: Who was he seeing? What did he think of his latest hit/flop? How was it working with so-and-so? What was his role in the next movie?

At one point he'd amused himself by guessing the questions and the order in which each journo would ask them. He'd said the same things so often, he could have given perfectly satisfactory answers even if somebody woke him up in the middle of the night. He had never stopped being amazed at the public's sustained interest in the exact same things year after year.

From the looks of her, this one wasn't going to be any different – and she wasn't even a regular film journo.

Maybe he should cut her some slack. They had been locked in, after all. It hadn't been her fault. And she hadn't made any moves on him. He could try for some civility.

Anjali made the introductions. He could see it was costing her to be pleasant. 'Nasser, this is Sitara Gopalasundaram from *Homme*.' She gave the woman a thin smile. 'But you've probably finished your introductions in the room earlier.'

'Not really,' Sitara murmured. She didn't want to rock the boat with this woman around. Even with the minimum interaction they'd had she could tell the manager had big troubles. She didn't want to be the one who sent her over the edge.

'*Homme* had a last-minute change of interviewer,' Anjali continued, 'remember, I told you – Mukul couldn't make it?'

'That's okay. It's nice to meet you too.'

Sitara bared her teeth at him – it wouldn't pass for a smile in any culture – but she couldn't do any more. 'I'm so glad.'

Uh oh. Someone in this room was seriously pissed off. Nasser shrugged. Her bad.

Although, maybe it would be a good idea to keep all liquids out of her reach.

He reconsidered. Or he could charm her into a better mood and save himself the trouble of staying on guard against her. Probably easier.

'I must apologize about getting off on the wrong foot, but–' he flashed a smile '–as I'm sure you've heard, I've had a trying day.' Ruefully boyish. 'And I'm usually quite punctual, but I'm off on holiday and my director really wanted to finish up. If I hadn't completed the shoot it would have meant a two-month delay for the film. You can understand that I couldn't let that happen.' Nasser congratulated himself on his sincerity.

'What a lot of crap we do by way of work, huh?' Sitara said blandly. She barely restrained her lips from curling into a sneer. Did he think she couldn't see through his act? That one fake smile would dissolve her to mush?

'Hmm.' Nasser was distracted by the ringing of his phone. He offered the woman – what was her name? – a distracted smile as he looked at it. Welcome, media invasion. He flashed his screen at Anjali, gave her a meaningful look and switched it off.

Anjali stepped in without missing a beat. 'I was just telling Sitara about the awards ceremony and that she might have to do the interview in the car...'

'I know that's not fair and I'd totally understand if you don't want to do that,' Nasser said hopefully. It wouldn't be his fault if she backed out of the interview. And he could do this over email. Or rather Anjali could write out the answers and send them to him for approval. Or maybe they would cancel the interview altogether.

Anjali quelled his hopes with a look. She smiled at the woman; a rusty effort but better than whatshername's. 'Any other time I'd just tell Nasser to sit here and do that interview, but this is an event he has promised to attend. They're giving him an award and it would be really rude if he weren't there after he promised. *And* the publication that's hosting the evening has a time constraint on the venue. I honestly think you'd get a better interview in the car – Nasser's already switched off his phone, and he won't have anywhere to run when you ask him the difficult questions. *Ha ha.*'

This was *his* employee? This was her idea of looking out for his interests? The journalist had looked ready to back off; now she seemed intrigued.

'I'll just take that call,' Anjali said sweetly, before leaving him alone with the reporter.

'It's totally up to you,' Sitara said indifferently. 'We're going to the other end of town so that'll give me enough time. I doubt it will make much difference to the answers whether we do the interview here or in the car. Unless you are a nervous traveller?' The words were inoffensive enough but her tone managed to imply that she expected only such poor-spiritedness from him.

Nasser refuted it instinctively. 'I travel just fine,' he said, and was immediately annoyed with himself. Why was he letting – whatever her name was – reduce him to defensiveness? Okay, this name thing couldn't wait any longer. 'What was your name again? I don't think I caught it earlier.'

'It is hard to remember, isn't it? So many syllables,' she smiled forgivingly. 'It's Sitara Gopalasundaram.'

Her tone was so matter-of-fact that Nasser almost nodded his agreement before her words sank in. His brows snapped together and he gave Sitara a hard look. Had she just implied that he would have difficulty with any word that had more than two syllables in it?

Sitara tried for wide-eyed innocence, surprised he had registered the insult. Well, that he was obnoxious didn't mean he didn't have the smarts.

One brow shot up. 'Do you find that works for you?' At her puzzled look, he elaborated, 'Taking digs at the intelligence of the person you're interviewing?'

'It's been known to happen,' Sitara said with a brilliant smile. Damned if she was going to let him make her defensive.

'Interesting. I'm not a fan, so let's hope you won't have to disembark midway through the ride. Shall we?'

'Right away?' This was more shocking than his threat.

'Yes. Is there a problem?' Now that he was ready to go, he wanted to go right away.

Was there a problem? Only the empty gnawing of her stomach. 'I'd ordered something from room service...'

'When?'

'What? Oh. Around ten minutes ago.'

'After you came out of the room? Well forget it then, it'll take at least another fifteen minutes for anything to get up here.'

3

He had made a bad decision, Nasser acknowledged. He should have let Sitara Gopalasundaram eat. Maybe she wouldn't have been as mean as a one-eyed dog then. He'd regretted it almost as soon as they'd pulled away from the hotel, but before he could make reparations, she had swung into action.

He shuddered.

It hadn't been an interview. It had been war. He would never have guessed that someone with all that wild, soft hair, and soft lips (where did *that* come from?) housed the soul of a Spanish inquisitor.

She was smart, she was funny, she was quick. And she was out for blood. He'd been taken in by her laughing and fluttering at the beginning of the interview and he'd relaxed his guard. That's when he'd told her – thankfully in general terms – about groupie sex and how common it was. He'd caught himself before names and numbers tumbled out. He'd been on his guard after that but the woman didn't know the meaning of 'no comment'.

She had displayed no respect for the rules of engagement with Bollywood: thou shalt not dig, deep or otherwise. Thou shalt not try and report on what stars are really doing. Thou shalt get by on platitudes, obvious untruths and worn-out stories. Thou shalt not burst the public's bubble about your nice guy image.

Forget respecting them – she hadn't even heard of the rules. He'd called off the interview at one point only to have her so apologetic and upset and ready to respect his boundaries that he'd given in. Which is why she now knew that he was as surprised as the next person to have cola flung in his face.

A little more than surprised, actually, since it had been his face that bore the damage. And Richa had cut his call when he'd demanded an explanation. He briefly considered telling her that was off the record, but didn't expect her to respect that.

She was now sitting across from him looking so much like the cat with the cream that he wanted to throttle her.

Then a better idea struck him.

Sitara didn't like to say it, but damn, was she good! And didn't he know it. He'd think twice about depriving anybody of a meal from now on. And keeping people waiting or laying into them with undeserved sarcasm.

Though to give him his due, he was pretty quick too. He had been far smarter than she'd expected. Hardly given anything away. Funnier, too. Sexier.

Whoa! Whoa, whoa, whoa! Sitara screeched to a mental halt. Where did *that* come from? This was taking her lust for brains too far. Or not far enough. Whatever.

'So what award are you getting this evening?' Sitara said the first thing that came to mind.

'I like the element of surprise when they announce it,' Nasser replied glibly.

Translation, he had no idea. Not that she could blame him. There were too many awards out there to keep track of.

'But you'll see soon enough.' Nasser smiled at her warmly.

His smile did rather lovely things to his face, Sitara thought. She closed her eyes briefly. She would not be a groupie, she would not be reduced to mush like all the others. When she opened her eyes, the flash of lust had been banished and she reprocessed his words. When they sank in, Sitara kept her face blank with an effort. Did he think she would be glued to the TV waiting for him to receive his award? 'Yes, I'll be watching the awards show on television to see what you win,' she said, not even trying to hide the fakeness.

'TV! No, no, you are coming for this awards ceremony with me.'

'God no,' Sitara exclaimed before she could stop herself. She'd seen enough clips on TV to know that she would rather pull out her own fingernails than sit through one. 'Uh, I mean, we're done with the interview. I knew I had to wrap it up before the show. I don't want to take any extra time.'

'That's all right. I think readers should get a picture of the real me and they can't get that from half an hour spent in the car. You need to spend at least a few hours with me.' Nasser almost smiled at the dismay written across her face. He cut in as she began to protest.

'You're an international publication, right? I believe the best magazines abroad always meet their star a couple of times. They spend quite a few hours over the cover interview. I thought those were the standards you were planning to set in India – am I wrong?' Let her get out of that!

'Of course, those are the standards we want to set,' Sitara began, buying time as she tried to figure out a way out of this disastrous turn of events. 'And I'm–' she choked the word out '–honoured that you would think of giving me this opportunity, but I don't really know whether I would get too many inputs now. I mean, you are going to be busy with your awards ceremony and it would be awfully rude to talk in between.'

'You're right,' Nasser answered, and Sitara felt a wash of relief. 'I won't be able to answer any questions, but consider this more in terms of background material. See whether what I've told you is really who I am. And you can ask me all the questions you want at the after-party.'

'*After-party*?' She would rather be boiled in oil. 'I mean, ask you questions at the after-party? I would hate to spoil your fun.'

'That's too nice of you,' Nasser's tone was patently insincere. 'But I think if something has to be done, it should be done right, don't you? I'm very happy that your magazine is setting such high standards in journalism and I'm not going to back off from that because of a little inconvenience it causes me. And what timing, here we are!'

'Won't it be awkward to have a woman trailing you after the incidents of today?' Sitara made a last ditch attempt to save herself from the nightmarish evening that suddenly loomed ahead.

Nasser smiled grimly. 'Not at all. It should really distract them. Make them wonder whether you're the reason Richa went off the deep end.' He found himself humming something peppy under his breath. Revenge could be so sweet.

Two and a half hours later, Nasser guided an unresisting Sitara back to his car. He calculated that it would take another half an hour for her to rise out of her zombied stupor. At the moment, she was a glazed-eyed, slack-jawed poster child who had just been introduced to an 'awards night'.

Over the years he had conned a series of unsuspecting people into accompanying him to the ceremonies – an unending round of uninspired dances, unrehearsed emcees, blatant sucking up, relatives accepting awards and prolonged speeches – and he had the routine down pat. Walk in with real live people, exit with the walking dead. He'd hastened this one into zombiedom by pointing out that a lot of cameras would be turned his way and it would be really rude if they caught her on her phone. Switching it off would be the best thing. She'd had no escape.

And he couldn't rustle up the slightest twinge of remorse.

Anjali had messaged him during the ceremony to let him know somebody had caught the entire Richa assault on video and the clip was on YouTube and all the news channels. Some smartass news channel had already dubbed it Colagate. And they'd been flashing images of him from the awards ceremony alongside a slow-mo clip of the cola hitting his face. They'd also started speculating that it was the unknown woman at his side who had prompted the entire episode.

He was going to get grilled by Abba when he got home. Which was a sad state of affairs for somebody who had reached the ripe old age of thirty.

He looked consideringly at his silent companion – should he let her go? Send her off home with his driver? A voice, which sounded remarkably like his father's, succinctly told him what he could do with that idea.

And was he going to listen to it? Nasser wasn't going to think about that.

It would be too bad to turn her loose in her present state. He'd get her back to normal and send her home, he decided, leading her into the hotel towards the hall where the official after-party was being held.

Sitara spluttered alive after a shot of tequila.

'Want another?' Nasser held out another glass.

She downed it before the words were out of his mouth.

'That was vile. Horrible. Terrible.' Sitara stopped a passing waiter and picked up a few more shot glasses. She could vaguely feel her brain awakening, but she was pretty sure some vital bits had curled up and died from the torture she had been subjected to earlier.

Nasser didn't pretend she was talking about the drinks – it would have been hard to when she was downing the other two at the speed of light.

'It wasn't so bad. I thought Aunty's speech was great, didn't you?'

'Aunty' had accepted the award on behalf of her brilliant daughter, who was unfortunately away on an outdoor shoot. And since an award wasn't enough proof of her child's brilliance, Aunty had hit the high points of her daughter's genius.

From the time she was five.

The emcee had unsuccessfully tried to cut her off. She had scolded him for trying to interrupt. The organizers had tried to get someone to escort her off. She had moved around the stage dodging them. Then she'd told them to wait till she finished up. Torturously she had progressed to her daughter's first movie. Which only left another dozen or so. The organizers had finally gathered their wits and gone into action with a three-pronged approach: drowning her out with a burst of her daughter's song and a two-person ambush – one to grab the mike from her and the other to lead her off stage.

Sitara shot him a look of loathing.

'Where's your sense of humour?' Nasser asked. It really had been funny. Then again his senses might be blunted by the number of awards ceremonies he was forced to attend.

Sitara choked. '*Sense of humour?*'

'Yes. Very important to survive these things. The secret is to grab your enjoyment where you can at these events. I should know – I go to a dozen every year. Or at least I used to,' Nasser said, with some satisfaction. This year he would be away in Tuscany. Where he was going from star to *bawarchi*. He'd get his revenge on Shiv somehow.

'Or you could get trashed,' Sitara suggested, hailing a waiter. 'I think that's a damn good idea.'

'That might work for you,' Nasser told her austerely. 'But it's a little more difficult for public figures.' He should know; he'd tried it. Not that he was ever going to tell her. 'Your magazine is planning one of these too, you know,' Nasser reminded her. 'I've been approached to confirm attendance.'

'Don't expect any sympathy from me,' Sitara muttered. You are a...' A tray of wine glasses intruded on her field of vision and Sitara stopped from slagging off the actor to grab two glasses. She bottoms-upped one.

'Hey! Go slow on that. You haven't eaten anything for a while, remember.' Crap. Wrong thing to say.

'And we all know why,' she looked at him narrowly. A finger poked him in the chest, and he looked at it in surprise. 'You. You are the one who wouldn't let me get something to eat.' She gave him another poke for emphasis. 'Now I'm going to get dunk – drunk, I mean – and it will be your fault.' He caught her hand as she made to poke him again.

She was going to have to go, Nasser decided. He refused to deal with another woman-related incident today. He called his driver and told him to come up, snatched the glass of wine out of her hand and steered her out of the way of the alcohol-laden staff. Five minutes. He should be able to keep her out of trouble for that long. Then he could hand her over to his driver and have her dropped home. He kept an eye on the entrance.

The woman at his side suddenly started to talk. 'Wow. Doesn't she look so much like–' she named one of Bollywood's top actresses. 'Except for the nose. And the lips–'

Nasser turned. And was horrified to find himself face to face with said actress. Who'd had work done on said parts of her face.

He hugged the actress, and complimented her effusively on her last movie. She barely acknowledged him. She was gone in sixty seconds. Maybe less.

Meanwhile, his burden had managed another glass of wine from somewhere. Nasser summoned the waiter and took another as back-up. He had changed his mind about the drink. Anything that kept her from talking was good.

He turned around and bumped into Bollywood's power couple. He shoved the drink into Sitara's hand as he did the meet and greet, ignoring the knowing looks they were giving him. He was not going to be drawn into any talk about Richa and the faceful of diet drink. He cast a look over his shoulder to check whether his burden was occupied and was alarmed to notice that she was staring, glass lowered, at the actress-wife.

The actor-husband followed the direction of his gaze and surprise flickered in his eyes. 'Aren't you going to introduce us?'

Nasser didn't have the chance.

'Call me Sitara. You won't be able to say my surname. It's too long and complicated for you all.' Sitara beamed at him warmly. 'And I know you. I mean, not Biblically or anything. From the movies,' she clarified to his girlfriend, laughing at her own joke. She received a flat, dead stare in return. All actors might be used to nutters; that didn't mean they had to encourage them.

Nasser interrupted with a remark designed to exclude her from the conversation. But it became clear that he didn't have their complete attention; the woman with him was staring at them intently. Finally, despite his best efforts, they fell silent.

'Sitara's just leaving–'

'Has anybody told you that you should stop doing things to your face?' Sitara directed the question to the actor-husband. 'No? I've surprised you?' She giggled. 'You can't even look surprised,' and burst into a peal of laughter.

Nasser muttered something incoherent and hustled Sitara away into the darkest corner he could see nearby. He'd never ranted before, but he obviously didn't need practice in the art. He was in full flow when his phone rang. His driver had better be outside 'Are you here?' he snapped.

Silence.

'Hello? Can you hear me? Where are you?' Nasser was hanging on to his patience by a thread.

'In a bar,' said an American accent.

'What the...' Nasser looked at his screen. Why? Why today? What alignment of planets had given him this day? What had made his brother pick today, now, to call him after they hadn't talked for, what, six months at least?

'I'm shoshed,' the voice said. 'Slossed,' it tried carefully. 'Slo... I'm very drunk.'

'Naeem.' Nasser kept his voice even with an effort.

'Yes.'

'Did you call me for a reason?'

''Swat I said. I'm drunk. Very drunk.'

'God give me strength,' Nasser muttered.

'What did you say?'

'I said why are you drunk?'

'I'm celeblating,' his brother informed Nasser. His brother, as far as he knew, was a teetotaller.

'No. No more drinks for you.'

Sitara had taken advantage of Nasser's distraction and grabbed a glass.

'How did you know?' Naeem sounded astonished. 'Are you watching me? Big brother!'

'No. I'm...forget it. What are you celebrating?' Nasser was beginning to feel out of control.

'Yes, I'm cel'bating. What? Yes, I'm cele... celbl... cel...'

Nasser looked around for a wall to bang his head against. 'Celebrating,' he snapped. 'Just tell me what.'

'Freedom.' Naeem intoned solemnly.

'Freedom?' Why was he even trying to talk to a drunk?

'Yes! From work. Woman. Responsibitties. 'Sis the nest of my life. I'm...oh, okay I'll pay the bill. Gotta go, okay.'

The phone went dead in Nasser's ear. If he were able to give it his full attention, Nasser knew he would be worried. Instead he was thankful Naeem had hung up; he could now stop Sitara from singing. Rather loudly.

He caught the eye of a waiter and beckoned him.

He had company by the time he looked back.

B'town's biggest gossip, the director of his last movie, and sort-of friend, Puneet Saldanha, appeared in front of him, accompanied by his chaddi-buddy and man-about-town Anurag Mehta. They were blocking his exit. He was enveloped in a man-hug before he could think of an excuse to move past them.

'Something to drink, sir?'

'Duck, Nasser!' Puneet said urgently. 'I hear these things are flying in your face today.'

Nasser shot a baleful look at the two who were laughing madly in front of him.

'He has no sense of humour,' Sitara said.

Anurag and Puneet stopped laughing, registering her presence for the first time.

'And no manners,' Anurag, the ladies man, cut in suavely. 'He hasn't introduced us; I'm Anurag and this is Puneet.'

Sitara ignored him. 'He thinks only awards are funny. Aunties receiving awards for their daughters. But I find his friend's face funny. Don't you think it's funny?' she demanded of the two in front of her. 'He can't even look surprised. And surprisingly,' she controlled a giggle, 'nobody had told him he had to stop. Not even his girlfriend.'

'Friend? She can't be talking about,' Puneet began, awe in his voice. He read the answer in Nasser's face. 'She is? Oh my god. She told him?' He looked at Nasser again for confirmation.

'Of course, I told him. I just told you, didn't I? You can ask me directly.'

Puneet and Anurag looked like they had been handed the keys to heaven. They would be able to live off the gossip for the whole evening at least.

'Who are you?' Anurag demanded. 'Why haven't I met you earlier?'

'Her name is Sitara Gopalasundaram,' Nasser snarled. 'She's a journalist. She's interviewing me.'

'I finished the interview three hours ago,' Sitara cut in. 'He wouldn't let me go home.'

'*Ohh*,' Puneet said meaningfully.

Nasser stared him down. 'I thought she could appreciate the chance to...to gain some insight. Some background material.'

'Is that what they call it these days?' Anurag asked slyly.

'Shut... No! No more drinks for you,' Nasser grabbed the glass Sitara had taken off a passing tray. 'You're plenty sloshed.'

'Not yet,' she disagreed.

There was a short undignified struggle for the glass of champagne, which Nasser lost on account of being a little more in a position to care about appearances.

'You charming devil,' Puneet murmured delightedly. 'You really know how to show a girl a good time.'

'Go away,' Nasser growled in frustration to both of them.

'Not in a million years.'

'Salman's coming our way – shall I introduce the two?' Puneet was all innocence.

Nasser was halfway across the room with Sitara when their laughter reached him. He'd had it. Where was his driver? He called him again. Phone unreachable.

He was going to sack him.

If he had to stay at this party, he had to do something about *her*. And he still had to make nice with the organizers. His eye fell on his burden who was humming loudly now. He definitely didn't want Sitara with him when he met them.

A strikingly fit older man caught his eye. The very man. Aman Sinha. The man who had taken over from Subhash Ghai as Bollywood's showman, an old-school independent producer but with the new business-like way of making movies, as renowned for his unmatched instinct for movies as his ability to talk about himself. Every director he worked with had at least one assistant director whose only duty was to attend to the man when he came on the sets. It was a full-time job. Nasser had no fear that Sitara would utter anything embarrassing; nobody ever managed to get a word in sideways.

Nasser paid his obsequies to the man and rattled off an introduction to Sitara insinuating that as a *Homme* staffer nothing could interest her more than 'Sir's amazing body' and his health secrets; nobody noticed when he slunk away.

Sitara looked in horror at the man in front of her, so buff that he had waxed his chest and was showing it off with a clinging, plunging T-shirt, the neckline showing off a cleavage that must be the envy of his heroines. She took a step back as he turned all his evangelical attention upon her, took a deep breath and started to talk.

She supposed it couldn't have been the lifetime it seemed, but she couldn't cut that timeline down no matter how hard she tried. At the end of it, she knew all about his three hours at the gym, his exclusive contract with his trainer and his healthy eating habits. He had dozens. She even knew how many eggs he ate for breakfast. Aman gave her no opportunity to slip a word in – turning up the volume whenever she so much as opened her mouth, and clutching at her hand if she so much as attempted to shuffle. He shooed away waiters bearing alcohol – 'calories, empty calories!' Sitara could feel her indignation building. What a dirty trick to have played.

Nasser looked disgustingly cheerful when he reappeared. He had another man in tow. 'And here you are!' he exclaimed.

Sitara looked at him balefully. Like there had been any chance of escape.

'I was wondering where you'd been.'

Sitara's palm itched to smack him.

He was making introductions before she could act.

'Sitara, meet Siddharth, he's a very talented director who has promised to make a film with me. And you must know Aman Sinha.'

It seemed he knew him pretty well because Siddharth the director immediately tried to leave. No luck. It was Nasser 2, poor suckers 0.

'I'll tell your wife where you are,' Nasser consoled him. 'Sinha sir was saying just a while ago that he wanted to produce something with young blood, didn't you, sir?'

Sitara watched the director's sense of self-preservation battle it out with his ambition. Ambition won.

'We'll leave you two to talk about it,' Nasser said rather indistinctly, dragging Sitara off with him in almost indecent haste.

Sitara waited till they were out of sight of the two. Then she whacked him on the head.

'Hey!' Nasser exclaimed, more surprised than hurt.

'You deserved it. Leaving me with that man.' She thought about it for a minute and thwacked him again.

'*Hey*! What was that for?' Nasser rubbed his head.

'It felt like the right thing to do.'

Nasser gave her a narrow-eyed stare. 'We'll let that

go. But don't do it again. I've had about all I can take today.'

She didn't look particularly intimidated. Probably because she'd got her hands on a glass of wine and was throwing back its contents in a manner that would have sent any oenophile into an early grave.

'Right. Let's go.'

Sitara chose that moment to lose her balance on some unseen obstacle and Nasser found himself with a soft body in his arms.

'Did you hear that?' Nasser said.

'What?' Sitara looked at him questioningly.

'It sounded like...' Nasser trailed off. He'd been about to say 'a crackle of electricity'. This was no good. He didn't want to feel any zings for journalists with attitudes, pudgy journalists with attitudes and uncontrollable hair and that invitingly full upper lip... No! Journalists who had unfriended half his friends for him. Still...there was an answering awareness in Sitara's eyes. She unconsciously swayed closer. Her eyelashes lowered, her lips parted...and she burped in his face.

It was quite a ladylike burp, Nasser conceded. That didn't detract a whit from its strong alcoholic aroma. He moved away double quick. She lost her balance again and her head hit his shoulder.

When he got her upright again, he found her laughing. 'Did I just burp in your face?' She doubled up again.

Nasser found himself grinning along even as a part of him noted that this wasn't something any other woman of his acquaintance would have done. Or found funny, if they'd done it.

He realized that Sitara had stopped laughing and was staring at him. 'What?'

'You laughed.' She looked amazed.

'It's been known to happen,' he said wryly.

'And not your movie star laugh.'

'That's been known to happen too.'

'I would never have thought you'd find it funny.'

His amusement fled. First family, then friend, and now an independent indictment on his sense of humour. He was getting a bit sick of this. He gritted his teeth to stop himself defending himself. 'Did Shiv put you up to this?'

'Who?' Big puzzled eyes stared at him.

'Nobody.' This had gone on long enough. He didn't need to feel any attraction for pesky journalists and he didn't need to listen to them. Why was he spending the evening with her anyway? Okay, stop. He didn't want to hear the answer to that. 'Do you live alone?' he asked abruptly.

'Yes. Why?'

'To see whether there's anybody who will feed you when you get there.'

'Oh.' Sitara had a feeling she'd sounded rather disappointed. 'Nobody has to feed me,' she tried to cover up. 'I'm a big gi–' that didn't sound right – 'woman' – no, that didn't sound right either – 'adult,' she produced triumphantly, 'now.'

'And big adult, do you have anything to eat at home?' He was pretty sure about the answer but found himself crossing his fingers anyway.

It took her a minute to process that. 'Oh. No.' Another minute. 'I'm hungry.' She looked startled at this revelation.

Of course she would be hungry. And of course she wouldn't have anything to eat. 'You don't even have Maggi?' Nasser was incredulous. What single-in-the-city type person didn't have Maggi? Well Shiv, but he didn't count; he was odd.

'Maggi?' She repeated it like he'd thrown something at her in Russian.

Which meant more time in her company. Somebody up there was really getting their kicks from this. Fine, he would feed her and do something about her drunken state before dropping her home. And as for the publicity, since she'd spent the evening sitting next to him, it couldn't possibly hurt to be seen at a restaurant with him.

Forty minutes later, he guided a very silent Sitara into the car. He was about to shut the door when she uttered a low, anguished, 'Nasser'.

'What?' He leaned in to hear. And became intimately acquainted with the contents of her stomach.

4

Sitara slunk into the office on Monday without making eye contact with anybody. Maybe if she ignored them, they would ignore her.

'Goodness! Look who's here.'

Damn. All that slinking wasted.

'Reporter *or* romantic interest?' Martin intoned, doing a fair imitation of the news channels. Sitara could never shake off the surrealness of having a man who looked like a hairy biker talk to her like he was her maiden aunt. From England. From the last century.

Sitara groaned. 'Please. Not that.'

Martin continued as though she hadn't spoken. 'Is she the new woman in Nasser Khan's life? The woman who made Richa Bali angry enough to assault the actor...' He paused significantly. 'With a weapon of mass reduction – a diet soda?'

'Har, har.' Sitara plonked her bag down, and switched on her computer, turning her back on Martin, hoping he'd get the hint.

'The last bit is from me. Ankur's been telling me that if I were on Twitter that would get me a lot of retweets.

Followers too. I'm considering allowing him to use it; he says his followers are at an odd number and he really wants to round them off,' he continued chattily. 'And turning your back on me won't make me go away.'

'I was afraid of that. I should warn you I haven't had my coffee yet.' Sitara didn't function well without her caffeine. If you were being blunt, she didn't function at all. Everybody in the office was well versed with that fact. And she was usually worse on Monday mornings; nobody approached her till after lunch.

'Ishan!' Martin yelled.

A dressed-to-the-nines intern arrived bearing two cups from her favourite coffee shop. He placed them carefully on the table, along with a couple of sachets of brown sugar on the side, interpreted the nod from Martin as both approval and dismissal and took off.

'Americano with milk on the side,' Martin announced with a flourish. 'Ishan just got back with it so it should still be hot.'

'You're sending interns to get me coffee?' Not that she cared, Sitara thought, as she poured in a careful measure of milk and sprinkled a hint of sugar. She took a sip; her eyes closing in pleasure. 'Oh, excellent. Just what I needed.'

'I don't know how you can drink that sludge,' Martin shook his head in disbelief. 'You may as well have an espresso. You're supposed to put in a drop of milk into tea, not coffee.' He shook his head again, this time in disapproval.

'You like coffee machine coffee, Martin, and I am descended from generations of filter coffee connoisseurs.' Sitara took another sip; she could actually feel the caffeine coursing through her system, waking her up. 'Where's Prabhakar, anyway?'

'Prabhakar, my dear, is an office boy. He has a lot of work to do. Interns on the other hand know nothing and can do nothing – their only expertise lies in hanging about coffee shops. May as well exploit that.'

'That's...uh, true,' Sitara was forced to concede.

'Yes. And unimportant. Tell me instead how you ended up lovingly nuzzling Nasser Khan's armpit?'

Sitara choked on her coffee. Martin slapped her back cheerfully.

It wasn't enough that the weekend news had spent an inordinate amount of time speculating about the Richa–Nasser fracas; unfortunately, some enterprising photographer had had his camera trained on her when she had stumbled against Nasser at the party. You couldn't see much of her face, since, as Martin had so succinctly mentioned, it was buried in said part of the actor's anatomy, but you could see his face, and some trick of lighting made it seem as though he was very interested.

Fortunately Nasser's disappearance on holiday and Richa's unavailability for comment and the fact that nobody wanted to give *Homme* free publicity meant she had got away lightly.

If you could call a dozen phone calls from her parents and another dozen from her extended family, three of which had included telephone numbers of her nearest Alcoholics Anonymous chapter, getting off lightly. All of them had been more concerned that she seemed drunk than that she was consorting with somebody from another religion and an actor to boot – she wondered what that said about her chances of marriage.

There'd been only one small, almost insignificant, aspect of the entire affair that had worried her – the location where her face had mushed up against Nasser. She'd been right to worry from the looks of it. She looked at Martin, dismayed. 'Oh no. It wasn't just me then!'

'There was an orgy of armpit nuzzling? I didn't know Bollywood was so kinky.' Martin's animation levels shot up.

Sitara ignored him. 'Damn. I was hoping I was the only one to think it looked like that. Has anybody else mentioned it to you?'

'No,' Martin said consideringly, smoothing down his handlebar moustache.

Sitara's relief was short-lived.

'But I mentioned it to a lot of people. Ankur was one. I believe there's already some talk about "Sitara the Armpit Nuzzler" on Twitter,' Martin added cheerfully,

'You're kidding, right?' Sitara demanded.

'Of course, of course,' Martin assured her hastily. 'Just pulling your leg. Would I do that to a friend? But tell me, why were you armpit-to-cheek with him in the first place?'

Sitara caught movement from the corner of her eye and fell silent. She watched the nattily dressed duo of Mukul and Sandeep approach with trepidation. They came to a halt in front of her.

Mukul gave Martin the thumbs-up. 'You're so funny, man!' He smiled at Sitara. 'Love your new title.' The smile slipped. 'I hope you're satisfied. You have destroyed the magazine's reputation. Nobody in Bollywood wants to work with us anymore. I had lined up three stars for interviews. All of them have cancelled. Others are avoiding my calls. I'm having a meeting with Debashish and Anil to bring them up to date. I don't know if anybody else in the publishing world will want to hire you.'

The ringing of her phone cut him off. He looked in the direction of the noise but wasn't able to locate the phone amidst the mess on her desk. 'I wonder if you're getting fired on the phone? Come on, Sandeep.'

Martin and Sitara watched them sweep away to the sound of the ringing phone.

'Turn down the volume,' a disembodied voice yelled from a few cubicles down.

Sitara reached under a stack of folders and turned off the ringer.

'I think you're supposed to answer it,' Martin sounded shocked.

'I never answer the landline. I'm not starting today. What did Mukul mean by "good title"?'

'How can you bear to let it ring?' Martin shuddered, avoiding her question.

'Journalism 101. Now–'

'Maybe you'd like to let the rest of us know how to get in touch with you then,' said a familiar oily voice. 'Your cell phone also seems to be switched off.'

'Debashish!' Sitara was treated to the lean, linen suit-clad magnificence of her boss. 'I didn't know it was you.'

'Hello Debashish, off to the races? But aren't they in winter?' Martin said innocently.

Debashish spoke to Sitara first. 'You might have if you had answered it.' He smiled genially at Martin. 'Martin, I haven't seen the redesigned cover yet. I think we all heard what Paris thinks of the attempts of your excellent team. I fear you will have to do it yourself. I know you're too senior to actually work, I said so to Anil, but he wouldn't listen to me. Is the deadline today? We can postpone it, I'm sure you'll need the extra time; I can explain it to Anil. I don't want to keep you from all your other important work. Or talk.'

The office waited with hushed expectancy for the next salvo in the long-continuing skirmish. They weren't disappointed.

'I shouldn't stand here talking to you then, should I? I don't want to waste any more time,' Martin said equally pleasantly. 'I'll go work on the cover.' He strolled away before Debashish could answer.

Debashish turned to Sitara with a smile. Sharp intakes of breath sounded loudly in the silence. 'Congratulations on getting Nasser Khan's interview. And so sensationally. Since you seem so comfortable being in the news, Anil and I decided that you should front the publicity for the Nasser Khan issue. We've arranged a couple of exclusive interviews with newspapers and news channels and you can share all the details of your historic evening. I believe you're going to be a celebrity.' He paused to give her a critical once-over. 'I'm sure we could swing in a diet plan and trainer from the budget. The camera adds a lot of weight, and you can do without it.'

Sitara looked at her keyboard in frustration. She switched her gaze to the monitor. She drummed her fingers restlessly.

It had been almost two weeks since she had interviewed Nasser Khan and Sitara was still having a tough time writing her piece.

In fact, she was having a tough time doing anything. Sitara looked broodingly at her cell phone: five unread messages and three missed calls. Her family was becoming unbearable. Kamala chithi wanted her to meet the sleazoid suitor again. Her parents thought it was a good idea. Of course, they also thought it would be a good idea if Nasser Khan visited them, which they had been letting her know for the past two weeks. Interspersed with these requests were fascinating nuggets of information: the age and viability of her eggs and the deadline on reproduction (her father), the rituals she should be doing as prescribed by their guruji (her mother), how she should be exercising (Kamala chithi) and the awesomeness of motherhood (her sister).

She had had to take her office phone off the hook and put her mobile on silent to escape this familial harassment.

She had thought being in the public eye would be difficult, but after overcoming the fear that somebody would uncover the ignominious ending to her evening, her two interviews with the press had been easy. She'd plugged *Homme* so shamelessly that the channels had been eager to get her off air. Even the office was more bearable. Getting the cold shoulder only helped get work done.

Well, all work except for the article. Two thousand words had never seemed more intimidating.

'Madam, there's someone for you at the reception.'

Sitara drummed her fingers on her desk. A wisp of thought had been floating her way just at the moment Prabhakar had spoken. Now it had completely vanished from her mind.

Finally, she looked at Prabhakar. She couldn't pretend he didn't exist. But she could get rid of her pesky visitor. She hunted out her landline from under a stack of magazines and called reception. 'Who's waiting for me? PR?'

'He said his name was Karthik Iyer,' the well-modulated voice informed her.

Sitara almost fell off her chair.

'–says he will wait till you can meet him,' the receptionist relayed in bored tones.

Prabhakar watched with interest as Sitara first did a credible impression of being turned to stone, then lifted off from her chair like a rocket only to turn back a few paces later, panting, to grab her bag. This time the progress towards the restrooms was far slower.

He made a mental note to keep an eye on her; he could always do with some entertainment.

Sitara looked at her reflection in the mirror. She'd cleaned up the smudging of kohl around her eyes, wiped up facial shine, deodorized, and finally run a hand through her hair. Was that good enough to meet a former fiancé? Good enough to make him regret dumping her?

She took a deep breath. She'd just have to find out.

'Karthik.' Sitara shot him a quick look and was disappointed to note that he still looked good. In a not-too-tall, have-to-wear-flats-when-out-with-him way, but still.

'Sitara.' His tone held the barest inflection of pleasure; his eyes were determined.

Sitara was further disappointed to note that the strong, silent, man of suppressed emotion and plenty of decision continued to be attractive, despite her eight intervening years as dumpee.

She stiffened her spine. She would not be a flower; she had her pride.

Somewhere.

'I think we should get married,' Karthik announced.

Sitara gaped at him. Gobsmacked sort of hinted at her state of mind. Long moments later, coherent thought continued to remain out of sight.

He led her to the reception's faux-leather sofas. She did not resist. He sat down across from her.

'I see I've surprised you,' his voice held the slightest note of satisfaction.

Sitara gathered her wits and managed a 'Yes'.

'I'm ready for marriage now, ready to settle down,' he said simply, as though that explained everything. 'You're still single. Our parents have already done all the preliminary work, our horoscopes match, I even have your engagement ring,' a slight dip around his lips indicated that this was a joke. 'It's a sign. We are meant to be together. We should get married.'

'But...' Sitara's mental facilities seemed to have gone blue screen. 'You dumped me,' she managed weakly.

'Dumped. Ugly word.' He sounded sorrowful at having been subjected to it.

Sitara caught herself before she could apologize. It was a near thing.

'As I explained then, I was not ready for marriage.

There was nothing wrong with you. Is six weeks enough?'

'Six weeks?' Sitara parroted.

'For the wedding. End of next month. I'm coming back for some work then. I can take a few more days off. And you can fly up to San Jose when your visa is done. We can take our honeymoon then.'

'No,' Sitara denied finally. Then with a little more vigour. 'This is not happening.'

'I know. It is hard to believe. But I knew when I saw you on TV,' He leaned forward, displaying a screaming amount of expression for him, 'I knew. The universe wants us to get married. Otherwise, how would you appear on TV just when I'm in India? And then I fly for some unexpected business to Mumbai. *And* your office is next door to my hotel. Too many signs to ignore.' He patted her arm in a feather-light motion. 'Take your time. Meanwhile, I'll tell my parents to start the preparations. It'll be the 28th of next month, I think. You should give in your notice at the earliest.' He looked at his watch and stood up. 'I have a lunch appointment now. I'll be in touch with you on email...'

Sitara came to life with a rush. 'Hang on. When I said this is not happening–'

'I understood perfectly. No need to explain.' Karthik cut her short. 'And I must leave now. I don't like being late.' A bell dinged outside the reception, signalling the arrival of the lift. 'I'll mail–'

'No,' Sitara said, 'wait. I'm not–'

'–you.' Karthik seemed to fly into the lift. He raised his hand in farewell. 'Bye.'

The lift closed. '–marrying you.' She was talking to thin air.

Sitara shoved her way into the office elevator, pushing aside a soul or two, waiting for somebody to take umbrage. She could do with a good fight. Nobody said a word. She was even more frustrated when she emerged. She got into a cab, and slammed the door shut. The driver didn't say anything. Where were Mumbai's balls today?

How could her parents have disappeared? Her father should be working at least. Answering his cell phone. And fine, so what if her parents weren't available, where was her sister? The mother of a one-year-old baby wasn't supposed to be gallivanting about.

Sitara looked at her phone. She was itching to talk to somebody. If only Maya were around. But no, her best friend had gone off to the US on work, blast her. She hadn't called once, Sitara contemplated, injured. Maya was going to have a lot to answer for when she returned.

Sitara looked at her apartment door with dislike. She needed to pace. There was no way she'd get more than eight steps in her one-BHK apartment. She shoved the key into the lock and was contemplating taking her half-yearly walk, when her phone rang. For once, her phone was where it was supposed to be – in her bag – and she answered on the second ring.

'Nithya! Where were you? Why didn't you answer my call? Where are the parents? And what is all this noise?' Sitara shut the door carelessly and flung her bag on the nearest surface.

'I was sleeping,' her sister said unapologetically.

'For five hours?'

'I wish,' her sister's tone was wistful. 'No, Sangeeta still doesn't nap for more than two hours. Gautam just got home so I'm on a one-hour "me" time. I've come to the mall.'

'Mall?' Sitara shook her head. 'And Appa and Amma?'

'No idea. Not answering their cell phones?'

'Not even land lines. Appa's taken off from his work?'

'No idea.' Her sister sounded distracted. Sitara found out why immediately. 'Do you think I could wear sleeveless?'

'What?'

'A sleeveless salwar kameez. There's a really pretty one in this store. I could cover up my arms with the dupatta,' her sister sounded amazed at her own temerity.

'Aren't you an adult? Married? A mother?' Sitara said impatiently. 'Just buy it. Anyway, listen, guess–'

'Yes, but I'm an adult in Chennai,' her sister snapped back. 'As it is I married before you. I don't want to shock the maamis any more by wearing sleeveless. You still have to get married. And it's difficult enough with that broken engagement. And now you and that actor. You're all over TV, you know.'

Sitara exercised her rights as an elder sister and told her to shut up. 'Stop talking like Paati. One psycho grandmother is enough to deal with. Now will you please listen to what I have to say? Karthik came to the office today.'

That got her attention. Her sister exclaimed satisfactorily. Sitara told her about the marriage next month. The exclamations were even more satisfactory this time.

'Why? He said he saw one of my interviews and said it was a sign he couldn't ignore. He knew we were meant to be together. Please note he's not put off by my notoriety,' she added. Petty was so good sometimes.

'Yeah, he was always weird,' her sister said dampeningly. 'I remember he said something about signs when he broke up with you too, didn't he? Anyway there's no question, you can't get married--'

'Exactly!' Sitara exclaimed.

'–by the end of next month. It's not a good time. I think early the month after–'

'What! Are you mad? I'm not marrying him!' Sitara couldn't believe her ears.

'Why not? Has he become gross?'

Had her sister lost it? 'That's got nothing to do with it. He dumped me. Now he wants me back. What am I – a plaything?'

'So you don't want to marry him to prove a point? Or is there any other reason?' It was her sister's turn to sound impatient. 'Because that would be a really silly thing to base your decision on.'

'No less silly than his signs,' Sitara retorted, nettled. 'What if he sees a sign to divorce me?'

'His parents will stop him,' her sister answered with certainty.

'They didn't stop him when he broke off the engagement,' Sitara pointed out.

'That's different.'

'How?'

'It created less of a splash for him. This will be too much. Most of your trousseau's still intact, I think. We'd just need to get you some salwar kameezes,' her sister mused.

'I'm not marrying him, so you can stop planning my trousseau,' Sitara said angrily.

'You'll thank me when you think about this,' her sister said, infuriatingly. 'Do you want a sleeveless salwar kameez?'

Sitara hung up on her.

Her phone rang less than five minutes later. Sitara rolled over to glance bad-temperedly at the screen. A call from home. Her parents were back in civilization. She sat up to answer it.

'Did you just speak to Nithya?' Sitara began truculently.

'Hello. Sitara?' her mother answered, sending her daughter's temper ratcheting up. Who else was going to answer her phone, for heaven's sake?

'Yes,' Sitara gritted out.

'Is everything okay? You sound odd.'

Sitara inhaled deeply. Her mother spoke before she could respond, finally processing her daughter's opening words.

'Why, what has happened to Nithya? Isn't she out shopping?'

'Yes, she's out shopping. Nothing's happened to her.' Then because she was still irritated with her sister – 'She's buying sleeveless.'

'Oh. I didn't think you would have a problem with that. I think it's fine. She's married, and the mother of a child. I don't think you should worry about it,' her mother sounded censorious.

'What? You're blaming me? I don't have a problem with it.'

'You brought it up,' her mother pointed out with inescapable logic.

'Forget it,' Sitara snapped. 'Where have you been? I've been trying to get in touch with you all afternoon. You haven't been home?'

'Oh. When did you call?' her mother asked curiously.

'From one onwards.'

'Yes, ma. You are right. We were out,' her mother confirmed.

Red spots danced in front of Sitara's eyes. It took a while to get herself under control, and consequently a little longer to process what her mother had said.

'Wait! What? What did you say?'

'We met your Girish's parents,' her mother repeated slowly, using her idiot-daughter voice. 'They wanted to talk about the marriage date.'

'Marriage date!' Sitara was outraged. 'I'm not marrying him. I told you that already.'

'Don't be silly.' The idiot-daughter voice had taken off ten points from her IQ. 'He's very eligible, he's well educated, he has a good job, he comes from a good family. There's no reason to not marry him.'

'He's a slimy–' Sitara groped around for a parentally acceptable insult, '–snake.' She couldn't help a feeling of dissatisfaction at the lukewarm description. She forged on nevertheless. 'He thinks that because I work in a men's magazine, I'm...loose.' Again, dissatisfaction.

'Yes, ma,' her mother said unsympathetically. 'Your father and I told you everybody would think that when you wanted to take the job. As usual you didn't listen to us. Now you have to live with your decision.'

'You–' Sitara began. Then controlling herself. 'I don't want to talk about it. I'm not marrying him and that's final. What I–'

'Your father and I like him. And we had your horoscopes matched,' her mother continued relentlessly. 'The priest says you can get married in six to seven weeks. End of next month or beginning of the month after.'

'Oh,' Sitara said, with the beginnings of malicious enjoyment. 'That might be a bit tough. Karthik has set our wedding date at the same time.'

Sitara was still grimly satisfied with the result of that announcement the next day. She ran through the conversation once again as she doodled in her notepad. Her parents were now faced with a situation they had never anticipated – two eligible men wanting to marry their older, way-past-her-expiry-date daughter at the same time.

She cast an eye in the direction of her boss. Still yammering on about timings. To her right, she heard a stifled yawn; at her left, somebody was surreptitiously typing out a text. Sitara shifted into a more comfortable position.

Some people got work done at meetings. Nobody at her office had quite mastered the knack. Especially not on Tuesdays, officially declared editorial meeting day.

Sitara hated Tuesday noon even more than she hated Monday mornings, and that was quite a feat. Not only did the meeting mean Sitara had to come in early to work, but it also meant an agonizing start to her day, and little hope of being able to raise herself out of the resultant stupor.

And though the noon timing was supposed to ensure that they didn't run over two hours, lunch was always, always a delayed affair on Tuesdays.

Her phone beeped: 'Is this love?' Sitara saw the text, looked up at an expectant Martin and gave him a withering glare. Martin smirked and gestured towards her notepad. Sitara looked down and was horrified to see that Martin had been correct – she had been drawing hearts with Nasser Khan's name in the middle. She scratched them out vigorously and put the pen down.

Her name caught her attention, and Sitara looked up. What now?

'Are you sleeping with Debashish?' Martin asked casually as he walked out of the conference room with her.

She didn't blame him. She bet the others were thinking it too. She was the newest employee in an office full of insecure, easily threatened divas. And not only had Debashish handed her the magazine's plummest story, but he had also given her a travel assignment when she wasn't next in line. And what an assignment. Ten days in Tuscany on a food and wine trail.

'He's messing with me,' Sitara said.

'That's not his usual modus operandi,' Martin commented.

'He's changed it then,' Sitara said flatly.

'Hmm,' he looked thoughtfully at Sitara, who waited for any explanation he could offer about Debashish's behaviour. 'I wonder who he's sleeping with. Canice says he's been hearing the seductive tone these days.'

'Your concern for me is stunning as usual.'

'Why should I be concerned? You are going off in ten days to some fabulous vacation and by the time you return, Debashish will have found somebody else to torture. No reason for concern. The only problem I see is that you won't miss our beautiful party on Saturday.'

'Ugh. Don't remind me.'

'Also, the next ten days,' Martin added, 'you'd better stay away from anybody with a sharp object in their hand. Or a blunt, heavy one. And don't eat any food they offer. Or drink...' Martin laughed, ducking the press release she threw at him.

5

Richa Bali posed graciously for the photographers. She parted her lips a fraction and turned her right cheek to the camera, one hand holding a glittering Leiber clutch, the other at her hip, in the barely flown-down-from-Italy dress. Paired with nude Manolos, pretty coral lipstick and a few baubles she had picked up over the years, she could say she'd nailed the look.

Or at least that's what her highly paid stylist had told her. She'd better be right. This was her first public appearance after Colagate and she wanted to make maximum impact. Her stylist would be sorry if she messed up – even if she had captured that excellent video of Nasser Khan. Richa banished the thought from her mind; she didn't want her smile looking less than genuine. These party pictures were too important.

Ever since Richa had glimpsed the end of her career on the horizon, she'd known the only way to ensure a continued presence in the magazines was through a stylish persona. She'd hired a stylist immediately. She could now talk knowledgably about vintage and high street and how she mixed them with designer labels for her particular brand of effortless style.

Effortless style.

She spit on effortless style. She didn't want to wear second-hand clothes and call them vintage; she didn't want to wear fake jewellery and call it costume; she didn't want to hide her body in acres of cloth and call it volume. She liked big shiny diamonds and good shiny clothes, and after paying a bomb for a body like hers, she wanted to wear tight short things and make all the men sit up and take notice and all the fat cows jealous as hell.

But she'd chosen style as her calling card and here she was, at a magazine–designer-brand co-hosted cocktail evening. She watched the man who had convinced her to attend rush to her side.

'Mukul! How lovely everything looks,' she said, over the prerequisite air-kissing.

She listened to his effusiveness with half an ear, scanning the crowd for her target. She allowed herself to be escorted toward the top men from both brands and accepted their heartfelt professions of delight at having her at the party.

Of course they were delighted. Her presence had just taken their party into prime-time territory.

'TV channel? Sure. I'll speak with them,' she smiled at them. Wouldn't she just. Not that she would have to say much, a few half-sentences, a few insinuations; the media was well able to jump to conclusions all on its own. Nasser and his 'no comment' policy were going to get a workout before she was done with him.

Sitara watched the media circus around Richa with a jaded eye. Her gaze wandered onto the phalanx of little black dresses and teeteringly high heels and she was depressed anew. Magazines should be all about the articles, she thought. Not about throwing parties. And socializing. And TV coverage.

'Your pink dress doesn't exactly blend in with the foliage,' a familiar voice said.

Sitara controlled her start of surprise as she turned her back on the inadequate cover provided by the fronds of potted plant. 'There's nowhere else to hide, Martin. Those loo attendants are already giving me suspicious looks.'

Martin gave her an exasperated look. 'You don't have to hang out with the office crowd, you know. You can schmooze with your contacts.'

'I don't feel like schmoozing,' Sitara said. She repeated hollowly, 'Hang out with the office crowd.' She followed it up with a hollow laugh. 'That's a joke.'

Debashish obviously had a 'screw Sitara' schedule drafted out. The dust had barely settled on the news of the Tuscany trip, and this morning Debashish had announced that she would be doing the next cover story too. Nothing major, merely Tendulkar's long-awaited interview. The entire office was giving her the cold shoulder. Only the fact that she was off to Italy the next day was making the entire situation bearable.

Martin didn't bother to deny it. 'I don't suppose you can go home,' he suggested.

'Right,' Sitara scoffed. 'And give Debashish something else to jack me with.'

'Seriously, Sitara, are you going to stay here for the rest of the evening?' Martin's eyes wandered through the crowd. An improbably social animal, he was obviously itching to circulate.

'Not at all,' Sitara was all dignity. 'There's another plant down the room. I'll divide my time between the two.'

Martin gave her a pitying look and walked away. He knew a losing battle when he saw it, even if it was hiding behind an inadequate plant.

'Hello. Sitara, isn't it?' said an unfamiliar voice to her right.

Sitara pasted on a smile and turned towards it. Whoa! Hottie introducing himself to her. She couldn't remember the last time this had happened. And this on top of two men wanting to marry her.

She sucked in her stomach reflexively, not that it made much of a difference, and fluffed out her curls. Maybe the evening wouldn't be such a dead loss after all. 'Uh yes...'

'I guess you don't remember me,' the stranger smiled slightly. His hot factor zoomed up when he did that. Oh no, was that a ponytail he had? Please, please let him be straight. 'My name's Anurag. I met you with Nasser at the awards after-party.'

'Shhh. Not so loud,' Sitara gave a furtive look around to check that nobody had heard. 'There are TV people here.'

Anurag laughed out loud. He was even more attractive when he did that. Of course, he seemed pretty damn attractive when he wasn't smiling too. She was leaning more and more towards him playing on her side. And he either looked interested or it was his default expression with females. It didn't matter which it was.

It had been a long, dry run for her love life and Sitara wasn't going to waste any interest that came her way.

'But at least your advice to a certain film star hasn't become media property,' his voice theatrically lowered.

Sitara cringed. That was one bit of the evening she remembered. 'I told you about that?'

'I think we managed to look surprised,' Anurag teased, leaning in on her, his vibes definitely interested.

'Did I say anything else?' Sitara asked. Her memory about a large part of the evening was hazy, and she'd had nobody else to ask about what happened.

'Well you also told us that Nasser had no sense of humour,' he obliged.

Sitara waved that away. 'That's okay. Nothing else damaging?'

'That's okay? Is that what you tell all your interviewees?'

'As it happens, Nasser was the first,' Sitara admitted.

'And did he take it well?'

'To be honest, I can't remember,' Sitara confessed, ruefully.

He laughed again, but persisted, 'You looked like you knew each other quite well.'

'I think that was my low tolerance for alcohol. I only met him that evening. I barely know him from Adam.'

'So you go around whacking men you've just met?' Anurag asked, eyes sparkling.

'Oh no!' Sitara groaned. 'Did I do that?'

'You hit him on the head,' Anurag grinned. 'That's my last memory of you. I would have been happy to unleash you on a bunch of others, but Nasser disappeared with you. Where did you go?'

'Is this quest for information personal? Or professional?' Sitara asked him suspiciously.

'Very personal.' Anurag dropped his voice and leaned in further.

A man with moves, Sitara noted approvingly. A man to be cultivated.

His arm joggled as somebody bumped into it and a spatter of wine hit Sitara.

There was a chorus of 'sorrys' but it was the signature husky voice that came out on top. Sitara looked up to see the woman she had been watching just a short while ago.

'Hello Anurag. Sitara,' Debashish greeted them from the actress's side, taking the situation from bad to worse. His eyes gleamed as he made the introductions. 'Richa, I'd like you to meet Anurag Shah, once again the city's most eligible bachelor, and our arts editor, Sitara Gopalasundaram. She did the Nasser Khan interview.'

'Your bad luck entirely,' Richa said.

Braced for an attack, or at least some bitchiness, Sitara was surprised into a burst of laughter at the actress's comment.

Richa's eyes sparkled with humour. She made an enchanting picture as she turned to Anurag. 'Once again? Is that the usual "once again" or have you moved back to the city? I don't think I've seen you before.'

'Both once agains,' Anurag admitted. He sounded a bit wary. 'I've been in Brussels for the past few years.'

'Actually, I'm wrong,' Richa said. 'I *have* seen you before. Gayatri's party. I can't remember names but I never forget a face.'

Was there a man who could resist a beautiful, famous woman who seemed to remember him? Sitara watched as she immediately became chopped liver to Anurag. So what if Richa looked beautiful and thin, all shiny and sheeny, with taut, seemingly poreless skin, artfully tumbled hair and an impossibly impossible chest, he didn't have to sound so dazzled. Men were so easy, Sitara thought, as the buzz of their flirtation vanished in a puff of smoke.

There was a lull in the conversation and Debashish jumped in. 'I didn't know you and Sitara knew each other,' he commented to Anurag.

'We met at the awards after-party,' Anurag answered, bestowing an intimate look at Sitara. 'It was a memorable encounter.'

Uh oh. Sitara looked at him warningly, but the mischief in his eyes did nothing to reassure her. Her glass tilted dangerously towards him. Luckily for the well-being of Anurag's clothes, Richa chose that moment to speak.

'Oh, *you* were the reporter with Nasser! It must have been odd to be on the receiving end of media interest,' she said sympathetically.

Sitara nodded warily.

'And I had to choose that day to throw things at Nasser,' Richa said ruefully.

The interest levels of her audience spiked a hundred per cent.

'But you spent the evening with him, I'm sure you felt like throwing things at him too,' Richa said.

That got a laugh from everybody.

Was this woman for real, Sitara wondered? Because she was finding it hard not to like her. Did Mukul have it wrong when he referred to her as Richa the Bitcha?

'It was really lucky that you were with him that night,' Richa continued. 'The new romance really cut down how much they wanted to chase me.'

Sitara sputtered into her glass. 'What! New romance? There was no new romance. I was meeting him for the interview.' She saw Debashish watching her speculatively. 'He's the one who assigned the story to me the day before.'

'Hmm,' Debashish had turned on his unfathomable look. It won him a second glance from Richa.

'The touchy-feelyness was a dead giveaway,' Anurag teased.

Sitara gave him a quelling look.

'It's okay sweetie,' Richa reassured her. 'We've all been there, done that. Just don't tell anybody you're only friends. That's a dead giveaway.' Richa chuckled infectiously; Debashish and Anurag joined in.

'Ha ha. Very funny,' Sitara forced a smile, hoping to put an end to the conversation. 'I hate to think what you'd have done for entertainment without me.'

'I could have thrown more drinks at people,' Richa took her cue and ran with it successfully.

When they stopped laughing, there was a light in Anurag's eyes that was impossible to miss. Richa turned to him. 'I'm dying for a drink. Want to risk getting one with me? I promise not to throw anything around.'

'You can throw things at me any time,' he reassured her gallantly.

A blinding smile rewarded him; he was practically putty as he walked away with Richa.

Sitara heaved a sigh of relief.

It seemed to echo.

Sitara looked around startled and was reminded of the unfortunate fact that Debashish had not taken himself off.

Another sigh.

Sitara rolled her eyes. She didn't want to hear any lovesick mooning from Debashish.

'What a woman!' Debashish's tone was frankly admiring. 'I've never seen anyone like her.'

Sitara gave him a look of dislike. He didn't notice it; he was too busy watching the two get a drink.

'I think I...' Sitara began excusing herself from her boss's vicinity.

'She's an artist. Today's manoeuvres would have done any general proud,' Debashish continued, ignoring her. 'What precision. What planning.'

Sitara stopped edging away. 'You mean this conversation was planned? But she was so funny. And charming. All that was fake?'

Debashish dragged his gaze away from the couple to look at her pityingly. 'Right up there with the boobs and nose, darling. Did you actually think she found the situation amusing?' He laughed derisively.

Action at the other end silenced him temporarily. Richa was leaving. She was being walked to the exit by Anurag and Mukul. Sitara could see Debashish didn't like that. She began edging away again. Alerted by the movement, he turned back to her. He smiled. 'So you and Nasser, huh? How interesting.'

'Of course not!' Sitara exclaimed. 'She was just kidding. You said she had this all planned out. Is this all some Machiavellian scheme?' Sitara stopped abruptly. Debashish's infuriating smile hadn't budged an inch through her protests.

'Methinks the lady doth protest too much,' he said predictably. 'I wonder whether any whispers of this have reached Mukul. I must go find out.'

By the time Sitara got home she was fighting an infrequent but vicious headache. She reached to put her phone on silent when it rang.

She looked at the name flashing on the screen – Nithya – and contemplated not answering it. Wishful thinking. She answered reluctantly.

Her sister didn't bother with a hello. 'Are you seeing Nasser Khan?'

'What?'

'It's on TV. In the news. People have been calling me all evening.'

'In the news,' Sitara repeated stupidly.

'Yes. His ex-girlfriend let it slip. I hope Karthik hasn't heard this. Do you think we should advance the wedding before he calls it off?'

'My head is killing me,' Sitara said in a controlled voice. 'I'll talk to you tomorrow.'

'Wait! Are you dating Nasser Khan? Amma and Appa–' Sitara disconnected with exquisite softness. Then she turned off her phone and got ready for bed, resolutely keeping her mind as blank as she could. She popped a headache pill designed to knock her out and went to sleep.

She was feeling much better the next morning. Even more so after a lazy, leisurely breakfast. Then she girded her loins and turned her phone on. She winced as the list of missed calls flashed. One number elicited a more positive reaction – a dial.

'Maya! Finally! Where have you been? When did you come back?'

'Early morning,' replied a voice she was almost as familiar with as her own. 'And obviously I've been too far away, if you've become Nasser Khan's main squeeze in the meantime.'

No beating about the bush for Maya. Expected, Sitara supposed, from your best friend, and the last of the single sisterhood, the person who probably knew her every last secret.

'Uff, not you too.'

'Me? I'm only repeating the news.'

'It's that Richa. What did she say? I can't believe I thought she was nice,' Sitara wandered restlessly around her hanky-sized apartment. Her parents, who lived in a two-storey bungalow with a garden, front and back, in the middle of Chennai, would have called her one-BHK a storage cupboard, but Sitara counted herself lucky to have found it. It was in Colaba, on the third floor in a nice apartment building – a sunny, friendly space with a balcony that looked out to the sea. It didn't matter that it took ten steps to get from balcony to front door; what did matter was that it took her exactly fifteen minutes to get to office, less if you didn't catch any signals.

'She didn't actually say anything; she caught herself just in time. It was beautiful. Haven't you watched it? Let me send it to you.'

Abruptly Sitara was left listening to empty air; Maya was presumably turning her computer on. She looked down and discovered she was staring at a hip-high pile of newspapers with a book and two mugs on it. When had she started to use old newspapers as a side table? She must remind her maid to sell them tomorrow.

'God, the internet in India is so slow,' Maya complained.

'Shut up, America-returned. You were only there for a month.' The newspaper stack was forgotten. Sitara wandered to the balcony, her gaze absent-mindedly fixed on a ship moving across the horizon.

'Yes, but things there are so much more organized. I mean, it's not just that the internet's faster, the boys are so cute too.'

Sitara shook her head in resignation. Could there be a Maya story without a cute boy? 'You sound like the guy who wants to marry me. "Everything's better in the States."'

'Ah, sent you the link,' Maya said over some disturbance. 'And now who is this man who wants to marry you that you've casually inserted into the conversation?'

'His name is Girish Murthy,' Sitara said loftily. 'He's looking forward to some world-class head from me.'

There was a moment of silence. 'Huh?'

'Not that he's going to get it,' Sitara continued. 'Now that Karthik has set the date of our marriage for next month, I don't have to settle for him.'

'Sitara Gopalasundaram,' Maya said sternly. 'What have you been up to in my absence?'

'Nothing much. Just two good horoscope-matched Tam-Bram men ready to marry me, which they may not want to after this news of my affair with Nasser Khan reaches them. Oh, and everybody in the office hates me, my parents think I'm an alcoholic, and there's also speculation that I'm an armpit nuzzler,' Sitara said. She didn't want to sound immodest but as a list of woes this one had unbeatable appeal.

'Right, begin with Karthik, then go on to the bonking man. We'll get to Nasser after,' Maya commanded.

Sitara was only too happy to follow.

'I should have been there. I could have kicked him off the balcony,' Maya interrupted her. 'But not bad. Turning down two eligible men at one go.'

'Well, Karthik didn't stick around to listen to me reject him,' Sitara said. 'And my parents think that Girish is amazing so they're really pushing that marriage. Even though I've said no a hundred times.'

'That's because they are picking up this lack of conviction in your tone. Do you want to marry that dumper?'

'No, not really,' Sitara said weakly. 'He still looks hot though.'

'Sitara! As the person who had to pick up the pieces after that idiot broke off your engagement, stop it! Grow a backbone. Karthik Iyer is not the man for you. Don't think that getting back with him will turn your one big failure into success. It will just be another big failure.'

'It wasn't my failure,' Sitara protested. 'He broke it off without a reason.'

'Yeah, then why are you the one who thinks there's something wrong with you when it comes to men? Why are you the person choosing morons and losers to date ever since?'

'I haven't dated morons and losers,' Sitara said affronted.

'Two words: Dharmesh, Irfan.'

'They were nice guys.'

'Uh huh. That's why you went to movies and plays and concerts with one, so you wouldn't have to hear him talk, and...let me think, what did you do with the other one?'

'I made out with Dharmesh,' Sitara said.

'Oh yeah. If that's what you call lying back and thinking about the necklace you had seen in Pahargunj?'

'Oh shit. Did I tell you about that too?'

'Honey, you tell me everything.'

'God, I'm heartless,' Sitara said remorsefully. 'Poor Darshan, he was trying so hard.'

'His name was Dharmesh, Sitara, and if you can't even remember his name, how can he count as a man? Actually, don't tell me. I'm not interested. I only want to know about you and Nasser Khan.'

'Okay, okay. Basically, it's all Debashish's fault. He assigned me to do Nasser...Khan's interview,' Sitara added hastily.

'The rat-bastard's sending you off to do good-looking single straight men?' Maya knew all about Debashish.

'He said it was because Paris wanted me to write it. But basically he's got it in for me now. And you know he hates Mukul. This was his genius way to piss us both off.

Deprive me of my one shot to interview Blake Gregory. I can't believe he gave that to Mukul. Like Mukul knows anything about design. And to waste a genius...'

'Sitara,' Maya said warningly.

'Yeah, okay. So Debashish – he's totally making me a target of office hate. He's given me Sachin for the next-to-next issue, and a travel assignment out of turn.'

'So you actually didn't do the Blake Gregory interview?' Maya was suitably shocked. She had only been hearing about him for the past few years.

'No. And Mukul did such a bad job of it,' Sitara wailed. 'I can't tell you how bad it is. I almost cried when I read it. And for what? So I could do the sadist.'

'Sadist? Nasser Khan? The normal kind?'

'There are abnormal sadists too?' Sitara asked after a moment of consideration.

'You can be so slow. I mean like an S&M type.'

'You think underarm nuzzling is S&M? Can I send you a link to clear up this gap in your knowledge?'

'Darling, I know more about S&M than you with your two-and-a-half men.'

'What do you mean, two-and-a-half men? My past may not contain all the straight men in Delhi, Bangalore and Hyderabad but it's got more than two-and-a-half men.'

'You're so easily distracted. Can you just get back to Nasser the sadist? We'll get back to the two-and-a-half later. So, Nasser,' Maya prompted.

'Where was I? Oh yeah, Debashish sent me for the interview. And then he was late. By three hours. And I was bored so I went to the bathroom to put on some make-up.'

'Sitara,' Maya interrupted. 'Is there a story in here somewhere?'

'Yes. And can I tell it the way I want? I'm giving you the background before leading into the good bits. Umm... You've distracted me now. Yeah, So I went to the loo, and dropped the eyeshadow on my shirt – stop sighing – and I had to wash it. Then I had to dry it with a hairdryer–'

'Sitara,' Maya said threateningly. 'It's a simple question – why was he a sadist?'

'Fine, if you don't want to hear about me and bare-chested Khan locked in a bedroom, I won't tell you. He's a sadist because he made me–'

'Wait, wait, wait. Bare-chested. Locked in room. This is serious. Tell all to Aunty Maya. Don't leave anything out.'

It took her approximately fifteen minutes for a detailed retelling. Neither of them considered a second of it wasted.

'Why don't these things happen to me?' Maya moaned. 'Did you make out with him? And where does the sadism come in?'

'No. I threw up all over him. But it served him right for taking me to the awards ceremony. That was the sadism part.'

'You threw up over him?'

'Yes. I got totally drunk at the after-party he dragged me to – I also told some actor to ease up on the Botox – and then he made me eat something before leaving the hotel.'

'Hotel?' Maya interjected

'Where the party was happening – and a few minutes

after we left I knew I was going to throw up and I turned to tell him and it sort of happened.'

They both fell silent. Even in her life as a klutz, this stood out.

'And then you were caught nuzzling his underarm too? That's an impressive downward spiral.'

'No, that was before.' Sitara agreed gloomily. 'And yes, it is.'

'Anything else?'

'You want more?' She crossed her fingers hoping that Maya would move on. Her friend knew her too well. But Sitara didn't feel like telling her how the night had ended. How her last memory was of being in Nasser Khan's car. And that she had woken up in her own bed. In a T-shirt.

'Yeah, that's bad enough. So your parents think you're an alcoholic because...?' Maya probed.

'Because the nuzzling photo appeared in the papers. And on TV. And I had to tell them it only happened because I was drunk. They've sent me the numbers of three AA chapters in Mumbai. It's not that funny.'

'Oh it is,' Maya choked. 'They weren't bothered about your notoriety? That you were with an actor? A man of a different religion?'

'Well, this was before Karthik and Girish, so Amma called the next day to say she and Appa had watched a movie with Nasser Khan. And he was quite fair and handsome. And that Chithi had told them he was a nice boy. And single also. And my age. She told me to tell him he could call on them if he was in Chennai.' Sitara was obliged to stop because her friend was laughing too hard to hear her. She joined in a moment later.

'This is too good. I love it,' Maya went off into another peal of laughter. 'And now?'

'I think they've got him on the backburner if the other two don't work out. Amma told me she was adding some sets of precious stones because Chithi said North Indians prefer stones to gold...' Sitara had to stop because her friend seemed to have gone into hysteria.

6

Nasser added a glug of olive oil to the chicken, tossed in a few extra cloves of smashed garlic – he still couldn't believe he'd got to the ripe old age of thirty without realizing how divine garlic was – and put the bird into the oven to roast. His dinner would be ready in another thirty minutes.

Who would have thought that he would take to cooking like Harry Potter to Quidditch? From the first toss of the salad he'd become a convert. After spending two weeks at the hotel next door training under a Michelin-starred chef, he'd wanted to put his lessons in action and hired a cottage in the village next door. He'd been enjoying experimenting with a bunch of recipes from the dozen-odd cookbooks he'd bought off Amazon, and it had also given him the time to do some serious thinking. He hadn't come to any conclusions yet, but he wasn't rushing it – he had another month of holiday left.

He turned up the radio and the strains of an Italian ballad filled the little cottage and poured out into the garden. He picked up the bottle of wine and took it outside where he'd set up a table to make the most of the view -- the fairy-lit speck in the distance that was Florence, the lovely lines of a villa-turned-luxury hotel that was his nearest neighbour, and a bunch of rolling fields, their lines broken by stands of olive trees.

Not a hint of civilization, Nasser thought with satisfaction. Just the way–

His cell phone shrilled from his pocket.

Fate should do something about its self-control, Nasser thought ruefully. It was too easily tempted.

'Hello Abba. Does Amma know you're violating the one-call-a-week rule?'

'You are my son. I will talk to you when I need to talk to you. I am not ruled by any woman, even my wife,' Bashir declared.

Nasser knew that line. 'She's still at work then.'

'Yes,' his father replied sheepishly.

His mother had announced the once-a-week call rule to him before leaving, and told him it worked both ways. They wouldn't answer more than once a week and nor would they call. 'You don't need the distractions,' she'd said.

His father had taken the rule hardest. Ayesha enjoyed her space, and unusually for Nasser, he had craved it. Bashir, who liked to talk and was used to daily chats with Nasser, had manfully attempted it. He'd managed two weeks. Last week, he'd sneaked in another call. Now, it seemed, he was upping it to three.

'So, what's up?'

'What's up?' His words had the effect of a cattle prod. His father's voice rose with indignation. 'I'll tell you what's up.'

That's what he'd been afraid of. 'Okay, but my chicken is going to be ready in twenty minutes, and I don't want to eat my dinner cold,' Nasser cautioned. He could almost hear his father battle it out between telling him off for giving him a time limit and not wanting him to have a cold dinner. Nasser had no doubts which would win. 'Fine,' Bashir barked. Then curiosity got the better of him. 'Are you making this chicken?'

'Yes. Roasting it.'

'You're still enjoying this cooking?'

'Loving it.'

'Hmm. Chicken with some vegetables, I hope?'

Nasser rolled his eyes. 'Yes, Abba. A salad. And bread. So we've got the carbs covered. And all my meals are equally balanced. So you don't have to worry about my health.'

'What about–'

Nasser cut him short. 'And I'm exercising regularly. Running. Swimming. I also sleep early and wake up early. I'm the very picture of health. Surely you didn't call to talk about this?'

'Humph. Good, good. You must take care of your health while you go through this phase.'

'What phase?'

'This...your midlife crisis.'

'Ha ha. Very funny.' There was no answering laughter from the other side. 'That was a joke, right? Because I'm not having a midlife crisis.'

'Of course you are. Breaking up with long-term girlfriend, shunning publicity, questioning your life, this new hobby, getting into a relationship with the reporter – all classic signs of a midlife crisis.'

'I am not having a midlife crisis,' Nasser gritted. 'I'm just taking a break. Wait. What reporter? What relationship? I'm not in any relationship.'

'Really? That's not what the newspapers are saying. According to them you are seeing this reporter, and that's why Richa was so upset.'

'What reporter? I haven't even met – oh no. No, no, no. They can't mean–'

'South Indian girl. She has a long surname,' his father said helpfully.

He conjured up a shock of wild curls, and a sexy Liv Tylerish overbite. He stopped abruptly – had he just said sexy? About the girl whose last encounter with him involved throwing up. On him.

The memory of that night sent a shudder through him.

He hadn't felt up to walking back into the hotel with sick on his legs so he had sat in the car and told his repulsed driver to make a quick getaway.

It had only taken two minutes before all three were brought to the awareness that Sitara hadn't emptied all at one go. There was still plenty where the first lot had come from.

Not only was his suit totalled, his car was totalled, and his driver, he had discovered, suffered from sympathetic retching, causing his foot to come down heavily on the accelerator. Nasser had given him money and sent him home. He had dropped Sitara – who had added insult to injury by falling asleep – and driven himself back.

He shuddered again.

'That's ridiculous. Nobody can possibly believe that.' Another thought struck him. 'And how come you're only telling me now?'

'Because it's on the news now,' his father said calmly.

'Now? But the interview was ages ago. How can they be talking about it now? That doesn't make sense.' Nasser shook his head, his eyes following the trail of a lone car down in the valley.

'Well, your reporter has appeared on TV a couple of times to promote that magazine, and Richa–'

'Richa!' Everything was illuminated. Of course Richa. Who else could spread such a ludicrous story so easily?

Nasser suddenly felt tired. Bollywood politics. Wasn't this holiday about getting away from them? Let Richa do what she wanted; he wasn't going to play.

'Don't tell me any more,' he told his father. 'I'm not having an affair, or relationship, or anything with the reporter. That's the end of that. Now–'

'Oh. Are you sure?' his father sounded disappointed. 'She looked nice. But you're right; you should marry a good Muslim girl. Abid was saying–'

Nasser gave a bark of laughter. 'Abba. Give it up. You're getting one Muslim daughter-in-law, you be happy with that.'

'Hah,' his father's tone was suddenly bitter.

'What? Has Mr Perfect done something to upset his fiancée?' Nasser wandered back toward the kitchen.

There was silence from the other end.

'Okay, sorry. I shouldn't have said that.' Nasser kicked a pebble in his way. 'We'll keep our problems between ourselves.'

'Yes, do that,' his father was unusually short.

Nasser tried for conciliation. 'Anyway, what has he done?'

'He's also having a midlife crisis like you,' his father said.

'I am not–' Nasser took a deep breath. 'Why? What did he tell you?

'Tell me? Tell me?' The strain was buried under an avalanche of indignation. 'He didn't tell me anything. I got a call from Abid...'

'Of course, you did,' Nasser murmured. His cousin Abid's talent lay in being the repository of all information about the family, and he was continuing the good work in the US of A.

'...and he told me that your brother has quit his job.'

'Oh. Where's he going?' Nasser might be the older brother but he had never worried about Naeem. His brother had known exactly what he wanted to do the moment he had discovered physics.

'Going?' If it was possible to have set his father off any more, Nasser had just managed it. 'He's not going anywhere. Unless going around the bend counts.'

Strong words to be uttered by a loving father. He must be really worried. Nasser set his teeth and did what he'd never thought he'd have to do – defended his perfect, genius, prig of a brother. 'He's been at the job for years now; he was probably due for a change. It's not a big deal.'

'That's not all,' his father quashed his attempt. 'He broke off his engagement with Zara.'

'Is Amma throwing a party for him too?' Nasser asked, before he could stop himself.

'Do you think this is funny?' his father practically yelled.

'Relax, relax. You'll give yourself a heart attack. I was just checking about family traditions. Since my broken engagement got a party it was a reasonable question to ask.'

His only response was some heavy breathing from the other end.

'So when did he break off the engagement?'

'Yesterday. He called Zara at the clinic, and dropped the bomb in the middle of a perfectly ordinary conversation. Zara didn't believe it. Khurshid Ansari told me she still can't. He called to ask what was happening. Why was my son playing with his daughter's life? What could I say? I didn't even know.'

Nasser's eyebrows shot up involuntarily. Whoa. This was serious. 'Over the phone? He broke up on a call?' He made no effort to hide his disdain.

'Yes. The way you broke up with that hand-in-the-hair girl,' his father leapt to his son's defence.

Oh crap. He'd forgotten that. 'I was a kid,' he defended himself. 'Not thirty.'

'Is that why Richa is going around throwing things in your face?'

'That has nothing to do with...' our break-up, he'd been about to say. But how could he be sure? '...with this. Anyway, I guess this is what he meant by freedom–'

'Huh? Freedom? You know about this? You spoke to him? When did you speak with him? Why did you speak to him? Why didn't you tell us?'

'Relax Abba, it was nothing. He called me the night I was leaving–'

'That long ago! And you're only telling me now?'

'I forgot about it, okay? It was a stressful day if you'll remember. Where I was getting puked on, and thrown things at, and losing half my friends in the industry, *and* almost missing my flight. A two-minute conversation with a drunk man didn't exactly–'

'Drunk?' his father said in an awful voice. 'Your brother was *drinking*?'

Nasser cleared his throat, hoping that would be considered a response.

'Your brother was drinking?' his father asked again.

There was no escape. 'Yes.'

'Drinking. My children drinking. What will I tell my maker?' A lot of muttering followed, thankfully undecipherable.

Nasser didn't make the mistake of interrupting.

'So your brother has quit his job, broken off his engagement, and turned to drink,' his father said heavily. 'And he told you all this?'

'No, no, no, no.' Nasser disclaimed all knowledge. 'No. Not at all,' he added for good measure. 'He only told me he was celebrating his freedom. And then, I think, he was getting chucked out of the bar, so he hung up to pay his bill.'

'He's getting thrown out of bars also?'

Nasser's lips twitched. He controlled himself; his father wouldn't think it was funny. He tried to think of a way to rescue the situation and settled for distraction. 'But what did Naeem say? He might have a perfectly reasonable explanation for all this.'

'He might. Except that his cell phone number is no longer operational. His home number goes straight to voicemail.'

'He's disappeared? Without a word?'

'No, no. Not without a word. He sent us an email. To tell us not to worry; he has decided to take some time off so he can go backpacking around the world.'

Whatever Nasser might have expected, this wasn't it. 'Backpacking?' he repeated blankly.

'Yes.'

'Naeem?'

'Yes.'

'Isn't he a bit...'

'Yes.'

Father and son shared a moment of complete communion. The last time Naeem had roughed it out was a trip home five years ago. He'd immediately fallen sick and stayed that way till it was time to return to the US. Ever since, Bashir and Ayesha went to spend time with him in the summer. Naeem stuck to his first-world life, and last heard had gone the first-world way in terms of weight and exercise.

Nasser spoke finally. 'I think you're right about the midlife crisis. For him. I...he's gone backpacking? Around the world? Backpacking! I can't believe it. And that's all he wrote?' Nasser looked around. Why was he standing in front of the mirror in the dining room? He made his way toward the oven.

'No. He also said he won't be checking his mail much, so he may not be in touch. Your mother's very worried.'

Since his mother thought worrying a complete waste of time, and, as he knew from experience, was more likely to bet on her sons than wring her hands, Nasser knew exactly where that was coming from. 'What did he tell Zara? What reason did he give to break off the engagement?'

'Some mumbo-jumbo about finding himself and setting himself free and living it up... Khurshid Ansari said he didn't understand what that meant, except that it was a mighty poor excuse. Do you know what that means? Is that what you are doing?'

Ouch. Low blow. 'No,' Nasser answered shortly. It wasn't, was it? A midlife crisis. He stuck a fork into the chicken with rather more force than necessary and shut the oven with a bang. 'Abba–'

'Anyway, what I wanted to say was that most backpackers end up in Europe. And you're already there. Why don't you ask around? See if you can find him.'

Ask around Europe? Nasser bit his tongue. Abba was just worried.

Find Naeem. Right. He was more likely to run in the opposite direction. Nasser couldn't think of anything more uncomfortable than having to struggle for conversation with an almost stranger. Unless that man also happened to be your brother with whom the last real conversation had been... Nasser couldn't quite remember. What was it – three years since they met? All they had in common anymore was the accident of their births. Nasser returned his attention to the call. His father was finally winding down.

'And–'

There was some clearing of throat.

Nasser gave the call his full attention. He was going to enjoy what was coming. 'Haan, Abba?'

Bashir cleared his throat again. 'Ah. Hrmph. Yes. So. This is a conversation between men. There's no need to worry your mother with it. You know how she is.'

'Don't you think she might be reassured that we were discussing it?' Nasser suggested innocently.

'No, no. No need to bother her with speculation. Unless we have something concrete to offer her,' his father rushed to disagree. 'So, you agree then? There will not be any necessity to mention this conversation to her when we talk to you on Sunday?'

Sitara cranked up the volume on her iPod, hoping to drown out the voices of her fellow journalists. She stared out of the coach windows and tried to concentrate on the scenery – on the twilight that hit the groves of some very pretty trees that weren't olive, on the vineyards that were probably responsible for the superlative wine she had drunk... No, it was no use; she still couldn't drown out the voices.

She'd been trying to tell herself for the past week that her present company was better than being in office. After seven days, she wasn't so sure.

Whoever had chosen the group had gone to a great deal of trouble to get a good representation of all the print media. Two of them were from national newspapers, a writer and photographer from a travel magazine, the writer-editor of a trade magazine, a freelance-writer couple, and Sitara from the men's magazine. The same person had also managed to get together a group that would rub each other the wrong way.

Sitara was ticked off with the others on too many counts, but a biggie was how they bitched incessantly about the food. On a food and wine trail! 'Why don't they use spices?' the trade mag man had asked at dinner last night, at a Michelin-starred restaurant, causing her vision to haze over. The freelance couple had gently harped on how the standard of accommodation and arrangements didn't compare to their earlier trips to such and such place, uncaring that their organizers and hosts could hear as well as anybody else. The newspaper man had only come to shop, and as a result hadn't arrived on time to even one of the planned activities. The travel writer refused to walk or explore, complaining bitterly or bluntly refusing any expedition that required non-motorized movement. Her photographer and the other newspaper person seemed vaguely normal; they just seemed to not like Sitara.

Perhaps because she had finally lost her cool this morning and said a few things about what a travel writer's job entailed, like trying new things, and eating strange food, and maybe, radical thought, sightseeing. They had retaliated with what they thought of a journalist having an affair with a subject and things had quickly deteriorated after that. Their guide Luca had had to do some quick talking to stop any bloodshed.

She was going to have a serious talk with Luca about branching off on her own. This couldn't continue.

Nasser had an uneasy feeling in his spine. Like he was being watched. He looked around but all he could see were rinds of cheese, a whole lot of sausages and even more people. Nobody seemed to be obviously Indian. That had been why he'd picked this food market in Florence to begin with.

But maybe this was a signal to stop loitering about, sampling all the food, and get a move on. Nasser bought some fresh mozzarella and two other cheeses that looked interesting, and moved through the crowd swiftly. A minute later, he found himself in the fruit section of the market.

Had he lost the starer? He thought so.

Satisfied, he turned his attention to the fruits. Who knew it could be so much fun?

'Hello Nasser,' a voice rasped behind him.

Nasser turned around slowly. The scruffy backpacker he had noticed earlier stood in front of him. Although, stood wasn't a correct definition. Doubled-up coughing was more accurate. It wasn't fun to watch. Nasser grabbed a water bottle from the pack and handed it to the man. It seemed to settle him somewhat. He looked at Nasser expectantly.

Nasser looked back at the face which hadn't had any recent acquaintance with razors or scissors. Not much soap or water either. The honest smell of sweat was perfuming the air gently.

'You don't recognize me,' the man said.

Nasser bristled at the amusement in his voice, quashing the polite response he'd been about to make. 'No. Maybe you can jog my memory,' he said crisply.

'Here's a hint. *Bro*.'

It took a moment for Nasser and he stared at the man incredulously. 'Naeem?' Of course it was Naeem. The eyes, the ears, the nose. It was like one of those hidden pictures; once it had been pointed out the distractions vanished and only the familiar remained.

'Have I changed so much?' his brother asked, as Nasser gazed at him open-mouthed.

'Completely.' Gone was the tubby, pasty-faced man his brother had turned into over the years of academia and a steady diet of American-sized portions. This man was a little too lean, a little harder and that beard – Nasser had no words for it. 'What happened to you?'

'That could take a while. Why don't I tell you over coffee?'

Coffee? Well, he could stand that, he supposed. Nasser nodded. His OCD sibling was backpacking across the world without a bath. His father had been right. This was a midlife crisis of Richter magnitude. 'We can grab a table there.' He gestured towards a café a little ahead of them.

They sat down at a street-side table, not too far from the end of the market. Nasser watched his brother arrange himself and his belongings around the table. The backpack was neatly placed out of the way of anybody walking past, the chair pushed back in at some magically correct angle, the water glass upturned and placed exactly so.

'It's an oxymoron to backpack and be OCD,' Nasser commented.

There was a pause as Naeem refolded a paper napkin into more accessible accordion pleats.

'It's a challenge, definitely,' Naeem said. 'But I strive.'

'Strive, you say? Can't say I remember the last time anybody strove.'

'Strived,' Naeem corrected, absently trying to catch a waiter's eye.

'Master's in English as well as Physics? This brilliance is too much.'

Naeem focused on Nasser. 'I thought you had outgrown that. And if you haven't, please try. You aren't twelve any more.'

'Your brilliance? It did pall.' But Nasser avoided his brother's eye, hailing a waiter instead. 'Do you need a menu?' he asked as the waiter approached.

His brother seemed willing to be distracted. 'No. I know what I want.'

'Fine. Go crazy,' Nasser said, then listened as his brother took him at his word, ordering an espresso, a couple of croissants, an omelette and a couple of sweet rolls.

'Are you sure that's enough? You might have missed a few crumbs? Sure? Or I guess you can always order later,' Nasser said, asking for a cappuccino and croissant.

An itty-bitty breeze touched them gently. Downwind from Naeem, Nasser was assaulted by his brother's new unbathed avatar. 'Phew. When did you last have a bath?'

'Is my smell offending your sensibilities bro?'

'It's overturning them,' Nasser said brutally. 'And what's with all this bro-ing?

Naeem laughed. 'Just something I picked up from my students.' He paused as their waiter returned to serve them coffees and croissants. 'Quick service,' he said approvingly. He inhaled a croissant. He brushed at his beard to rid it of the crumbs.

Nasser watched with horrified fascination.

Naeem took a chunk out of his second croissant. 'I hitched from Milan but the guy dropped me a couple of miles out of town. I worked up a sweat getting myself here.' The croissant disappeared the way of its brother.

'Why are you hitching? Don't you have money for the train? Do you need any money?' Nasser caught himself. He sounded like his father.

Naeem thought so too. 'You need to guard against sounding like Abba,' he advised Nasser. 'And I hitched because I am backpacking and that's what backpackers do.'

'They also take the train. Haven't you watched *Before Sunrise*?' Nasser added, feeling the need to back up his assertion with something,

'Why don't you tell me when you've done it, bro?' Naeem said provocatively.

Some patterns were so easy to fall into. If they acted any younger, they'd be drinking milk from bottles. Nasser took a deep breath. The waiter's arrival with the rest of their order provided a welcome distraction.

'I fell sick in Milan and it blew my budget. So any way I can save money I will,' Naeem offered the explanation as a peace offering. 'Like letting you pay for breakfast.'

Nasser ignored the distraction. 'You were sick? Nothing serious I hope?'

'You're an actor. You should be able to do concern better, bro,' Naeem mocked.

'We can't all be geniuses. I am just a ham,' Nasser said, unable to stop the edge creeping into his voice. 'I do what I can.'

'You know life would be easier all around if you could get that chip off your shoulder. Anyway, don't worry yourself to the bone. It was just fever and this blasted cough and cold. Nothing serious. Just left me a bit weak. And before you ask again, I don't need money. I've just set aside a certain amount for this backpacking and want to finish within it. I have savings if I need them.'

Fair enough, Nasser told himself. Still, he took a sip of cappuccino before he spoke. 'You've lost a lot of weight.'

'That's not because of this fever. Maybe a little, but most of it was already gone. I've been working out for a couple of months.'

'How come?'

'Is it so inconceivable that I should do it because I wanted to?'

'Yes. And for future reference, you only start in on the big words when you're trying to hide something.'

'I had the beginnings of cholesterol. Don't,' he warned his brother, 'don't say it's all that beef.'

'Wouldn't dream of it,' Nasser reassured him. 'I was going to say it was the steaks.'

Naeem gave him a disgusted look and turned his attention back to his omelette.

'So how come you're–'

A loud crash from a nearby stall distracted him, and the voluble burst of Italian that followed had the brothers swivelling to see what had happened.

Somebody had crashed into a container of peaches, scattering them faster than billiard balls. A crowd had gathered, some to help pick up the fruit, others to not miss the action. A man was placating the fruit seller, who was pointing at the peaches on the ground and talking loudly.

Their waiter appeared at their table. To get a ringside view, from the looks of it. He shook his head. 'Bad luck.' His relish was hard to miss. 'Antonio, he will take money.'

Hands were waved. People expostulated. And in the middle of this spoke a female voice in English: 'I'm so sorry; it was really clumsy of me. I don't know how I could have missed the box. I am so, so sorry.'

'I don't believe it,' Nasser exclaimed, as a familiar figure appeared in the crowd.

'*Assurdo*!' The waiter exclaimed at the same time.

Neither of the brothers needed any translation for that.

'What?' they echoed.

'He is asking 200 euros for the box.'

It was obvious that the transgressor was as shocked as their waiter. Soon it became apparent that she didn't have much money on her either. But the stall owner wasn't letting her off.

'Oh for heaven's sake.'

Naeem watched interestedly as Nasser shoved his chair back and stalked towards the scene of the crime. His eyebrows touched his hairline when Nasser took out his wallet, overruled the woman who didn't want him to pay, firmly told the stall owner to pack up the peaches and deliver them to him, and took the woman by her elbow and propelled her to their table.

'Sit. Try not to break things. Or drop them. And if you feel the urge to throw up, turn that way,' he said pointing at Naeem. 'He hasn't had the pleasure yet.'

The woman looked almost as cross as Nasser. Crosser. 'You shouldn't have paid him. Now he'll make a career out of extorting tourists.'

'I don't think he has that many tourists who walk into his fruit,' Nasser said dryly.

'You should have let me finish bargaining with him. What kind of mug pays 200 euros?'

'The kind who thinks he's helping you out of an unpleasant situation. And you're most welcome.' Nasser hadn't expected Sitara to fall at his feet in gratitude but he'd thought a thank you would be forthcoming.

'I'm not some helpless female who needs mighty man to step in and smooth her way. I could have handled it.' Sitara told him.

Naeem took pity on his brother. 'Damsels in distress aren't what they used to be,' he said.

Two pairs of furious eyes turned on him. One nose wrinkled in distaste.

'Phew. What's that smell?' Sitara said.

Nasser laughed. 'Meet my brother. Naeem, this is Sitara Gopalasundaram. Remember her last name, or she'll accuse you of being an idiot who can't speak words with more than two syllables.'

Sitara looked down her nose at him. 'I won't have to accuse you. You would be an idiot.'

'Nice to meet you Sitara,' Naeem spoke before things could escalate. 'And just to clarify the issue, I'm not anti-baths, but Nasser caught me before I could get one.'

Sitara gave him a rueful smile. 'Forgive me if I don't say much. I've got a few feet taking up an awful lot of space in my mouth.'

Naeem laughed. 'Swill them down with some coffee then. What do you want? Order the best. Nasser's paying.'

Sitara pokered up at the words. She turned to Nasser and said stiffly, 'I'll pay you back, of course.'

'I don't want to be paid back,' Nasser snapped.

'That's too bad. I'm still paying you back.' It was a bad time for the contents of her wallet to flash through her mind. She bit her lip. 'I'm not carrying the money on me right now, but I'll find an ATM.' She made a motion to rise.

Nasser grabbed her hand and thunked her back. 'For the last time, you are not paying me. Read my lips. I am not taking money from you. Now, do you want an espresso?'

Sitara looked at him mutinously.

Nasser glared at her, willing her to bring up money again.

Naeem watched, fascinated.

'Can I look at the menu or will you also tell me what coffee to drink?' Sitara asked bloody-mindedly.

Nasser wondered whether wringing her neck would be considered justifiable homicide.

Sitara finally looked up from the menu. There hadn't been much choice. 'I'll have an espresso,' she said.

'Sorry, what did you say? I didn't catch that,' Nasser said.

Sitara wondered whether braining him with a chair would be considered justifiable homicide.

'He used to use that tone when we were younger too,' Naeem told Sitara. 'It usually led to a split lip.'

'Really?' Sitara was insensibly cheered by the thought.

'All the time,' Naeem affirmed.

'Keep your imagination within bounds,' Nasser interjected. 'You could barely fight. I beat you all the time.'

'Aren't you the older brother? You should be ashamed of hitting somebody younger than you.'

There was the slightest pause before Naeem spoke. 'An espresso? Something else? I highly recommend the sweet roll. I find a good fight always does wonders for the appetite.'

Sitara acquiesced to a sweet roll and sat back while Naeem ordered. She looked between the two and wondered at the contrast. Nasser with his movie-star looks was hot but despite the hair and the scruffiness, and the smell, Naeem was equally attractive. She frowned – no mention of a brother had come up in all those interviews and background searches she had waded through. And why had she assumed that Naeem was younger? Not that either of them had denied or confirmed it.

'How've you managed to hide your brother all these years? I didn't see a single mention of him in any interview,' Sitara asked Nasser. 'Or are you a cousin?'

'Sadly, he's my own,' Nasser replied. 'And you haven't read anything about him because I haven't spoken about him. None of us talk much about the black sheep in the family.' He shot an amused look at Naeem.

'Oh. Well. Erm.' Sitara was dying to ask questions but politeness kept her quiet.

A minute tilt of the head acknowledged Naeem's appreciation of Nasser's master stroke.

'So from an early comment, I gather you've thrown up on Nasser?' Naeem continued smoothly.

'Don't think I'm embarrassed by it. In fact, after today, I'm glad I did,' Sitara told him Naeem. 'He deserved it. He was being a...a...'

'Prick,' Nasser supplied helpfully.

'Yes, prick, because I did a brilliant interview,' Sitara said.

'You know, that is true. And you wrote it very well too. Anjali mailed it to me yesterday. Not many people can tell the world how strange and debauched I am while making it sound funny.'

'Err,' Sitara was discomposed. It wasn't often she came face to face with people she had dissed. Subtly, but dissed nonetheless. She slid a look at him. He didn't seem too upset. He was always doing that – being nice when she didn't expect it. Like putting her to bed. She ducked her head and willed her blush away.

'So we're even now,' Nasser continued. 'I took you to the awards–'

'You took her to an awards ceremony,' Naeem broke in, sounding genuinely shocked.

'I have to get my thrills somewhere,' Nasser replied.

'I can understand the throwing up. Brilliant. A reporter who can throw up on command,' Naeem said.

'Arts editor,' Sitara thought she sounded normal. 'And I only throw up when I get drunk.'

'Arts editor? Sounds serious. For whom?' He didn't wait for her to answer as another thought struck him. 'And you got drunk at the awards? Do they pass the booze around these days?'

'No, they don't,' Nasser replied for her. 'She got drunk at the after-party.'

'I'm quite capable of answering questions,' Sitara said coolly. 'I got drunk at the after-party,' she said. 'And I work for *Homme* India.'

'You took her to the after-party too?' Naeem looked half-shocked, half-awed at his brother's gall.

'Yes, and he handed me over to this gasbag and disappeared.' Sitara still hadn't recovered from that episode.

'Gasbag?' Naeem raised an eyebrow. 'Could she mean Aman Sinha?'

'How do you know?' Nasser asked, diverted.

'Amma...met him.'

'Oh yeah, she met him at *that* party.' He'd had his ears blistered for not rescuing her sooner.

'And then he saw her at the hotel and renewed his acquaintance,' Naeem said.

'Really? How come I didn't hear about that?'

'You were shooting somewhere without a signal. I heard rather a lot about it.'

Nasser laughed. Aman was funny when he happened to other people.

'So you haven't met him?' Sitara asked Naeem.

'I haven't had that particular pleasure... Somewhere in my youth or childhood I must have done something good,' he sang softly.

Sitara gave in to her laughter. The waiter arrived

with the coffees and rolls. When he left, Nasser turned to Sitara. 'So, what are you doing here?'

'Stalking you, of course,' she said limpidly.

Nasser looked at her levelly.

'Falling over herself to get to you,' Naeem added, a thread of laughter in his voice. He earned himself glares from both his table mates for his efforts.

'It's an official trip,' Sitara said. She explained about the food and wine familiarization trip for media.

'This falls under the arts?' Naeem asked curiously.

'No,' Sitara said flatly. 'This falls under m–' she remembered just in time that Debashish was a friend of Nasser's and changed it to '–a perk,' she finished rather lamely.

'Come on, what were you really going to say?' Naeem asked. 'I don't know anybody at your office, and you can just ignore him,' he said nodding at his brother. 'Go on.'

'It's my boss's idea of a reward for doing a good cover story,' Sitara said, hoping the explanation would get him off her back. She looked at Nasser to see how he'd received the news and found him looking at her far too perceptively. She quickly shifted her gaze to Naeem.

'Nasser's?' he asked. 'The cover story that you did well?'

'Yes.' Sitara replied, taking a sip of her coffee. 'Why did you say espresso?' the words spilled out involuntarily.

Both brothers looked at her strangely. Nasser raised an eyebrow.

'I mean, most people order a cappuccino. Why did you think I'd order an espresso?' Sitara elaborated, knowing she was asking to be slapped down. They were in Italy, after all. It was a figure of speech.

'Your many-syllabled surname was a clue,' Nasser replied dryly. 'And you didn't seem the type to care about softening things up with milk and sugar.'

'Oh,' Sitara said, trying to sound like it explained everything, while also trying to figure out whether he had just insulted her or complimented her. He definitely seemed to have spent some time thinking about it, about her. Whoa, she had to stop that. Get serious, Sitara! She warned herself.

'Are the rest of your journalist friends here, too?' Nasser didn't give her much time to think. He looked around reflexively at the thought. He didn't want his holiday disturbed by a bunch of Indian journalists. Especially not when he was with Naeem. And Sitara. The woman he was supposed to be having an affair with, he remembered belatedly.

'At a food market?' Sitara sneered. 'Don't be absurd. They're more likely to be soaking in the local flavour of the Golden Arches. I'm flying solo. Though I've got to head back up shortly for a cooking lesson. Learning from a Michelin-starred chef,' she added, unable to resist the temptation to show off.

Michelin-starred chef. Head back up. Cooking lesson. Things were sounding horribly familiar. 'Head back up?' Nasser's tone was ultra-casual.

'Yes, I'm staying at Fiesole. Do you know it? It's not far from here. We're staying at this posh hotel there. I keep forgetting its name. Hang on, I think I have my itinerary with me...' There was a lot of fumbling in the bag, some of its contents necessarily had to be kept on the table, and finally... 'Here it is. Okay, where am I staying... Yup, it's a place called Villa Brunacello.'

'Isn't that where you're staying?' Naeem asked Nasser with an expression of extreme innocence.

'Not any more,' Nasser was glad he could say that truthfully.

'But you're close by, no? That's what Abba's mail said. Rented your own cottage, I believe.'

Nasser had no choice but to nod.

'Excellent!' Naeem turned to Sitara. 'We'll give you a ride up–' He smiled sweetly at Nasser '–since I'm accepting my brother's invitation to host me.'

7

An open-topped car, the wind in your hair, the sun on your back, and a view of Florence straight out of Merchant–Ivory on either side – it was hard to feel anything but alive.

Even if you were driving two people who were more irritating than anyone had the right to be.

Nasser shot a glance at the woman at his side – he had flatly refused to have Naeem smelling up the seat next to him – and found her, eyes closed, face turned up, almost greedily, to the sun. An uncomfortable, unwanted flare of attraction did a quick skitter down his spine. He quashed it immediately, concentrating on overtaking a tourist bus ahead of him.

The silence in the car stretched on. Nasser's brow creased into an unconscious scowl. Surely – after not letting anybody get a word in edgeways, and manoeuvring them into this uncomfortable situation – the least his brother could do was gab on during the drive. But no, he seemed to have fallen into a brood. His head might be turned towards the scenery but Nasser would bet that he wasn't seeing anything.

'So–'

'So–'

Nasser and Sitara laughed.

'Ladies first,' Nasser gallantly told Sitara.

'No, no. You go on.' Sitara was equally accommodating.

Since Nasser had been about to make a comment about the weather it was with complete truth that he could say 'it was nothing important.'

'I was just going to ask you whether you'd been enjoying weather like this for a while,' Sitara said reluctantly.

Nasser controlled an impulse to laugh. 'Yes, it's been rather glorious. I believe such a long spell is unusual at this time of year,' he felt obliged to add.

'Yes, it's almost too good to be true,' Sitara said stiltedly.

'It is, isn't it?' Nasser agreed. 'Though Mumbai's not bad at this time of year either.'

'Still raining a little, though.'

'Yes, it's good to be away.'

'God, yes,' Sitara agreed. 'Especially given that–' she came to an abrupt halt. Was she just about to blurt the news of their roaring affair?

'Yes?'

'–how humid it is,' Sitara recovered quickly.

This was ridiculous, Nasser thought. Surely two reasonably intelligent adults could come up with something better.

'So–'

'So–'

Nasser and Sitara laughed nervously, again.

A noise faintly reminiscent of steam kettle going off emerged from the backseat. Naeem was with them again. Nasser shot him a grateful glance.

Too soon as it turned out.

'Please spare me,' Naeem entreated. 'I'm used to conversations of a slightly higher intellectual level.'

'Can't expect smarts from Bollywood,' Nasser drawled, stung. 'Don't you know we're all brawn and no brains?'

'No need to get defensive, bro,' Naeem sounded amused. 'It was just a comment–'

'To tell us what a sub-par conversation we are having. Sorry, my quark theory's on vacation. Just like me, in fact.' He resisted the temptation to honk at the passenger coach in front. 'The vacation you're crashing.' Nasser knew he was overreacting but could do nothing to stop it.

'Oh come on, relax,' Naeem said, but there was an edge to his voice. 'You were having a retarded conversation about the weather. Given that the two of you are having a flaming affair, I was only going to say it smacked of a certain lack of intimacy.'

'We are not having an affair!' Sitara exclaimed.

'Retarded,' Nasser could feel an unaccustomed pressure at the top of his head. 'So glad to know what you think, O Great Mind.'

'Why are you blowing this up into this big a deal?' Temper was evident in Naeem's voice. 'I was just being smart–'

'And there's that word again,' Nasser cut in. 'Is it a coincidence that it keeps popping up? Or does it mean you can't control how superior you feel?'

'While you're displaying a classic inferiority complex,' Naeem shot back.

'Uh, excuse me–' Sitara tried and failed to be heard.

'Inferiority complex? Of course! I'm sure everybody you meet has an inferiority complex. How else can you continue to be so superior?' Nasser narrowly overtook a car on the road, ignoring the gasp from the passenger seat.

'Look, we all know what this is about. There's no need to drive like a maniac and scare Sitara,' Naeem controlled his temper.

'Oh so reasonable, so caring, and smart too,' Nasser gibed. 'A superior human being all around.'

'Fine,' Naeem sounded fed up. 'You want to hash it out–'

'Oh yes–'

'–your problem is that you're jealous.'

'Jealous! You don't–'

'Oh yes. Because of the physics–'

'Oh my god!' Nasser exploded. 'Get over yourself!'

Naeem raised his voice. 'But you're the one–'

'You have no idea–' Nasser yelled.

'–who acted like a petulant child–' Naeem met yell with yell.

Sitara covered her ears and fixed a dread-filled gaze on the road.

'–your psycho babble–'

'–and I'm sick of it–'

'–patronizing me–'

'–selfish, whiny, child–'

'Can you stop the car if you want to fight?' Sitara interjected without much hope of being heard.

Nasser came to a screeching halt on the shoulder and jumped out. He stood outside the passenger door. 'Get out,' he commanded Naeem.

'This is not what I–' Sitara could have been speaking to herself for all the attention she received.

'You want to fight?' Naeem said. 'Fine. Let's brawl in front of the reporter.'

'Arts editor,' Sitara corrected automatically. 'What do you mean brawl?'

'No brawl,' Nasser denied. 'I'm going to beat you to pulp, is all.'

'You can't fight–'

Naeem ignored her. 'It'll be fun to watch you try.'

'I'll do more than try. But you'll have to get out first.'

'Stop it right now!' Sitara made a grab for Naeem before he could follow his brother's instructions. She looked around the road wildly. Where had all the other cars disappeared to?

He shook her off effortlessly, and swung out of the car. He raised his fists. 'C'mon bro,' he taunted, 'I'll try not to spoil your movie star face too much.'

Sitara scrambled out of the car inelegantly and put herself in front of Nasser. 'Stop it right now. I'm not going to let you two fight.'

Nasser didn't bother to reply. He picked her up and deposited her out of the way. In a silent rush, he tackled Naeem to the ground. They hit the dirt with a satisfying thunk and rolled about in a flurry of arms and legs, each trying to get enough leverage for a solid hit. Nasser managed a couple of glancing blows, then sucked in his breath sharply as Naeem got in a couple of his own. He was vaguely aware of Sitara yelling in the background. She was going to get the cops on them, he thought muzzily, and was glad when she fell silent.

Something small and hard and cold hit him. It was followed by a trickling down his back. His lack of concentration earned him a blow that rocked his head back.

'What the–' he heard Naeem exclaim. 'Hey!'

Something wet and pulpy hit him in the vicinity of his ear. Another hit him square in the face. He felt a trickle near his mouth. He tasted it tentatively. What the – He rolled away from Naeem and got to his feet.

'Are you done fighting?' Sitara asked in a deadly voice, looking from him to Naeem who was also struggling to his feet. She held a peach in her hand. The crate of peaches lay open with conspicuous gaps in the top row.

Naeem raised his hands in a gesture of surrender.

'You?' she gave Nasser a laser-like look.

Far from it, Nasser thought. He shot a look at Naeem. A small sound was the only warning he received before a peach smashed open against his cheekbone. Even before his 'ow' had faded, another hit the exact same spot. Who would have thought a peach could hurt that much? 'I surrender, I surrender.' A peach hit his chest. 'I surrendered,' he yelled, 'didn't you hear?'

'Just making sure,' Sitara said coldly.

There was a choking sound from Naeem. She turned to him, arm raised. 'Pax, pax!' he said hurriedly. 'It was just admiration for your arm. Where did you learn to throw like that? You've got great aim.'

'For a girl you mean?' There was a dangerous edge to Sitara's voice. Her arm trembled.

'Of course not,' Naeem denied roundly. 'I'm not sexist. Unlike others I know.' He looked at his brother significantly.

Sitara narrowed her eyes at Nasser. The hand shifted direction. 'He's just stirring up trouble,' Nasser said. 'Which is just about what you would expect from–'

'Stop it,' Sitara commanded. 'I don't care what problems the two of you have. I don't want to hear about them. I just want to get to my hotel but since I'm stuck with you,' – bitter look – 'you will both behave like civilized human beings. Now, shake hands.'

Two outraged denials rent the air.

'And apologize to each other,' she continued, hardily. 'Now!'

Neither brother made the slightest effort to move.

'I'm counting till three,' Sitara said. 'There are a lot of peaches in this crate. One. Two. Thr– '

'Okay, okay,' Naeem said. 'But I'm not going to make the first move.'

'I'm not either.' Nasser folded his arms across his chest. They came up against something sticky. Ugh. He unfolded them quickly.

'How old are you?' Sitara asked. Both men looked at her mutinously. 'Fine. I'll count from three. Both of you can walk together. Three, two, one, go.'

She watched as the two men took reluctant steps towards each other and even more reluctantly shook hands. 'Say you're sorry. Nasser, you first.'

'He started it,' Nasser protested.

'I don't care. Just say it.'

'I'm sorry,' Nasser muttered, looking at his brother's ear.

'You too, Naeem,' Sitara commanded.

'I'm sorry,' Naeem's voice trembled.

Nasser cast him a swift look before returning his focus to the ear. But it was too late. He'd seen the laughter brimming in his brother's eyes. The chuckles started off silently enough but soon they were laughing so hard they had to hold on to each other for support.

'It's not that funny,' Sitara said, which seemed to set them off some more. 'Men!' she muttered. She slumped back against the car. Now that it was all over, she was feeling a bit shaky; her hands were cold. Shock, she supposed. Sugar, she thought vaguely. She should eat something sweet. She took a bite out of the peach.

Nasser, who had regained his composure somewhat, caught sight of her and doubled over with laughter again. He poked at Naeem to direct his attention. It took a while for Naeem to catch on since Nasser was unable to say anything.

'You paid for it,' Naeem gasped. 'I can't take it. Stop her.'

Sitara finished with the peach, groped around for a tissue in her bag, wrapped the pip in it and deposited it neatly on the dashboard. Feeling better, she gave them a measuring look, and must have been convinced about their harmlessness, because she climbed back into the car and sat down.

'If you're done wasting time, I have class to attend,' she threw back at them. 'You can pack the peaches and we can move on.'

Attractive, angry and angst-ridden. Bold, beautiful and brooding. Cute, complex and...

Sitara paused in the middle of chopping up tomatoes and tried to think of something alliterative with 'C' that also described The Brothers Khan. Sometime in the past hour, between getting out of a rather peach-perfumed car and starting her culinary class, they had become the lead characters in a soap opera she couldn't wait to get her next fix of. They were a perfect fit. The estranged brothers meeting after years, good-looking, tormented, unhappy, the reasons of their separation shrouded in mystery...Ekta Kapoor couldn't have done better. In fact, maybe she should make that Kute, Komplex and...

Somebody poked her. Sitara looked up to realize the chef had been talking to her. 'Uh sorry, my mind was wandering...' she muttered, and tried to listen to what the chef was saying.

Komplicated! Ah ha. She had it.

D was easy – dashing, difficult, dodgy – but it was with E that trouble started. First there was some spoon dropping. Then right about the time she rejected Eerie and Eager, she misjudged the distance between a dish and the table, and in rapid succession her elbow hit a jug that took down a couple of glasses, she lost her grip on the plate of bruschettas she had made, causing them to rain down on the heads of the reluctant walker and the female half of the couple, and then she backed into the trade mag man who had bent down to cut some herbs causing him to slice open his finger.

There was calm after the storm in which the complete extent of her damage was borne upon Sitara.

Where do I begin? Sitara thought. Horrified at her irreverence, she turned to the man with the bleeding finger. 'I am so sorry.' Sitara said, moving to help him staunch the blood.

'You...stay away from me,' the man howled, shrinking away from her, protectively holding his finger to his chest. Another victim shot her a look of loathing and moved to console him while the female half of the couple bowed her head for her husband to remove the tomato from her hair. The rest of the group closed around them protectively.

Sitara tried to say that it had all been an accident but the words stuck in her throat as the full glory of her absent-mindedness struck her. The kitchen looked like it had been hit by a tornado. She looked at Chef Sebastian, and found her distress quite eclipsed. The man had gone from suave to shattered, and was staring at the ruins of his kitchen uncomprehendingly.

There was some quiet whispering in one corner and their guide Luca materialized next to her, gently but firmly leading her out of the kitchen.

'It is okay, it is...how to say...not big thing,' he lied soothingly, wondering how on earth was he going to square this with the hotel. He had no doubt that the fallout would be fierce. A sound drew his attention back to his charge and the whiteness of her face. He sighed inwardly and drew her out towards the terrace. He'd better tend to her first; he'd know soon enough how bad the rest of his problems were.

They were worse than he could have imagined. Her group had refused to go further with her. No amount of cajoling or threatening or appeals to their professionalism had moved them. If she was part of the rest of their itinerary, they weren't going to be.

The hotel had been easier. If you discounted the fact that the chef refused to serve her food – the manager had assured Luca she would be able to get him out of that snit by tomorrow. Most likely. He didn't have the budget to hire another guide especially for her, and he could not make a separate itinerary for her. He'd been at his wit's end till one of the staff had told him the lady seemed to have a couple of friends staying close by. Maybe they could be persuaded to see the sights with her.

He sure hoped so. Luca said a prayer and rang the bell.

'Who was that?' Nasser asked his brother, as he lightly tossed the salad they were having for lunch.

In an unspoken agreement, they were pretending their earlier fight had never happened, despite sundry bruises that were blooming into existence on their countenances. They had reverted to the scrupulous politeness of the past few years. Nasser was playing host, and Naeem had a good line in playing the perfect guest.

It was excruciating.

Thankfully, Sitara's handiwork with the peaches had given them the perfect excuse for time off from each other. Nasser had quickly taken himself off to the kitchen on the pretext of making lunch and almost enthusiastically told Naeem not to bother with helping, and to just explore the place and relax.

The good thing about a smart brother was that he got hints. He had returned only a short while earlier. He'd gone into the kitchen to the sound of the doorbell ringing and had volunteered to answer the door.

'A tour guide named Luca.' Naeem propped himself against a counter and watched his brother set the table. 'Do you want me to do anything?'

'It's fine. I've got it.' Nasser placed two wine glasses on table and reached for the wine rack to pick out a bottle. He hesitated. 'Do you still drink?'

'Yes. I think so. But don't pour me too much.'

'You needn't if you don't want to,' Nasser said, pouring himself a full glass and his brother a thimbleful. He gestured for Naeem to take a seat.

'I know. One of the first things I learnt. And not so little. I want more than a sip,' Naeem said with an edge in his voice that he couldn't quite suppress.

Nasser gave his brother a narrow look. There was a charged silence as the brothers contemplated another bout of fighting.

'Lunch looks absolutely great,' Naeem said conciliatorily. 'All the food groups too. Salad and pasta and meat. Nobody would ever guess you didn't know how to boil water till a month ago.'

Nasser acknowledged the compliment with a nod, and passed the salad to Naeem. 'So what did he want?'

'Who?' There was some complicated juggling as dishes were passed around and things were served.

'The tour guide. What was he doing here anyway?' Nasser said impatiently. He took a longish sip of his wine. He needed all the help he could get.

'Oh, he's yo...' Naeem caught himself, 'Sitara's tour guide.' He forked up the salad gingerly. 'I've never been much of a veg... Oh! This is good.'

'No need to come up with excuses about how you're

not much of an Italian food person then?' Nasser said. A moment's thought and he add, 'It's a jo..'

'Please. I'm not that far gone. And I still have some allergies up my sleeve for the pasta and meat.'

Nasser relaxed. 'That's fine then. So what was Sitara's tour guide doing here? Wants to give us a tour?'

'Sort of.'

'Really?' Nasser's paused, fork suspended en route to his mouth.

'Yes. With Sitara.' Naeem polished off the last rocket leaf and reached for the meat. 'What's this called?'

'Not pork,' Nasser put his fork back down on the plate. 'Explain your cryptic little answer.'

'Beef?' Naeem made no move to serve himself. 'I'm really not into exotic meats. Or cuts.'

'Lamb. Concentrate. Explain.'

'That's fine then.'

Nasser watched impatiently as his brother took his own sweet time carving out a portion. 'You can talk *and* cut, you know.'

'I'm not good at multitasking,' Naeem replied, undisturbed. 'All done, anyway. So, Sitara. Remember that cooking lesson she was talking about, it seems she had a bit of an accident during it.' He looked at his brother expectantly.

Nasser raised an eyebrow.

'And she's fine, since you ask,' Naeem huffed.

'We're not having an affair. I hardly know the woman.' It was Nasser's turn to be exasperated. 'And can you please finish this story sometime today?'

'Whatever you say. Thousands wouldn't believe you,' Naeem shrugged, 'neither do I, but let's continue. So it turns out she wrecked the kitchen–'

'Sebastian's?' Nasser exclaimed.

'–and injured quite a few people in the group. Blood flowed freely, I am told.'

'In Sebastian's kitchen?' Nasser listened in horrified fascination.

'And now the group doesn't want anything to do with her.'

'And Sebastian?'

'The chef is refusing to serve her food, I believe. I gathered there'd been something of a tantrum.'

'Something!' Nasser breathed. 'That man throws things on good days.'

'He threw things at you?' Naeem asked, interested.

'His aim's bad.' Nasser had a memory of a bread roll sailing past. 'But what's that got to do with us? Why was the tour guide here?'

'Asking whether we would like to spend the next two days with Sitara and go to all the places on her itinerary – he gave us different times so we wouldn't run into the rest of the group.'

Nasser had lost interest and returned to his food. 'What did he say when you said no?' He forked up some pasta.

'Nothing. I didn't say no. Take a sip of your wine. It'll help with the choking,' Naeem instructed kindly. Nasser shot him a furious look, but followed instructions. Naeem continued, 'We're meeting her in another hour. There's a lovely vineyard that we have to see.'

'*We* are not seeing any vineyard,' Nasser said through his teeth. '*You* can do what the hell you want. Don't involve me.'

'It will be fun,' Naeem soothed. 'And you have to drive the car. Just think, you'd have to show me around–'

'I would?'

'–and now there's a third person who can be our excuse for not talking to each other. It's a great idea.'

Nasser looked at him, trapped. It made sense, in a warped kind of a way.

'Is that really why you agreed?'

'Of course. Did you think I would do it because it would annoy you?'

'Yeah.'

'Well, that would also be right. But of secondary consideration.'

Something vibrated against his leg and Nasser smiled for the first time all day. He answered the phone, 'Hello. Can you hear me? Here, speak to Naeem,' and thrust it into his brother's hands.

'Who? What? Hello? Abba. Shit. No, no, I didn't say that. I mean not to you.'

Good. Let Abba grill him. He deserved it. Nasser turned his attention back to his food, satisfied.

A suspiciously red-eyed and red-nosed Sitara met them in the driveway an hour later. Her eyes slid away from Nasser's searching stare and landed on the empty passenger seat in front. She pointedly shifted her gaze to Naeem.

'I'm a creature of habit. I get attached to seats on public transport too,' he answered her unspoken question. He said it easily enough, but Sitara could feel the tension radiating from the car.

'Annoying habits,' Nasser said. There was an edge to his voice when he spoke to Sitara. 'Are you going to get in the car anytime soon?'

'Look, I don't know what Luca told you,' Sitara began, her voice subdued. 'But you don't need to do this. I can go on my own...'

'Yeah, the way you did this morning. Sure. Now can you get in the car, since we've taken the trouble to come here and pick you up?'

Sitara drew herself up. 'I was doing fine. You–'

'Just get in the bloody car, will you?' Nasser exploded. 'I'm not going to stay here and argue with you just because you want to be all polite.'

'Don't yell at me,' Sitara's snapped back, recovering some of her old spark. 'I don't know why you're in a bad mood but don't take it out on me.'

Nasser gave her a long look. 'That's better. Guilty is not your best look.'

Sitara took a moment to digest that. 'You were deliberately provoking me?'

Nasser shrugged. 'It sort of kills the atmosphere. *And* I did want to know if you were getting into the car anytime soon. Which was a good question since you're still standing outside it.'

'You're a jerk!' Sitara pulled the car door open and dropped into the seat. 'But that was nice of you.'

'I was just going to say that,' said a voice from the backseat. His comment earned him a warning look in the rear-view mirror from Nasser. 'But I won't,' Naeem continued. 'Because Sitara has a much more interesting story to share, something to do with an accident in the kitchen.'

'Do the two of you have any friends?' Sitara jibed, but there was no tension in the car any longer. 'It doesn't seem likely.'

'Friends are overrated,' Nasser said, picking up speed now that he was out of the hotel's driveway.

'But then you wouldn't be here with your brother and this fair maiden on a warm autumn afternoon,' Naeem said.

'Exactly my point.'

Sitara huffed out a laugh then joined in with a few insults of her own.

Two pairs of eyes watched Naeem expectantly as he sniffed and swirled and finally sipped the wine. Naeem closed his eyes. 'Hmm.'

'Hmm? What's hmm?' Sitara demanded, incensed.

Right after they had arrived at the vineyard, Naeem had commented that he'd like to be able to discuss wine. From under the vines, down to the cellar, and up to the tasting room, Nasser and Sitara had given Naeem the benefit of their combined wine tasting knowledge – their guide from the vineyard had got in a few words whenever they paused for breath – and to receive a 'hmm' at the end of it was a bit much.

'Hmm is it tastes...sort of...'

'Yes?' Nasser, Sitara and the guide leaned forward.

'...winey,' Naeem finished.

The insults followed thick and fast. Their guide muttered a few things under his breath too.

'Okay, okay. Let's retire this wine thing,' Naeem held up his hands to stop the flow. 'My Muslim guilt is giving me hell for drinking. I'm going back to being a teetotaller.'

'That might be a good idea, signor,' their guide agreed, his voice expressionless.

'Thanks,' Naeem said undisturbed. 'But I know a couple of people who would love the wine. Can you pack me a couple?'

'Certainly,' the guide said. 'Please follow me.'

Sitara watched Naeem head to the cash counter, unconsciously still shaking her head.

'All that time wasted,' Nasser said disgustedly, drawing her attention back to him. 'If only his guilt had kicked in half-an-hour ago. I mean, winey! I don't think a lesson's ever fallen so flat!

Sitara couldn't help laughing at his expression. 'I have to say that was one comment I wasn't expecting.'

'Yes! Can you imagine if that poor guide got winey after every class? He would be ready to cut his throat.'

'Well, he looks a little less suicidal now that Naeem's buying some,' Sitara commented. 'Aren't you getting any?'

'I wouldn't be able to drink it without thinking "winey".'

'Aww, poor baby. Life's so unfair,' Sitara grinned.

'Don't make fun of me, woman. Or I'll abandon you without dinner.'

'Oh, please, no,' Sitara pleaded, taking hold of his hand. 'You can't be so cruel.'

Nasser caught her arms and tugged her in front of him. 'I'll consider it. But only after you've paid for your crime,' he growled in his best evil voice.

'Oh no, what do you have in mind?' Sitara said. She hoped he would put the huskiness in her voice down to the play-acting.

Nasser tugged her closer. 'I think you know,' his voice had dropped.

Sitara found herself transfixed by his lips. And was it her imagination or were they coming closer...

'Break it up you two,' Naeem said sternly, causing them to jump apart guiltily. 'I'm very sensitive to public displays of affection. Here's some wine for you. I'm sure you don't want to forget this vineyard.'

'Are we still going to the restaurant that Luca recommended?' Naeem asked once they were back in the car. 'Because he suggested that place would cheer Sitara up. Something about ogling Italian hunks. Obviously, she doesn't need them now,' he said meaningfully.

'Wow. You waited five whole minutes to bring that up. A new world record,' Nasser said. 'God, I'd forgotten what a pain you were.'

'All the good memories coming back. Excellent. My plan is working,' Naeem said, deliberately. And waited for a reaction from his brother.

Sitara turned her face back from where she had been blushing out the window and shot them both a quick look. Whatever she saw in Nasser's face had her concentrating on the road ahead.

'I'm guessing Abba told you where I was,' Nasser said finally. 'How many emails did he send you?'

'Eight. Ten, maybe.'

'But you couldn't have known I was going to be in Florence yesterday morning,' Nasser shook his head. 'That's pushing it.'

'I got lucky. I was going to take a bus up to Fiesole later.'

'Okay.' So Naeem had deliberately sought him out. He'd have to think about that. Later. A sudden thought struck him. 'Did you know I was going to be in Florence too?' he asked Sitara.

'What?' It took Sitara a moment to understand the implication. 'Of course! Don't you know I'm stalking you? That's what us crazy fans do.'

Did he really think that of her? Sitara wondered. Was she just another crazy fan to him? She'd thought they were getting to be friends. And more. Could her radar be so wrong? Damn it. All the fun just drained out of the evening.

'Brrr.' Naeem met a furious glance from Sitara. 'Nothing, nothing. Just ignore me.'

'You can drop the ice. I believe you,' Nasser said.

'I am so relieved,' Sitara exclaimed. 'Life is all sunshine and roses now. I want to go back to the hotel. Can you drop me back?'

'No,' Nasser said. 'I'm hungry. I'm driving. We're going to the restaurant.'

'Fine,' Sitara snapped. 'I'll just–'

'–walk it,' Nasser completed. 'Good idea. You can start from the restaurant.'

'You're an...'

'You wound me,' Nasser said, sounding anything but. 'And you did say you got this assignment out of turn. I was supposed to be staying at the same hotel till the end of this week, you know,' he mused, returning to their earlier discussion. 'It's a bit of a coincidence that you get this trip and land up at the same hotel with a bunch of journalists right after rumours that we are having an affair.'

'Hey!' Naeem protested. 'I thought we weren't talking about that. I've been cramping my style for nothing.'

Nasser ignored him, so did Sitara.

'Don't you think you're getting a little paranoid?' she suggested. 'Coincidences happen. That's why, you know, they're called coincidences.' But she had a sinking feeling that he was right. It was exactly the sort of thing that Debashish would do. But how could he have known?

'I do think it's a coincidence, but only the bit where your office got invited for the trip. You coming for it – sorry, too much to believe. Is this the place?' he asked Naeem.

It looked alike a nondescript shop front, glass windows curtained. There didn't seem to be too many people in it.

'The name is the same,' Naeem said doubtfully.

None of them made a move towards it.

'I think you'll just have to face it,' Naeem told Sitara. 'Luca was lying to you. This place isn't crawling with Italian hunks.'

'You think.' Sitara took a deep breath. 'Okay, let's go eat. We can come up with more conspiracy theories to pass the time.'

'I thought you were going to walk back to the hotel.' Nasser reminded her. He grabbed her arm as she turned to leave and pushed her toward the door.

'Get your hands off me!' Sitara tried to wrest herself free, but he was too strong.

'Nope. And it's not a conspiracy theory if it's true.' Nasser opened the door and shoved her in.

'How sweet. Any excuse to touch you,' Naeem murmured from behind, then had to jump back when Nasser let go of the door so it swung in his face.

'Does your editor know Richa?' Nasser asked Sitara, casting a look around the dimly lit room. There wasn't a single other soul there.

Sitara folded her arms across her chest and stared at the wall.

'Because I can believe Richa would figure out where I was staying. That woman's a whiz at intelligence.'

'I think you've lost your audience,' Naeem said sotto voce as Sitara continued to stare ahead unresponsively.

A woman materialized from a narrow corridor off the side and gestured for them to follow. Nasser moved to take Sitara's arm again, but she shook it off disdainfully and marched ahead. Nasser shrugged and followed, Naeem at his heels. The sound of noise and laughter grew louder with each step and Nasser looked around curiously. The corridor opened onto a big glass conservatory that had been converted into a warmly lit restaurant. And a popular one; every table seemed to be filled. The woman with them seemed to magically conjure up some space and an empty table where she left them.

'Well, let the dinner begin,' Naeem said, as he dropped into a chair. 'Are you going to stand there all night?'

8

She could have dinner, Sitara decided. She could also ignore creeps. She could do it very well.

'Don't you think you're being a little childish?' Nasser asked, over starters.

'This veal is really good,' Sitara commented to Naeem. 'How's yours?'

'It's artichoke. How good can it be?'

'Why did you order it then?'

'I like to see whether anybody can make it into something decent.'

'Are you going to keep this up all evening?' Nasser asked.

Naeem looked from one to the other and rose. 'I'll be back soon.'

'Where are you going?' Sitara asked in alarm.

'The bathroom, I assume, since he's given up drinking. Do you want to go with him, too?' Nasser asked.

Sitara gave him her best bored look and concentrated her attention back on her food.

'It's hard to believe this is the same person who was throwing peaches at me this morning.' Nasser lounged back in his chair and watched her. 'What sore spot did I hit?' he mused far too perceptively.

'You didn't hit a sore spot,' Sitara shot back. 'You pissed me off.'

'You know what, I don't believe that,' Nasser said, watching her closely. 'The last time I messed with your food, you chewed me up in your interview. None of this shrinking violet stuff.'

'You want me to throw stuff at you, I'm very happy to oblige.' Sitara reached for the bread basket; only Nasser got there quicker and placed it next to him.

'Now you're just trying to distract me. Hmm,' Sitara could almost see him replaying the conversation. 'Maybe it wasn't something I said. Maybe it was something you said.'

'I don't want to talk about it,' Sitara cut him off. 'Let's just pretend everything's okay and have dinner, and we won't have to see each other again after that. There's no reason for our paths to cross once I get back to India.'

'Maybe I want them to cross,' Nasser said.

The words fell into a pool of silence.

'Have you sorted–' Naeem appeared.

'Come back in ten minutes,' Nasser said without looking up.

Sitara barely registered Naeem's departure. She was still trying to come to grips with Nasser's last sentence.

'Is this–'

'Not a joke,' Nasser cut her off. 'Why are you so insecure? Don't you think I'd want to meet you again?'

'No,' Sitara said blandly. 'You're an actor. What would you want to do with somebody like me?'

Nasser's eyes glinted wickedly. 'I could tell you – in great detail – but Naeem might come back any minute.'

Sitara could feel herself blush, but refused to back down. 'That's not what I meant. You hang out with beautiful, slim, hot women; you were engaged to one. I'm nothing like them.'

'No. You're not. But it's you I want. To get to know,' he tacked on. 'Not them.'

'You mean a two-night stand?'

'That would be good start, I think.'

Sitara could almost taste her disappointment.

'But I'm afraid I'll have to decline,' Nasser continued. 'I don't want to shock Naeem, you see. He's young, innocent – and here he is.'

'Can I eat dinner now?' Naeem asked, taking his seat. He gave the bread basket next to Nasser's chair a suspicious look. 'I need to get my beauty sleep for the early start tomorrow.'

'What early start?' Sitara and Nasser chorused.

'I met a couple of backpackers at the bar. They're going to Turkey tomorrow. It sounded like fun. I said I would come along.'

'That's very sudden,' Nasser's brows drew together.

'That's the way it is with this backpacking business,' Naeem replied easily. 'You can up sticks anytime and go anywhere. And it won't make any difference to tomorrow's plan. Nasser can still drive you.' He gestured to their waitress. 'We're ready for the main course now.' He turned back to his companions. 'Did you know this restaurant has a Michelin star?' and moved the conversation determinedly back to more general matters.

When dinner was over, Naeem excused himself saying he was meeting up with the backpackers to thrash out some details. He hugged Sitara, told Nasser he'd see him later and disappeared from their table.

Sitara watched Nasser watch Naeem's departure. Maybe he felt her gaze because he turned his head and met her eyes.

'You must think we're quite odd,' he said with a twisted smile.

'Absolutely,' Sitara agreed with him, quelling an odd urge to reach over and hug him. 'Raving mad.'

Nasser laughed. 'Yeah. That we are. Shall we go?'

Outside, the street was even more deserted than when they had arrived. Fiesole obviously went to sleep early, Sitara thought. At her side, Nasser looked abstracted. Naeem's departure, Sitara guessed.

'Want to take a walk?' Nasser broke the silence.

Would she care for a walk on a moonlit night in a romantic little town with the most attractive man she knew, one who had also expressed an interest in her? 'Yes, that's fine,' she said sedately.

They walked silently for a while. Sitara didn't mind. It felt comfortable. Actually, everything about him felt comfortable, she realized, like there had been a connection from their first meeting. She had never spoken to another interviewee the way she had with Nasser; she would never have dared to. Or got drunk on the job and whacked people.

Oh god, had she taken one look at him and fallen hard? Sitara shied away from the thought. She hadn't fallen for him, he was just like a... Thankfully, the subject of her thoughts spoke before she was forced to classify him.

'I haven't seen him in almost three years,' Nasser said, almost to himself.

Sitara didn't say anything.

'We used to be inseparable. Then...we weren't.' Nasser thrust his hands into his pockets. 'It's good to remember that we used to have fun together.' He shook his head, glancing at Sitara finally, and made an obvious effort to lighten up. 'But at least I have a whole bottle of winey to remember him by.'

Sitara laughed. 'You should have seen your face.'

'I saw yours,' he retorted.

Sitara laughed again. When she sobered, 'It will be interesting to see what he gets you from Turkey.'

Nasser's mouth twisted, 'I don't know when I'll see him after Turkey. Enough about Naeem. Tell me about yourself? Do you have any siblings?'

Sitara told him about Nithya and her sister's marriage to her college sweetheart, her niece, her parents and their Facebook habit, their mobile phone phobia. They walked on, unaware how far they had come from the restaurant. In turn, he told her about his mother's betting and his father's worrying. She told him about Maya and he told her about Shiv.

'Aren't you afraid I'll sell all these tales to the tabloids?' Sitara teased.

'I trust you,' he smiled.

Sitara stumbled; Nasser caught her hand. 'Thanks,' she disengaged it. 'You trust me even though we're supposed to be having an affair with each other and I've been giving interviews about it?'

'Tell me the juicy stuff,' Nasser said.

'You're taking it very lightly,' Sitara was suddenly mad.

He gave her a half-smile. 'You would too if you were reported to have an affair every week.'

'Yeah, I guess you don't have a reputation to bother about. And now I don't either,' she said flatly. 'Can we go back now? I'm tired.'

Nasser caught her by her shoulders and turned her to face him. 'Why, Sitara Gopalasundaram, why do you really care what the papers say? Or have I scared you with something else?'

'What's there to be scared of?' Sitara made herself meet his eyes. 'These affairs won't affect your chances of getting married.'

'Marriage? You're doing the arranged marriage thing?' His voice was sharp.

'Yes. My parents haven't given up hope despite–' Sitara caught herself, '–despite the fact I'm over the hill. Thirty.'

'Ancient. But that's not what you were going to say, is it? You can tell me,' Nasser coaxed, 'in fact, you should tell me, you know everything about me. It's only fair.'

'Fine,' Sitara said, crisply. 'I'll tell you if you tell me why you're here learning to cook.' She looked at him challengingly.

Nasser met her eyes. 'I lost a bet to Shiv. Your turn.'

'That's not fair,' Sitara protested. 'You have to tell me why.'

'We can go another round after you tell me about your "despite",' Nasser said.

'I was engaged.'

Nasser gave a bark of laughter. 'This is your deep dark secret. And you were hiding it from me? Why'd did he break it off?'

'What makes you think he broke it off?' Sitara demanded.

'Because you would have an excellent reason if you'd done it. And you wouldn't be shy about telling it. Come on, tell me.'

'Not till you tell me about the bet you lost. And we should turn back. It's getting late.'

'If you insist.' Nasser took her hand and began to walk.

He was silent for so long that Sitara thought he wasn't going to tell her about the bet. He spoke just when she was writing off the conversation. 'Shiv bet me that I had ten expressions or less in my last movie.' He smiled wryly. 'He was right; I had to pay up.' He shook his head. 'I never bet against him; my mother has trained him too well. And I've always thought I could act–'

'You can. You're good.' Sitara couldn't let that assessment go. 'Except for that last movie. You were just going through the motions in that.'

'Oh thank god, I thought you'd been taken over by aliens, saying nice things about me. Give me some notice the next time. I may not survive the shock otherwise.'

Sitara punched him in the arm. 'Shut up. And I'm serious. I think you were just bored or stale. Don't let it get to you.'

'Do you realize you're beating me up all the time? If you want to get physical, we can do it more pleasurably,' he said suggestively. 'No? Oh well, I'll try again soon. And I came to the same conclusion. Now tell me about the break-up with whatshisname.'

'Karthik. Karthik Iyer. My parents introduced us. We were engaged for three months, another two to go for the wedding. He got a job in Silicon Valley. I lost my passport that week. You know how you misplace stuff around the house. Anyway, he said he had to listen to the universe; he couldn't dismiss the signs any longer. We weren't meant to be together.'

'What a man,' Nasser said reverently. 'He got away with that? Genius! No explanations required.'

'Shut up!'

'You shut up,' he rounded on her. 'Or don't. This should be your cocktail time story, you shouldn't be hiding it. It's terrific.'

'When you tell the world you got dumped without any ostensible reason, they look for reasons in you. They make them up,' Sitara said sourly. 'They don't laugh at it.'

'They do if they have the slightest sense of humour. If they don't, you shouldn't waste your time on them.'

'Easy for you to say.'

'No, actually. I learnt it the hard way,' Nasser said, silencing her. 'Chew on that tonight. I'd better head back. I've got tall, dark and bearded waiting for me.'

Where was Naeem? Nasser did a quick tour of the villa, ascertained that this brother wasn't there, and stepped out. He wasn't surprised to find Naeem occupying his favourite spot at the picnic table, holding a mug. Nasser didn't waste any time on preliminaries. 'What was all that about? Are you really going to Turkey?'

'Yep.' Naeem seemed loath to say more.

'Why tomorrow? You could have gone next week,' Nasser demanded.

'Yes. But this way, you get to spend a day with Sitara and no third wheel.'

'Ever heard of a day trip?' Nasser said.

'Same difference,' Naeem shrugged. 'How does it matter where I go?'

'The difference is you can come back after a day trip.'

'Why? Because we get on so well?' Naeem sounded distant.

'We got on okay for the past couple of hours. And you're the one who came here to see me,' Nasser sat down opposite him.

'Yes. Because Sitara was there. And I have seen you. And it's been,' Naeem paused, searching for a word, 'nice.'

Nasser swore under his breath.

Naeem turned to face him. 'No, really. It's been nice. Nicer than anything in the past couple of years. We can do it again. Soon. But not right away. Okay?'

Nasser looked at him for a long while. 'Yeah. Okay.'

'Great.' Naeem's teeth flashed in a smile. 'Want to make me some sandwiches for my journey?'

Sitara paced up her balcony and back. She was too wired to go to sleep. Nasser's words kept echoing in her head.

Had he really meant it? Was he interested in her? Or had he just been playing her because she hadn't fallen into his lap like all the others?

Uh, yeah, an inner voice mocked. *The way you didn't fall into his arms in the wine tasting room.*

That was just physical attraction, she argued. He seemed to have been talking about something more.

And that scares the shit out of you because of what happened the last time you cared, the mocking voice continued: Karthik and the broken engagement.

Surely she couldn't still be scarred by that, Sitara thought. That was eight years ago.

So?

So indeed. Maybe she had been playing it safe. Maybe she had been determined not to be hurt again after Karthik. But surely she didn't refuse to believe that anybody she was interested in was interested back in her as well? She thought of her last two boyfriends; she certainly had not been interested in them. Oh god, maybe Maya was right. But that didn't mean anything in this situation. It wasn't some ordinary man who was interested in her. It was Nasser Khan, movie star. He could have anybody he wanted. And had, according to Mukul. Even if he was interested in her now, he would soon return to thin young heroines, and groupies.

So based on what might happen, which you don't know because you don't know him, you don't want to explore this even a teeny-weeny bit, the inner voice demanded.

Sitara flopped down on her bed and lay staring at the ceiling. It was a long time before she went to sleep.

It was a silent duo that set off for San Gimignano the next morning. Nasser had been up early to see Naeem off, and make him sandwiches, and Sitara hadn't slept much.

'Naeem went off okay?' Sitara asked. It seemed the safest topic right now.

'Yes. Except for leaving at a disgusting 6 a.m., he went off fine.' Nasser didn't mention the relationship advice Naeem provided him at 6 a.m., as if he wasn't the one who'd broken off an engagement over the phone.

'I know you like smart women,' Naeem had timed his advice with the arrival of his bus on the horizon, 'but this one's a smart woman with issues – what? I'm sensitive – and you're a film star. So either figure out whether you want her permanently in your life or spare her a whole lot of publicity if you just want an affair.'

There'd been an awkward sort of hug before he'd boarded the bus and was gone.

'Yeah, he went off fine,' Nasser repeated moodily. How was he supposed to know whether he had long-term plans for Sitara? He'd just met her twice, for heaven's sake. It seemed longer. Possibly because the two days had been so eventful. He glanced at Sitara and found she had thrown her head back and was letting the wind stream through her hair. He looked away abruptly, startled by a tightening in his gut. He turned on the radio for distraction. After a moment's consideration, he turned up the volume. He could do without conversation right now.

What was the point of flying business if the attractiveness quotient of your fellow passengers didn't go up in proportion to the leg room and cost involved? Where were all the handsome, rich, available men you could spend eight hours getting to know?

Sitara smiled weakly at the distinguished-looking older man in the seat next to her, who promptly rolled up the partition between them. Not even her fellow passenger wanted to spend time with her. Sitara sank back dispiritedly. Over the past 24 hours she had gone from surprise to disappointment to bewilderment to anger, which had seemed ready to slip into depression at any moment.

She wondered for the five hundredth time what had happened to Nasser. She had spent all of last night coming up with reasons that would have led him to behave so.

Why would the warm, flirtatious man from the night before turn into a stone? He hadn't spoken a word on the drive to San Gimignano, and once there he had treated her like his maiden aunt, politely and distantly. At their farmhouse lunch, he had been an attentive and interested guest, and asked a million questions of their hosts. He had talked so much that nobody had noticed he had barely spoken to her.

He had been silent on the drive back again. Sitara had been furious by the time they reached the hotel, unwilling to trust herself to talk, and had thanked him curtly for taking her around and walked away. To her surprise, he hadn't even said bye.

She was not going to waste one more minute on him, Sitara resolved. But even the airline was conspiring against her. They had Nasser's last movie as an option in the Bollywood section. It would be incredibly masochistic of her to watch it when there were dozens of other choices.

Three hours later she had fresh self-knowledge. Not only was she a masochist, but she also had decidedly obsessive, stalker-like tendencies. She had watched Nasser and not the movie, analysing his every expression, pausing the video at times, rewinding at others. Then she had brooded over him for the next couple of hours, coming to no helpful conclusion.

9

This was the worst jetlag she had ever had, Sitara thought, as she dragged herself out of bed and into the kitchen to set the coffee to brew. Thank god it was a Sunday, and she had a day to recover before facing the rest of the office.

She was stirring her coffee when the phone rang. She looked at it uninterestedly. Maya. She took a sip and contemplated answering it. She answered on the eighth ring, since Maya showed no signs of hanging up.

'I could have been sleeping,' Sitara said by way of greeting.

'Hello to you too!' Maya sounded nauseatingly cheerful. 'Guess what?'

'Just tell me.'

'I'm coming to Mumbai!'

Sitara felt a faint stir of spirit. 'Cool,' she managed. 'When?'

'Next week. The dates aren't confirmed yet.'

'Okay. Great,' Sitara said feebly.

'Why are you sounding like death warmed over?' Maya demanded. 'Haven't you just come back from ten days of food and wine under the Tuscan sun?'

'Jetlag.'

There was silence at the other end. 'It's got to be a man,' Maya said, finally. 'Who did you meet? What happened?'

'Why does it have to be a man? I didn't meet anybody.'

'You can't lie. Never could. Now tell me.'

'Fine. I met somebody. I don't want to talk about it right now.'

The silence at the other end was even longer this time. 'You're already in the licking-your-wounds-in-private stage? That's serious.'

'Not really,' Sitara said with some bitterness.

'But good. It's time you stopped using Karthik and the break-up as an excuse for other relationships.'

Sitara didn't say anything.

'So was Nasser good in bed?' Maya asked.

'We never... How did you know?' Sitara gasped.

'Doesn't everybody know? The papers are carrying stories about your affair,' Maya teased. 'Okay, okay. You were in Italy, only one of the three men in your life could possibly be in Europe at this time, and I'm smart this way.'

'It could have been a fellow journalist. Or my tour guide,' Sitara exclaimed.

'I've seen your fellow journalists,' Maya dismissed them. 'Tour guides are likely to be taken. Why don't you just tell me the story?' Maya coaxed, adding slyly. 'It will put things in perspective.'

'That's...slimy. I'll tell you when you get here.'

One week after Sitara flew out, Nasser was back home. It had taken him 48 hours after her departure to come to the conclusion that his holiday felt flat and four days before he had given in and done something about it.

He sent his luggage up to his flat with the driver with instructions to open all the windows, and went to meet his parents two floors below. He checked his watch again – 7.30 a.m.; his father should be awake, at least.

Nasser reached his parents' door at the same time as their maid. His father opened the door.

'Lata! You're back. Thank god. Oh hello, Nasser.'

Nasser's lips twitched. Sons rated far below maids these days.

'Don't smirk,' Bashir admonished, reaching out to hug him warmly. 'You try and survive for four days without somebody to clean up after you. And no cook and no driver.'

'Is that Lata?' a voice bellowed from within. 'Is she back?'

'Amma's awake early,' Nasser commented. Ayesha always woke up 45 minutes before work, which was more than an hour from now. He'd only known her to be awake this early if any of the three men in her life were sick.

'It's the anxiety of whether or not the servants will come,' his father said in all seriousness.

Nasser burst out laughing.

'Are you laughing at me?' Nasser turned around to see his mother emerging from her bedroom, still managing to look elegant in a nightie and robe.

'Of course I am,' he said, crossing over to hug her tightly. 'I believe you've been losing sleep for the first time in your life...over Lata and Anu and Ali.'

'Laugh now, but your time will come. When your maid's father will die for the fifth time and she will leave you to go to her village for a week-long funeral, and the driver will fall sick, and the cook will go all religious,' she told him darkly.

'Hai Allah, if only I had known such a fate awaited me,' Nasser hammed, following his mother into the kitchen, 'I would have stayed and cooked some more spaghetti.'

'Speaking of which, why don't you make some tea and breakfast for us?' Ayesha suggested, handing him the kettle. 'Show us what you learnt in Italy.'

So much for his plan to scrounge breakfast off his parents. 'Is there any servant who has stayed to work with you?' Nasser asked as he walked into the kitchen.

'The ironing woman has been coming in daily,' his mother replied without breaking her stride. 'If you want to make us omelettes, your father can't have the yolk. The teapot and cups are in the drawer under the microwave oven. You need to boil the milk. Now let me get to Lata and tell her what needs to be done on priority.'

He had to move away – far, far away – Nasser decided, as he took a look around. How could he get himself to believe that he was a famous movie star if he was going to be put to work at home in this fashion? He would have to get one of those big gas ovens, he thought absently, as he emptied the milk into its designated steel utensil and lit the stove.

'So your fancy classes taught you how to boil milk,' his father drew up a chair at the nook that divided the kitchen from the dining room. He'd come in to offer help, but his son seemed to be getting on quite competently with the preparations.

'And a few other things,' Nasser said, deciding to go with omelettes. Maybe with tomatoes and not mushrooms. 'Don't you keep any fresh herbs?' he asked, frowning into the fridge.

Bashir's eyebrows shot into his hairline. 'You mean dhania, pudina?'

'Of course n...' Nasser caught himself just in time. Asking for herbs was asking for a ribbing. 'They'll do.' He could feel his father's eyes on him as he rooted through the fridge.

'How was your break? Why are you back early? Weren't you supposed to spend a month doing nothing?'

No pussyfooting about with Bashir. No idle chitchat about the month that had been. He had to know about the month that hadn't. 'I just got tired of doing nothing. I'm not used to it.'

'Are you giving him the third degree?' Ayesha walked up behind Bashir. 'You could have waited for me to come.'

'Thanks Amma. I knew I could always rely on you.' Nasser poured the water into the teapot, settled a tea cosy over it, placed the entire thing onto a tray with cups and sugar and milk and plonked it down in front of his parents. He watched fondly as they went about their tea ritual. They were so British about it – a cup in the morning when they woke up, another around 6.30

p.m., after his mother returned from work. Seeing how his father had spent so much time on film sets drinking the milky special, Nasser had always wondered how he'd managed to hold on to this habit. He himself had converted to coffee when he realized that you could get decent coffee from cafés, but tea you had to make to get it right. Which brought up the question: 'Where have you kept the French press?' he said, rummaging through the shelf where the tea was kept.

'It's in the next cupboard, with the dals,' his father replied.

Dals. Coffee. 'Why is it with the dals?' he asked helplessly.

'Don't try and change the subject.' Bashir took a sip of his tea and turned his attention back to his son. 'You met Naeem?'

'Yes, we spent the day together,' Nasser said, finding the coffee maker exactly where his father had said it would be. 'He's grown a beard and become thinner than me. He seems to be enjoying his backpacking.'

His parents looked doubtful but were eager to know more so he launched into a description of the day, excising the fight. He sent them into fits of laughter with 'winey'.

'Good that he has stopped drinking,' his father said when he stopped laughing.

'You haven't mentioned anything about that magazine girl,' Ayesha said innocently. 'Naeem said you spent the day together. And the next day alone.'

He would have a few things to say to Naeem when he met him next. 'Because of him. He stuck me with her.'

Bashir dismissed Naeem with a wave of his hand. 'He knows you have trouble asking women out. He was just helping. All this stardom has stunted your ability to make the first move.'

Parents never stopped astonishing you. 'Thanks for the dating advice, Abba. I'll keep it in mind.' He poured himself his coffee, and sat down.

'Here,' his mother handed him the milk.

'*Nahin* Amma, thanks. I like it black.' Nasser ignored his father's snort.

'So what's been happening? Besides the lack of servants?'

Bashir started to speak, but subsided at his wife's look. For the next fifteen minutes, Nasser heard all about his cousins, her colleagues, Shiv and the new girl he had a crush on, and the havoc the hotel prankster was continuing to wreak. He was just thinking how wonderful it was to be back home when Bashir moved in for the kill.

'Why don't you invite this girl over for dinner?'

'Amma, can you please control your husband?' Nasser exclaimed.

'*Theek hai, theek hai,*' she held out her hand placatingly. 'What is your hurry?' she scolded her husband. 'She's coming for dinner next week.'

Both his parents sat back and looked at him smugly, and refused to tell him anything more about that.

10

Anjali was not happy. Harsh had still not lost the weight he was supposed to. His sherwani would have to be let out. Worse, he had stopped his diet. He wasn't even trying. He had also refused to go for a detox holiday to Thailand, reacting rather wildly to the idea of flushing out his insides with water.

They had argued over it. It was par for the course. These days, arguments burst forth whenever they opened their mouths. And Harsh seemed to have adopted 'relax, chill' as his mantra. She was going to hurt him if he said it one more time.

All the things that had attracted her to him in the first place were driving her up the wall now. He didn't seem to realize what a disaster it was that Sunita Jain had a slip disc. Instead of doing her wedding decorations, the woman was lying in bed somewhere nursing her back. Harsh had suggested that her assistant would be able to handle it.

Anjali's blood boiled at the memory. She didn't want assistants when she was paying for Sunita. She wanted Sunita. And her dream décor, every detail of which she had perfected with Sunita. They had been at it for months and now there was no Sunita. Now she couldn't even approach her second choice. It was far too late. She was stuck with the assistant. An assistant who was far too young, far too inexperienced and far too casual about it.

And Harsh had suggested that she should concentrate on work and he would deal with this. As though she wasn't concentrating on it. It was galling that Nasser hadn't given her a phone number where he could be reached. She'd tried to get it from Shiv and from Aunty but both of them had refused. She'd had to mail him. Pepsi wanted him. They were dying for him. They were prepared to shell out huge chunks of money for him. So what if they also wanted Richa in the advert? That was a minor detail, and she'd said as much in her mail to Nasser.

And Nasser had not replied.

It was the biggest ad deal ever and he was holidaying. How was anybody supposed to believe that he wasn't even answering mail when the news was so big?

Men, Anjali fumed. Cannot communicate. Cannot lose weight. Didn't they realize that every extra pound would show up in the photos? And in the video? She would be able to Photoshop the official ones, but what about the ones her friends took? The ones that would go up on Facebook? Didn't Harsh know that nothing could ever be deleted from Facebook?

Her wedding was heading towards disaster, and her groom was fat.

Anjali rang Nasser's doorbell. She still couldn't believe she had to learn of Nasser's return from his driver. That too after he had been in town for a week. The man was getting too full of himself.

She rang the doorbell again. Why was Radha taking so long to open the door?

She had her finger ready for a third jab when a grumpy, rumpled Nasser opened the door.

'Are you still sleeping? It's 11 a.m.'

Nasser yawned, and morning breath had Anjali taking a hasty step back. 'No. I *was* sleeping,' he said, his voice still husky from sleep. 'Now I'm standing here talking to you. Why are you here?'

'What do you mean why am I here?' Anjali dug out a mint from her bag and held it out for Nasser. 'I'm here because a whole lot of work needs to be done. Because you haven't done a thing on your holiday. Can we go inside and talk? Why don't you take the mint, you know how sensitive I am to smell. I could get a headache.'

Nasser took a deep breath, and pondered letting it out on her face. He decided to be adult about it. 'A holiday is for not doing anything,' he ran an impatient hand up his stubble. 'And I'm still on holiday till the end of the month, so email me if it's urgent. That way you won't get a headache.' The door shut with a click.

Anjali looked at it stupidly for a minute. Then she could have sworn she heard something snap and a second later she was pounding on the door like a woman possessed. Doors flew open on the floors below, and a few maids and their mistresses made their way up.

Nasser had just thrown himself back in bed when he heard the racket, and almost fell off in his haste to get back. A scatter of thoughts went flying in his head. Had Anjali fallen, hurt herself, was there a hostage situation, danger, the underworld, should he call security? When he opened the door, a leg kicked him in the shin. Hard. 'Ow. Anjali. What are you doing?' She raised a fist to hit the non-existent door and Nasser caught hold of her hands. 'Stop it, stop it. What is wrong with you?'

'Don't you ever, ever shut the door in my face,' Anjali panted. 'And nothing's wrong with me, you jerk, you're the one who's shutting doors in people's faces.' She raised a fist to hit the door.

Nasser twisted out of the way. It didn't take a genius to figure out that Anjali had lost it. 'I'm sorry. I apologize. That was very rude of me. I shouldn't have done it.' His soothing best didn't seem to be getting through to Anjali. She had a blank, fixed stare that was even more disturbing than the pounding.

'Come in, let me get you a glass of water,' Nasser urged. He gave her a nudge in the direction. She took a step inside and he loosened his hold. She took another step and he turned to tell the audience that the show was over. And Anjali turned and slipped by him, running full tilt at the stairs, pushing past the crowd and leaping down the stairs. She was gone by the time he'd closed his mouth.

Nasser ran after her, but she had too much of a head start. She had disappeared by the time he arrived in the car park.

He called her the moment he got back to his flat, but her phone was switched off. Very worrying. He called her home, but her parents were out on wedding-related business. He asked the maid to call him when Anjali got home. Then he called her parents. They said they would go home immediately and check.

Richa's intelligence network had found out that Nasser had cut short his holiday and was back in Mumbai. (Her spot boy had got it straight from Priyanka's hairdresser who had it from Nasser's make-up man who had it from his driver. Her spot boy also thought there was something brewing between Priyanka's hairdresser and Nasser's make-up man; she'd told him that bad things happened to people who gossiped.) But he still hadn't replied to the Pepsi people. She didn't like waiting. She could bet the Pepsi lot didn't either.

Nasser almost killed himself getting to the phone. How was it that mobile phones always found themselves in a place that was furthest away from you when they rang? This time it was under the newspaper on the sofa.

'Hello. Anjali, are you okay?' he said, rubbing his knee where he had banged it against the sofa in his haste.

'Hi Nasser,' replied a familiar voice that wasn't Anjali's.

'Richa?' Nasser's eyebrow shot up. 'This is unexpected.'

'Yes. I like doing the unexpected. It keeps things interesting.'

'Not so much when you're at the receiving end of a can of cola,' Nasser said easily, one part of him noting how he felt nothing for his former fiancée. No anger, no guilt, no disappointment. He could be talking to any acquaintance. Not the woman he'd fallen in love with, or proposed to or held through bad drug trips and rehab visits.

'But the results are excellent – Pepsi wants us for an ad,' Richa said.

Nasser couldn't help but admire her sangfroid. No apologies, no embarrassment, they might have been the best of friends. 'Did you do it for the ad? Or because you were pissed?' he asked curiously. Neither seemed in keeping with her personality.

'It was an impulse,' Richa said. 'You know how you used to tell me to take life as it comes; it just seemed to ring through my ears at that moment.'

'I was wrong,' Nasser said. 'Ignore it next time.'

Richa laughed. 'It felt really good. Addictive,' she taunted.

'I'm sure,' Nasser said, dryly. 'Shall we cut the chit-chat? Why did you call?'

'When are you going to let the agency know you are doing the ad?'

She had always gone after what she wanted; it had been one of the qualities that had attracted him to her. That didn't mean he had to give in to her.

'I'm on vacation right now, Richa. I'm not thinking about work till it's over,' Nasser wandered over to his balcony.

'That's still three weeks away. They won't like being kept hanging that long.'

'That's their problem,' Nasser said.

'Well, I don't like being kept waiting,' Richa's good humour was slipping. 'And after what you did to me I think it's the least you can do for me.'

'Ah. Appeal to my guilt, I was wondering when you would use that,' Nasser said. 'The thing is, I no longer feel guilty.'

'You dumped me because I had a boob job and you don't feel guilty?' Richa demanded.

'To be specific, you're the one who broke it off.'

'Because you couldn't bear to touch me.'

'No. Because I could see you had a new addiction and I couldn't live through another one.'

'Very convenient for you,' Richa said scornfully. 'But these are just beauty treatments. All actresses have to do them.'

'Then I don't want actresses,' Nasser said. 'I can understand the Botox, and fat injections but I don't see a need for multiple boob jobs, nose jobs, chin paring, and some six other procedures.'

'That's because you are a man and you get author-backed roles, while we heroines are there for our looks.'

'Yeah, the industry's unfair, but it wasn't about the industry. It was about us. And we were over.'

'You know what Nasser, I don't give a shit about your reasons and explanations. I just want you to sign that contract.'

Nasser controlled his anger. Losing his control was just handing her a weapon.

'Tick tock, tick tock,' Richa said, giving him a rare glimpse of her ruthlessness. 'You're taking too long. Actually, what am I doing? You don't have to tell me. Just call up the agency and tell them that you're on.' Richa hung up.

Anjali's mother called. She had shut herself in her room and seemed to be crying. She was refusing to come out or let anybody in. They would keep him updated.

Nasser looked at the time. It wasn't even noon. That was already two too many women to deal with at this point of the day. Reaching for his phone and dialling a third would be just masochistic.

No, he decided. Having a conversation with a third woman would indeed be masochistic. Trying to call her, on the other hand, was just futile. She wasn't picking up the call and he was damned if he was going to send her a text identifying himself.

His phone rang and he felt a jolt of anticipation. Then he looked at the name of the display.

'Shiv. Hello.'

'You sound disappointed. Expecting your journalist?'

'Fuck off.'

'Yeah, yeah. Want to do dinner? There's a new place I want to check out.'

'Yeah, okay. The staff won't be all over me, will they?'

'No, no. No need for a disguise. Your crowd has already been there.'

'Fine. What food is it?'

'Ethiopian. And I don't want to hear any smart remarks about it.'

Sitara was absorbed in the last reading of a page before sending it to press when her mother called. 'They have sent some very nice designs for the wedding cards,' she said by way of greeting.

'For the last time, I am not marrying Girish,' Sitara exclaimed.

'He doesn't care about your broken engagement. Or you and the actor,' her mother said persuasively.

'I don't care about it either. I am still not marrying him.'

'Do you know how difficult it is to get single men at your age? You only get divorcees.'

'Divorcees are just fine,' Sitara snapped.

'Girish wants to meet you again. He is coming to Mumbai soon.'

'Enough Amma. Please say no to them. I am not marrying him. And I'm not going to discuss this anymore.'

Sitara had barely excised a couple of unnecessary commas when Prabhakar appeared at her elbow. 'Somebody to see you at the reception.'

'I'm busy.'

'He says he will wait till you come.'

It was no surprise when Sitara stomped out that she was faced with Karthik.

'What?' she demanded.

'Oh.' Karthik's smile faded. 'Bad time?'

'Yes.' Sitara said shortly. If he couldn't call before he came then he would just have to deal with what he found when he arrived. For the first time since she had known him she found herself unmoved in his presence. Perhaps she was finally over him. But right now, she couldn't care. She wanted to get back to the page she was reading.

'I'd come to discuss the wedding with you–'

'There is no wedding,' Sitara said, bluntly. 'You can't–'

He held up his hand. 'I know you're busy right now, I'll meet you after work. I'll be back at 6 p.m.'

'No.' Sitara gritted. 'I have plans for the evening.'

'Fine. Dinner then,' Karthik continued undaunted.

'My plans are for dinner.' She took great pleasure in informing him.

'I'll join you. Where are you going?'

Sitara looked at him in amazement. Had he always been such a selfish jerk? How had she not noticed? She had refused to notice, she realized. She had loved him and wanted to marry him and she had refused to acknowledge anything that interfered with her rosy picture of him. And when he had broken off the engagement, deep inside she had believed that it had been because of some deficiency in her. But it wasn't. He had just been a selfish jerk. Nasser had been right. How had she let him get away with it?

'It doesn't matter where I'm going. You can't come.'

'Are you meeting another man? Is that why you're behaving like this?'

Sitara looked at him, shaking her head. 'You're unbelievable.' She turned and walked back inside.

Sitara walked into the restaurant she had been asked to review and looked around with a jaundiced eye. It was the coolest new restaurant in Mumbai, serving the coolest new cuisine in town and filled with the city's coolest people. Did nobody think it was weird that they were eating Ethiopian cuisine?

'Hey Sitara!' a familiar voice greeted her.

'Hey Anurag! We meet again!' she said as they air-kissed. Ever since she had returned from Italy ten days ago, life had been a whirlwind of activity, as she had accepted every invitation she received. Most, reflecting the sad state of her personal life, had been for office events. Given the magazine's snob factor, they involved society people. She had run into Anurag at almost every one of them.

'I was hoping you'd be here,' Sitara said. Truth be told, she had gotten rather fond of him over the past ten days. 'The friend I was supposed to meet for dinner just texted to say he'd be a little late.'

'This new generation,' Anurag took his cue and comfortably settled himself at the bar next to her. He then proceeded, as he had at every opportunity, to flirt with her agreeably for a good half-hour. Then somebody with a short skirt and long legs greeted him and he regretfully kissed Sitara goodbye.

Sitara watched him flirt with the new girl with equal enthusiasm as she dialled Martin's number. She had to hand it to Anurag. He loved all women equally, though if rumours were to be believed he loved Bollywood actresses a little more.

'Sitara, my dear, I have some bad news,' Martin said. 'I won't be able to join you for dinner.'

'Why? And why didn't you tell me earlier?' Sitara demanded, most put out by this cavalier attitude.

Martin lowered his voice. 'Because this very hot girl hinted she'd like me to go home with her only minutes ago.'

'You're ditching me for some floozy?'

'A very hot floozy,' Martin said unrepentantly. 'She's coming back. Gotta go.'

Sitara took a sip of her wine, and pondered what to do. It was too late to ask anybody else to join her and there was no way she was reviewing this restaurant on her lonesome ownsome. But then what was she going to do for dinner? She mentally ran through all the restaurants that fell on her way home, trying to choose where she would like to pack food from.

'Hello Sitara.' She was greeted by a familiar voice for the second time in the space of an hour. This one was far from welcome.

'Karthik. What are you doing here?' He had dressed up for the dinner, she noticed. He looked good. He did nothing for her.

'I thought I would join you for dinner. We never finished our conversation in the afternoon.'

'How did you know where I was?'

'I called your office.'

'And they just gave it to you?'

'No. I told them I was meeting you for dinner, but I had forgotten where. Your colleague was very helpful.'

Sitara considered Karthik. She could get rid of him now, or she could brush him off after dinner and the review. She voted for post-dinner. Let him be useful for once.

'Fine. My reservation's in a couple of minutes. The maitre d' will call us. You want a drink till then?'

'Some water. I'll get it.' Sitara watched him order it and was once again struck by the fact that she was completely over him.

He got the glass and turned toward her. He raised an eyebrow. 'That's an intriguing look. Do I want to know what you were thinking?'

And there was why she'd liked him. He was smart. 'I was–'

'Ms Gopalasundaram,' a voice interrupted, before she could tell him. 'Your table's ready.'

As the two fell in step behind the maitre d' there was a stir in the restaurant. Karthik turned to look.

'Bollywood star?' Sitara asked, not really interested in the answer. She had heard enough from Mukul about how often he and his Bollywood friends came here.

'Yes,' Karthik said. 'Nasser Khan. Aren't you going to say hello?'

Sitara controlled the start, but she couldn't stop herself from turning around and seeing him again. 'Not really. We don't really know each other.'

'Sitara! Are you going for dinner?' Anurag rose from the table he was sharing with a brand new woman, a rather unhappy-looking one that too, and enveloped Sitara in a hug. 'You have to save me from her,' he whispered. More loudly, he said, 'You look more beautiful with every passing day. Let me kiss you.'

Sitara gave him a narrow-eyed look and fended him off with one hand.

He winked at her. 'Come join us, my lovely. Let me serve you in this fashion at least.'

There was the sound of some throat clearing; Karthik stood looking from Anurag to her. 'Aren't you going to introduce us?'

'I already know the most important thing,' Anurag declared. 'You are having dinner with this lovely woman, one of the loveliest people I know. Everybody who knows her loves her. I love her and I haven't even known her for long.'

'Excuse me. You're blocking the way,' a man said politely.

'Nasser,' Anurag hugged the man who had just spoken. Sitara's head whipped around so quickly she felt dizzy. 'You're the man. Sitara doesn't believe that I love her. Tell her.'

Sitara looked at Nasser coldly. He looked back at her equally unsmilingly.

'Yes, my fiancée is very lovable. I love her too,' a voice broke in, hand reaching out to Sitara's waist and drawing her possessively to his side. All eyes turned to the man they had forgotten.

'Fiancée? You're engaged? When did that happen?' Anurag asked.

Sitara's vehement 'No' collided with Karthik's equally loud 'Yes'.

'We are not engaged,' Sitara said.

'A couple of weeks ago,' Karthik said. He moved his hand down to her hip.

Nasser's eyes followed the movement. 'You seem a little confused about the engagement,' he mocked.

'Sitara's right. We were engaged a couple of years ago. This time we're getting married directly,' Karthik explained. 'The wedding is next week.'

'Congratulations.' Nasser said. 'My table's ready, if you will excuse me...' he edged away. The maitre d' followed solicitously.

'Bye Anurag,' Sitara gritted. She grabbed Karthik's hand and dragged him outside. 'Let's get this straight:

I am not going to marry you. I don't like you, I don't want you, I don't care about you. You wanted to know that look on my face earlier, I was thinking how over you I was. Just go away. Get out of my life and take your signs with you.'

Nasser's mood had gone from anticipatory to foul by the time he reached his table. If another person hugged him or tried to air-kiss him, he'd throw himself on the ground and drum his heels in a major tantrum. He'd forgotten why he didn't go out to restaurants – you ran into too many people who wanted to meet you and none you wanted to meet.

And there was Shiv, prattling on about people kissing and making out. Nasser caught three words in a dozen: 'girls', 'uninhibited', and 'public'.

All he could think of was that Sitara had been engaged when they were in Italy. And she hadn't once said anything. For possibly the first time in his life he had made the moves on a girl and she had already been taken. She'd been playing him.

She'd played Naeem too. What a laugh. Being told she was the marrying kind. Yeah, right! The marrying kind who had stray men declaring their love for her before the whole world.

He had given her advice on this creep. She had probably laughed herself silly behind his back.

He'd been kicking himself for getting cold feet that last day. It was probably the best thing he had done.

'What's the matter with you, dude?' Shiv asked. 'You're looking very screwed.'

Nasser grunted. 'What's good here?'

Shiv shot him an assessing look and decided he'd save his questions about the run-in with the reporter for later. 'Everything. Let's order some wine, and I'll fill you in on what's been happening while you've been away.'

By the time Nasser had finished his drink, eaten some excellent starters, got the latest updates on the hotel prankster – he'd hit F&B twice more, messing up deliveries and room service – he had regained the vestiges of his sense of humour.

'Isn't that the guy who's marrying Anjali?' Shiv had chosen the seat that gave him the best view of the restaurant, so he could catch all comings and goings. 'What does he do again?'

Nasser turned left to look at the man who was entering the restaurant. 'Yes, that's Harsh. Real estate. Very rich. Very low-key.' He noted the teddy-bearness to the man's outline. 'Doesn't look like the diet worked,' he said. Anjali had only mentioned it to him once a day for the past couple of months.

'He looks too good natured and laid-back for Anjali,' Shiv observed.

Nasser caught Harsh's eye and raised a hand in acknowledgement.

The smile slipped off Harsh's face. He turned to say something to his dinner companions, an older couple who looked most definitely like his parents.

'He's coming over,' Shiv said unnecessarily. After a beat: 'He doesn't look very happy.' Another beat: 'Should I call in some protection?'

'No,' Nasser said shortly. He rose to meet Harsh. 'Hi Har...umpf.' Nasser fell back against his chair rocked by a fist ploughing into his face. There was a starburst of pain. His face was on fire.

'Arghhh,' said Harsh, cradling his hand.

'You're bleeding,' Shiv said faintly.

Oh god. 'Look the other way,' Nasser said thickly. But he was too late. His friend had slid gracefully down to the floor, unconscious at the first sight of blood.

Sensation. A semi-circle formed. An inner ring of waiters, not sure what to do. A couple of rings of diners, all talking loudly, shouted instructions at the waiters.

Now that Shiv had mentioned it, he could feel the wet slide of something from his nose. His shirt now wore an interesting pattern of blood. Harsh must have hit his cheek and the blow had glanced off his nose. It hurt like the devil.

Harsh didn't look too happy either. Nasser didn't think he had ever hit anybody in his life and was feeling the pain of violence. Nasser watched him clutch his hand in satisfaction. Good. Between his own pain and the pain of Harsh, it took Nasser a moment to realize that he was being spoken to.

'Sorry. Sorry,' said Harsh, looking defiant, and attempting to not look shocked. 'But you had it coming, you know. You're a bastard.' It didn't have the ring it should have.

A waiter tried laying a tentative hand on his arm. He shrugged it off. 'Can you give me a moment here? I'm not going to hit him again. I just need to speak to him. Thank you.'

A thin voice from the outer sphere of the circle could be heard. 'Harsh? Harsh! Are you there? What are you doing?'

'I'm fine, mummy,' Harsh yelled over all the commotion.

Nasser snorted with laughter and was rewarded by a fresh flow of blood. He groped around for a napkin.

'Sir, please step away from there. We will call the police otherwise,' a more decisive voice cut through.

'Can I just speak? Oh don't cry, mummy, I'm fine. Can you get me some ice please?'

He turned his attention back to Nasser who was trying to stuff the napkin up his nose. 'I don't know what you told Anjali...' A waiter appeared with the ice. 'Oh thanks, could you put the ice in the napkin? That's great.' Two bouncers had a firm hold on him.

'Sir, please leave,' said the manager.

'Just one second. I need to tell him something... Ow, watch it. You're hurting my hand. Okay, okay, I'm leaving. I'll call you,' he flung back at Nasser.

Nasser nodded distractedly, occupied with emptying a glass of water on his friend's face.

11

Richa had watched the news all morning hoping to see if anybody had discovered who had punched Nasser. Nobody had a clue. Her delicate probing had revealed no results either. The man had been a first-timer at the restaurant and a walk-in customer. He'd given his surname to book the table, except that nobody could decipher what it was – not even the hostess who had written it.

Nasser was predictably keeping a low profile on it.

Nasser was an ass. An ass who was ruining her career. Did he think advertisers would want him if he kept getting beaten up every time he went out? Did he think Pepsi would want him? And if Pepsi didn't want him, they wouldn't want her.

Which she couldn't allow.

She was going to have to do something to give him back his cool. She'd better call that lying, cheating drunk to find out what he knew.

'Hello Anurag,' she cooed. 'I hope I didn't wake you up...'

She was exultant when she hung up. Anurag had

proved a fount of information. And he had finally picked up on her hints and invited her out.

Now she only needed to spread the story. She was going to entangle Nasser so deeply with the fat girl he was going to find it impossible to get out.

The day couldn't get better.

Nasser looked at the sorry sight in front of him and shook his head. A bad idea; he wasn't in any condition to be moving his face any more than required. He had a sore cheek and a swollen nose, and one hell of a headache. And he was holed up in a hotel room with his phone switched off.

The press would have staked out his apartment building. For all he knew they had staked out this hotel room too. He didn't feel like switching on the television. He had enough of a headache already.

Pity Anjali wasn't around for damage control anytime soon. But a woman had to do what a woman had to do. In this case, wallow in self-pity and refuse to take his calls.

He was talking more to her mother than to her. Maybe he should hire Aunty to be his manager. She listened to him at least. And gave him reasons why he was getting his daylights punched out by her future son-in-law.

Like the fact that the moron had come home, found Anjali crying, decided that Nasser had to be the reason, cast him as the villain, and–

Why wasn't anybody giving him any sympathy?

Wait a minute – everybody he had met since the day of the interview had beaten him up. Even Chef Sebastian had landed a roll on him in their last class. This couldn't be a coincidence.

He had to get Sitara out of his life.

Hmm.

Or maybe they just had to move on to the next phase of their...whatever it was, and people would stop hitting him. Nasser thought about that too.

For two seconds.

He should call her immediately.

Nasser reached to turn his phone on. Then hesitated. Maybe after the bruising faded. After he looked normal again.

Nasser walked up to the mirror and peered at himself. He did look a sight. But there was the entire sympathy card he could play.

Okay, that just sounded pathetic.

He flopped back onto the bed again and tried to reason with himself. The reason he had suffered cold feet in Italy was not so that he could come back and call Sitara.

Sitara was over because Sitara was a serious commitment. And he wasn't ready for serious.

Which was surprising for somebody who had been engaged to be married not so very long ago, a rational voice prompted. He acknowledged the hit. He had been ready to get married for a couple of years now. Why had he backed away from Sitara then? It wasn't even like he had spent that much time with her.

It wasn't the amount of time, but the way it was spent, the voice in his head held an annoyingly superior note. She'd seen more of the real you in two days than Richa saw in three years. And that scares the hell out of you.

A vision of Sitara and the short dweeb from last night chose that moment to replay in his mind, forcing Nasser off the bed. However much it scared him, he wasn't going to let Sitara waste herself on that...

A short rap on the door interrupted his search for the right epithet. It was followed by two longer raps and another shorter one. He rolled his eyes, winced, pulled the door open.

'Ayesha Bond, I assume?' he asked. 'What took you so long?'

'I've always wanted to try that,' Ayesha ignored his surliness and walked into the room. 'I loved writing with invisible ink too. Your father managed to burn every single note by overheating the iron.'

Nasser shut the door and followed her into the room, listening to her in disbelief. 'Amma! You're late! I'm hurt. And why are you telling me about your spy fantasies? What about sympathy for your son? Or apologies? Or food?'

'Oh, poor baby,' his mother said immediately. 'Does it hurt very badly? Have you seen a doctor? Have you eaten?'

'You are an unnatural mother,' Nasser said disgruntled, and his mother grinned at him.

'Sit down,' she said. 'Let me look at that. Did you put ice on it?' She smoothed a hand through his hair unconsciously as she looked at his face. 'You have a fat nose. Cheekbone hurts?'

'Yes. But it's okay, I can bear it,' he said heroically.

'What did the other guy look like?' Ayesha hugged him, pressed a kiss on his head and stepped back.

'Five kgs overweight,' Nasser said, dryly.

Two short raps sounded against the door. They were followed by a longer one.

'Your majesty's secret service?' Nasser asked.

Ayesha grinned at him and went to answer the door. She came back rolling in the dining cart. 'Can't be too careful with the paparazzi. Here you go. American breakfast with everything. Dig in.'

She kept up a stream of undemanding chatter till his intense concentration on food relaxed. 'A reporter called,' she said so casually that Nasser set down his fork and gave her all his concentration.

'She wanted to know whether it was true that you and the mystery man had come to blows over Sitara Gopalasundaram?' Ayesha looked at him expectantly. When Nasser didn't say anything, she waved a hand in front of his face. 'Nasser? They want to know whether the two of you are getting married. Seems they've heard it somewhere.'

'That doesn't sound like Anurag,' Nasser mused absently. 'Unless...hmm, I wonder.'

'Nasser,' his mother said sternly.

'Sorry, Amma. It's not a bad story actually. Better I was in a fight than that I was knocked down. By my own manager's fiancé. The guy's tamer than a pet dog. It'd look really bad on me. Where are you going?' he asked his mother as she rose.

'Nowhere. I just wanted to do this.' She smacked his head.

'Ow! Amma! I'm already injured, remember,' Nasser exclaimed rubbing his head.

'I did. It would have been harder otherwise,' his mother said grimly. 'You have now been having an "affair"' – she sketched the quote marks with her fingers – 'with this girl for over a month. Now you're getting beaten up by her boyfriend. Are you going to marry her? If you aren't, you'd better start dating one of your floozy groupies immediately.'

'Floozy groupies,' Nasser repeated. 'Is that what you think of my girlfriends?'

Ayesha shot him a look that had been putting him in his place for the past thirty-five years. It was as effective as ever. 'What are you going to do to fix it?' she demanded.

'Nothing,' Nasser said. 'Anything I do will only make things worse.'

Ayesha looked at him for so long Nasser began to get worried.

'What?' he asked, apprehensively.

'Nothing,' she said. 'Eat up.'

'Okay, Amma, you are scaring me. Are you just going to let the subject go?'

'Of course. Didn't you just tell me you couldn't do anything? And you also have Anjali to worry about.'

'I do?'

'Of course. I believe Harsh isn't answering any of her calls and nobody's telling her where he is. She went to his house, and he wasn't there. I think he's hiding somewhere. Like you.'

'I don't see any part in this that I have to be part of,' Nasser said.

'Not if they speak by tomorrow,' Ayesha said sanguinely. 'But–'

'Not ever, Amma,' Nasser said with some emphasis.

'Fine,' his mother agreed. 'I'm sure you are right.'

'Stop it!' Nasser exclaimed. 'This is freaking me out. Why are you agreeing with me?'

'I'm reading a management book–'

'Oh god, no. I don't want to know anymore. Have you got the stuff for my escape?'

Monday mornings were the invention of the devil, Sitara thought as she switched her computer on.

'Do you want to give a quote to *Hindustan Times*?'

Martin must have been watching to have arrived at her side with such speed. Sitara didn't even spare him a glance. She strongly believed that there was a time and place for everything and there was no place for conversation on Monday mornings. Not before her first cup of coffee.

'About your impending marriage to Nasser Khan. And the fight between him and your boyfriend last night,' he continued, unconcerned by her lack of response.

It took her a couple of moments to process it. 'Marriage? Fight? What?' Her voice sounded rusty.

'I had a feeling you didn't know,' Martin said with satisfaction. 'You and one boyfriend is difficult enough to believe. Two of them, fighting over you?' He shook his head to indicate his disbelief.

Sitara didn't know whether to be relieved or

insulted. She caught sight of the office boy and settled for shouting for coffee.

'No coffee yet?' Martin exclaimed. 'Prabhakar, *jaldi*. Very important discussion.' He perched at the edge of her table impatiently tapping a magazine against the edge.

'You can tell me,' she said, tartly. 'There's nothing wrong with my ears.'

'Only your brain. I know it doesn't work till it's got caffeine.' He resumed the tapping with the magazine.

'Stop it!' Sitara snatched the magazine out of his hand. Then she remembered. 'Ditcher!' She turned bad-temperedly to her computer and began checking her mail.

'I know,' he said unrepentantly. 'How could I have known that there was going to be a fight?'

Prabhakar arrived with her special brew, diverting her from replying to Martin. He handed her the mug and rushed away. Nobody in their right mind interacted with her till after lunch.

Martin waited till Sitara had taken a couple of sips before speaking. 'Has it reached your brain?' He peered at her to check.

Sitara gave him a baleful look.

'Okay, you seem more like yourself now. So, your new, unknown boyfriend punched your actor-boyfriend in the nose. He bled,' Martin sounded thrilled. 'Do you know why?'

'Because he was hit in the nose?' Sitara said sarcastically.

'Oh, drink your coffee,' Martin exclaimed. 'Not why he bled. Why he got hit.' He held up his hand. 'No, no.

No sarcastic remarks. I'll assume you don't know. Uh huh,' he cautioned. 'Don't say anything.'

Sitara took a deep breath and prayed for fortitude.

'Yes. So. Blood. All over the place. Took half a dozen guys to stop them. He didn't go home last night. Was he at your place? Asking you to marry him?'

'Who?' Sitara asked blankly.

'Prabhakar,' Martin yelled. 'Did you give Sitara coffee or water?'

Sitara smacked his arm.

'Nasser Khan, that's who.' Martin grabbed her mug and peered at it. 'Prabhakar, get one more. Can you imagine? Almost two years he goes underground. You enter his life and he's all over the news. So, are you marrying him? Do you know who hit him? You don't really have a boyfriend, do you?'

'No.'

'You sure?' he looked at her suspiciously. 'Are you hiding things from me? Because it's all over the news. What are your parents saying?'

Sitara shuddered. 'They haven't called yet. You sure it's all over the news?'

'Positive,' an oily voice answered.

Debashish. That was all she needed. Sitara turned to face him reluctantly.

The office had fallen silent behind her. Debashish didn't leave his domain unless he was stirring up trouble.

'I'm not sure that all this publicity reflects well on the magazine,' he said, shaking his head in disappointment, its effect spoilt by the glee in his eyes. 'I will have to speak to Anil about it. You should try and do some damage control quickly. Otherwise...'

Would she have to tell him how much he owed her or would Nasser have understood by now? Richa thought the latter. But it wouldn't be any hardship to explain it all to him just in case.

And get him to call Pepsi to pay off his debt.

Richa dialled Nasser's number. It was switched off. She had forgotten the Garbo thing their break-up had set him off on. Though she hadn't understood why he should be Garbo when she was the injured party.

She considered for a moment, then picked up the phone, her mind made up. Why stop at spreading one story a day when you could spread two? Especially when there was the possibility of causing trouble in paradise – if anything that included Nasser could be called paradise.

Martin was back at her desk.

'Don't you have any work to do?' Sitara snapped.

'What's the use of slogging it out to become creative director if I still have to work?' Martin cast a look of dislike at her work area, and gingerly perched on the edge of her desk.

'I'm busy.'

'On a Monday? Since when? But I can take a hint. So, what I wanted to know was...'

'The hint is that you should leave,' Sitara said, her tone of somebody goaded beyond endurance.

'...actually, *Hindustan Times* wanted to know what you thought of Richa and Nasser getting together again?' Martin continued unconcerned.

'What!'

'But since you are so busy–'

Sitara grabbed his arm. 'Tell me or die.'

Martin told her.

It wasn't much. Just a new rumour. But it had been repeated by a source with some credibility. There was most likely some truth in it.

Sitara listened to him with as much calm as she could muster. She even smiled and made some irreverent remarks before shooing Martin away to return to her work.

She was not upset.

She was just fine.

It wasn't like there had been anything between them. Just two days. She probably got on better with his brother than with him. Nasser was an acquaintance at best.

Asshole.

Good thing he'd watched all those Amitabh Bachchan movies as a kid, Nasser thought. How else would he have thought of pasting on a fake beard to disguise himself otherwise? His swollen nose was just what his make-up man had ordered. Change the nose and you changed the face. And he didn't even need the prosthetic. Some additional padding inside his cheeks, a hunch, a shabby shirt and shiny shoes and he was all set. He'd like to bet with somebody that the reporters wouldn't make him even in bright noonday light.

Nasser took a taxi home. The watchman stopped the cab officiously. Then: '*Oh sir, aap. Jaaiye jaaiye.*'

Nasser looked at him suspiciously. Had he recognized him? But that tone... He took the stairs up to his parents' place. Hopefully he would spot any lurking media before they spotted him.

There wasn't anybody.

He rang the bell.

Footsteps came around pretty quickly. Abba must have been waiting for him. Amma must have warned him.

The door opened.

'Oh god, no!' Nasser took an unconscious step back.

'Hello brother,' said the apparition in the doorway.

'What are you doing here?' Nasser looked resentfully at Naeem sprawled on the sofa in front of him. That was the sofa he had moved six times in a day last year, when his mother wanted to rearrange the living room. She had made Nasser and Shiv lug it back and forth till she was satisfied. He had wanted to call in the drivers to do this. His mother had called it an exercise in family bonding and refused.

His mother had some odd ideas. She wanted him to stay grounded, she had said.

What was the use? It wasn't like anybody in the industry was grounded. At least he didn't arrive at hotels with a staff of three and get them to rearrange the furniture according to vaastu and light up the aromatherapy before he would deign to step in. He didn't demand to travel by a certain class of car, or get his spot boy to dispose of chewing gum. Well, not often. Or ask for a cola-dispensing machine on set.

He didn't do drugs anymore. Hash didn't count. But even that was only on rare occasions. He didn't party wildly anymore. He hadn't done any floozy groupies in...three months. A lifetime. He should do something about that, he mused. And his present count was nowhere in the league of his past. Not that he was crass enough to count, but the number of women he had... slept with...was in the low hundreds. Compared to the rest of the fraternity, he was practically a virgin. And he had never cheated on his girlfriends. Except...but that didn't count. They'd been on a break. Moving on.

And when it came to work, he was a complete professional on sets, he didn't give his directors grief, he didn't make unreasonable demands. And he said 'please' and 'thank you'.

Mostly.

He gave to charities. He prayed. He fasted during Ramzan. And now he could cook.

He was the very poster boy of moderation. In fact, he was downright boring. If only his mother would see it.

He watched his father offer his brother masala chai, made with his own two hands. A brother who he was pretty sure wasn't told to stay grounded.

'Do you want some?' his father asked Nasser as an obvious afterthought.

Naeem smirked. Nasser met it with one of his own.

'No, no,' he replied with perfect truth. His father

couldn't make masala chai to save his life. He either boiled the tea too long, added too much milk, or too much sugar. Often he did all three. It could be worse. Sometimes he used perfectly excellent Darjeeling tea to make masala chai so you got a mixture of hot water and milk with a lot of sugar.

He watched Naeem raise the cup to his lips. He'd see who had the last smirk.

To his credit Naeem only betrayed himself with a quick gasp and a widening of eyes.

'There's nothing like a good cup of masala chai to make you feel at home,' Nasser said soulfully.

Naeem gave him the finger.

Bashir smiled mistily, happy to have both his sons in the same room and civil to each other.

'Yes.' Naeem took a deep breath and bravely raised the cup to his lips again. Nasser gave him one more sip. He settled back to watch which strategy his brother would use. Talk so much that the tea got cold and needed reheating, i.e., a quick dump into the sink, or become so absorbed in the task that he would 'forget' his cup. He could also spill it, but Nasser didn't think Naeem would do that. Yet. Nasser had done all three. Making coffee his preferred drink had been easier all around.

'Amma find you okay? She wasn't too late? She didn't feel like leaving me,' Naeem needled. 'You seemed surprised to find me here. She didn't tell you I'd come?'

'She wanted to surprise Nasser. She said so before she left,' Bashir said repressively.

'It's okay Abba, I know how memory goes as you age. And Naeem's got his midlife crisis to deal with too,' Nasser said, leaning back unconcernedly in his chair.

Bashir gave him a warning look. Then he switched sides to give it to Naeem. 'I'm only going to say this once,' he warned. 'I can't control what you do, but in my presence, behave yourself! Or...'

'Be careful of that or,' Naeem told Nasser, 'it might be Sitara.' Catching Bashir's puzzled look, he paused. 'You haven't told them?' he demanded of Nasser.

'I wonder why,' Nasser snapped. 'There's a concept called discretion I'd like to introduce you to at some point.'

'You're sacrificing a peach of a story to discretion?' Naeem said enjoying Nasser's wince at his pun. 'Any violence is strictly PG, no need to worry about it,' he warned Bashir before launching into a scene-by-scene replay.

'She didn't,' Bashir gasped, when the first peach had made its appearance.

'She did,' Naeem grinned and told him about the rest, sending him into paroxysms of laughter.

Nasser watched them sourly. 'It isn't that funny.'

'Yes, it is,' Naeem replied.

Nasser's expression lightened as he watched Naeem take a forgetful sip of the tea. He grinned as his brother launched into a fit of coughing to cover up his reflexive spitting out.

'Yeah, you're right. It is funny,' he agreed.

Bashir leapt to his feet in concern. 'Are you okay? Do you have a cold? Or sore throat? You're so thin. Nasser didn't tell us you had been sick. Drink up, drink up. Hot tea is very good. I'll get you another cup when you finish this.'

Naeem gave his brother a look of such horror that

Nasser had to do some coughing of his own to hide his laugh. He rescued a bottle of mineral water from Naeem's backpack and tossed it to him. 'Here. Maybe you should try some water first. And then you can tell us what you're doing here. Aren't you supposed to be sticking out your thumb in Turkey?'

Naeem abandoned his cup of tea with alacrity and grabbed the bottle of water gratefully. 'Thanks.'

Nasser watched as his brother set some speed records for downing water. 'I'm waiting,' he reminded Naeem when he finally stopped.

Naeem looked up from putting the cap on the bottle. 'I thought it'd be more fun to stick my nose into your affairs. It would really take my mind off my midlife crisis.'

How could she have missed seven calls in ten minutes of loo break? Sitara checked her logs to see who had been calling her. It was Maya, the psycho she called best friend.

The woman who was calling her back for the eighth time.

'Hello Maya–'

'Where were you? I've been calling and calling.'

'I noticed–'

'Do you have any plans for tonight?'

'No–'

'Cancel them if you do. We are going to party.'

'We a–'

'I'm flying in at 6 p.m. Come straight to my hotel after work. I'll message you the details. We'll have dinner and go to this party. Remember Lokesh? It's his thirtieth birthday and he's having this blast.'

'Who–wha–'

'Gotta run. Bye.'

'You're still here?' Bashir stopped at the foot of the couch in front of the TV where Nasser lay, a twitch of the thumb on the remote control the only sign of life. His son had been in the same position a couple of hours ago when Bashir had retired for his siesta, leaving Nasser with an ice pack and some pain pills.

Nasser grunted what sounded like an affirmative without taking his eyes off the screen.

'Where's Naeem?' Bashir moved to stand in front of the TV.

'Abba!' Nasser protested. 'I was–'

'Switching channels. Where's Naeem?'

'In hospital.'

'What!'

'He annoyed me, I broke his nose and–'

'You can stop with the wishful thinking,' Naeem strolled into the living room. 'I was sleeping too.'

'That's not funny.' Bashir glared at the supine figure on the couch and switched off the TV. 'Enough of this lying about. Make yourself useful. Go make some tea. Your mother should be home any – ah, there she is.'

She was, indeed. And she wasn't alone. She'd come home with a hairy appendage.

Nasser grunted a greeting at Shiv, which was ignored as his friend met his brother. Nasser muttered something under his breath and stumped away to make them all some tea, unaware of the eyes that watched his retreating figure.

'Shiv has come up with a plan to save your reputation,' Ayesha announced as she watched him carry in the tea tray.

'I don't need my reputation saved,' Nasser set the tray down in front of her and picked up the sole mug on the tray.

A chorus of 'Yes, you do' went up.

'Is your nose hurting you?' Bashir asked. 'Do you have a headache?'

'Hormones, Abba,' Naeem said. 'It's that time of the month.'

'Ha ha ha.' Nasser said wistfully, eyeing the couch his brother now occupied. He dragged a chair from the dining table and sat down.

'Naeem! Don't talk about things you know nothing about,' Shiv scolded. 'He's in a bad mood because he learnt about Sitara's engagement.'

'Enough teasing,' Ayesha said firmly, sensing that bloodshed was about to follow. 'Shiv's plan is that you go to a party tonight and have a good time. We'll put on some make-up to cover your bruises. You show the world that you are fine and if there was any fighting, the other guy came off worse. I think that sounds like a good plan.'

'I'm not in the mood,' Nasser said.

'What did I say about that time of the month?' Naeem whispered sotto voce.

'It doesn't matter,' Ayesha said, her tone brooking no argument. 'You'll go. Anjali would have told you the same thing if she was here. And you can have fun. Shiv and Naeem will go with you.'

12

Mumbai traffic could really kill your appetite for a good time, Sitara grimaced, as she walked into Maya's hotel an hour after she had got into the cab at Nariman Point. Her mood had spiralled further downhill after she'd spent the entire ride trying to convince her parents that she wasn't engaged to Nasser Khan, and though she and a man who thought he was her fiancé had been present at the scene of the crime, they hadn't beaten up a film star.

Her parents hadn't believed her. The only difference in their attitude was that from planning her wedding to the sex maniac – though from all reports he still held out hope for it – they were now planning it with Nasser Khan.

Sitara couldn't say that was an improvement as things stood.

Her mood dipped even lower when she walked into the hotel and the receptionist told her that Maya Dhillon had not checked in yet.

Sitara tried Maya's number. Switched off. Figured.

What was a girl to do when she was being stood up? Sitara did the only thing possible: she went to the restaurant and started ordering food. She was well on the way to finishing her gourmet burger when a woman walked up to her table, a trail of turned heads following every sway of an hourglass figure that was a miracle blend of North and South: honey-brown eyes and bosom courtesy Punjab; silky, dusky skin and hips courtesy Kerala – all adding up to five feet four inches of sex goddess.

'I knew I'd find you here!' Maya said, enfolding Sitara in a warm hug. Sitara was shocked to find herself tearing up and blinked furiously before she faced her friend.

'Idiot!' Sitara said, to cover up her emotional response. 'You're late!'

'I know,' her friend said. 'But I knew you'd have the restaurant to comfort you.'

Sitara laughed, recovering her composure.

'And boyfriend blazer,' Maya continued, giving her a once over. 'Very nice! Suits you. And does something to that blinding colour combination you're wearing. What do you call it? Neon and fluorescent? This magazine's making you very fashion conscious.'

'Shut up. It's only green and purple. The magazine's not making me fashion conscious, it's freezing me to death,' Sitara retorted. 'I've borrowed this to stay warm.'

'Borrowed from where? Or whom? Please tell me it's from one of your many admirers-slash-fiancés.'

'It's from the fashion closet,' Sitara said flatly.

'How *Devil Wears Prada* of you,' Maya said, lightly observing the tension in the figure opposite her. 'But we haven't talked about the most important thing – have you ordered anything for me? I need some fuel for the night ahead.'

Maya spent the next five minutes trying to dictate her order to a waiter too stunned by her to take anything in. Just when Sitara had relaxed, Maya turned to her and began the grilling. 'So are you engaged to Nasser Khan or is he back with that woman?'

'Who cares,' Sitara said as casually as she could.

'Hmm. If only you had told me you met him in Italy, I might be taken in by that answer. But it's very suspicious that you haven't spoken to me about that. By which I mean you're hiding things from me because you have things to hide. So, out with it. What happened?'

'Nothing.'

'Nothing?'

'Nothing,' Sitara affirmed, staring at her friend. Maya could do nothing about the truth. Except probe deeper.

'What happened before the nothing?' Maya asked.

'You're not allowed to know me so well, damn it.' Sitara stabbed a fry with her fork before proceeding to chop it into tiny pieces. Maya waited while she minced the fry. Sitara shovelled it onto her fork.

'Looks delicious,' Maya observed.

Sitara exhaled and put her fork down. 'He told me he was interested in me. There was some soul baring. Some physical attraction.'

Maya fanned her face. 'And?'

'And nothing. He behaved like a total stranger the next day,' Sitara said flatly.

'And then he's fighting with your fiancé? Sounds very cold to me. Completely uninterested.'

'He didn't have a fight with Karthik. I don't know where these rumours started – well, I know and I'm going to kill Anurag – but if he had a fight it wasn't with Karthik. I saw Karthik leave.'

'Which means he knows the rumours are untrue and he is happy to go along with them. Which, in case you are not following my reasoning, means he does not mind being linked to you. Which means–'

'Nothing,' Sitara supplied. 'Or rather, it means he doesn't talk to the press, so he can't be bothered to clear it up.'

'Yeah, you're right. He doesn't care about you. We're making too much of this.' Maya waited while her salad was served and the reluctant waiter had taken himself off. 'Plus he could be back with Richa.'

'Come on. You think I'm going to fall for that? I'm not jealous. I don't care.' Sitara reached for another fry.

'That's what I just said.' Maya didn't look up from her salad and missed the look Sitara flung her way.

'But he did do some good,' Sitara said, absentmindedly mincing this fry too. 'I am now finally over Karthik. You were right, I was letting him mess me up. Doing too much self-searching trying to figure out where I screwed up.'

Maya looked at her with interest. 'And now you know you didn't screw up?'

'Now I know that I might have screwed up but so did he. Which means I am no more wrong than him. Which means I have to stop beating myself up. And stop trying to think of what I might have done to put people off.'

'And what does this have to do with Nasser?'

'Nothing,' Sitara exclaimed. 'We're not talking about Nasser.'

'Anything to do with your sex maniac?' Maya looked at her expectantly.

'No. This is *my* epiphany. Big moment for me, you know?' Sitara said exasperatedly. 'For the future, when I meet men, and if anybody is interested in me, I am going to let them do all the work. And I'm going to take what they say at face value. If they like me, they have to come get me. I'm done trying to read between the lines and figure out their motives. And the motives behind their motives.'

'So you're saying you've thought endlessly about why Nasser turned cold and you haven't come up with an answer so this is your way of dealing with it,' Maya said ruthlessly.

'Yeah. Of course,' Sitara said sarcastically. 'That's what it is.' She shook her head in disgust. A waiter appeared at her side before she'd stopped.

'What can I get you?' he asked Sitara; his eyes stayed on Maya.

Sitara closed her eyes. It was always like this when she went out with Maya. She took a deep breath and ordered coffee.

Maya waited till the waiter reluctantly retreated before she spoke. 'And since the only people you obsess about are the people you have feelings for – please note, no obsessing about Karthik from now – I deduce you've gone and fallen for this guy.'

'Fallen!' Sitara snorted.

'Yes,' Maya agreed. 'Fallen.'

'He's a film star. I–,' Sitara ran a hand through her

hair, '–might be dazzled. But not fallen. And,' Sitara spoke hurriedly to forestall whatever Maya was about to say, 'even if I have, it makes no difference. Because he's a film star. Who'd want to get involved with one? He'll cheat. No future. I know it. I'll get over the dazzle.'

A cup of coffee appeared on the table in front of Sitara. The waiter must have broken all speed records to get it. He stood looking at Maya, his expression reminiscent of a puppy that had fetched. Maya smiled at him and indicated he could clear her plate. There was a sense of slow motion about that task, but finally he was gone.

'Why do you smile at them?' Sitara burst out. 'You know they can't function after that.'

'I'm searching for the exception,' Maya said. 'So. Let's go party.'

'That's it? You're not going to say anything else?' Sitara asked suspiciously.

'No. You did a good job with the summary. Let's go up and get pretty before we party. Come on.'

'So remind me again who Lokesh is?' It was an hour and a half later, and Sitara was certain that if she had had to watch another stroke of eyeshadow being applied or another strand of hair teased, she would have done a wolf-to-the-moon howl. Absence made the memory grow frailer because she had forgotten that Maya did not get ready in a hurry. And how aggravating that could be.

Time was not of the essence when hair had to be teased into the right shape, the right dress figured out, the right make-up put on. It was like being on a shoot, but without the sense of purpose, and no appreciable end in sight.

'Do you want me to put some make-up on you?' Maya said.

'Uh uh,' Sitara declined, while applying a coat of the red lipstick. Didn't look half bad, she thought. 'Can we go now?'

'You know what they say about New Yorkers being in a hurry – you're becoming like that in Mumbai,' Maya had told her as she finally started packing away the tools of her transformation. 'You've got to let yourself relax, settle back, take it easy. There's no hurry to get to this party – it'll be one of those that start late and end in the morning.'

Since it was already 10 p.m. and Sitara had to get to work the next day, all she felt was a sharp urge to get into bed. 'I'm already tired of hearing about it. Can I just go home?'

'Going home to bed early will make you old before your time,' Maya scolded her. 'All this routine will kill you. Do you think this dress works or should I wear the green one?'

Maya laughed at Sitara's sputtering. 'Sorry, I was just teasing you. Let's go.'

And finally, finally they were on their way.

'So Lokesh?' Sitara asked again when they were seated in the car; Maya had risen far enough up the corporate ladder to get one.

'I think I dated him for a couple of weeks – or was it weekends? – when I had that project in Pune. It was four or five years ago,' Maya reflected. 'He must have been nice, and normal, because I really don't remember anything else about him. In fact, I may not even have dated him. I think I dated his friend.'

Sitara looked at her friend silently.

'What?' Maya said defensively. 'I can't remember everybody I've met.'

Sitara shook her head, but didn't comment. 'So how did we get invited to the party?'

That turned out to be a task in investigative journalism. The story went that when Maya posted her imminent arrival in Mumbai on Facebook, one man called Lokesh had messaged with an invite to the party and its address. Maya being Maya was going whether she remembered the host or not.

Thankfully, Lokesh, whoever he might be, seemed to have a better memory than Maya because he had left her name with the muscle at the door.

Sitara looked around the penthouse in awe. It was decorated in the latest in rich and arty, and she could bet there was a swimming pool around somewhere. She wondered whether the mysterious Lokesh lived alone or with his parents, and where his parents were if he lived alone.

She looked around at the sea of faces. Everybody looked rich, beautiful, thin and facial-ed, and not a day over thirty-five. Sitara tried not to be insecure about her blackheads. She took a deep breath, and lowered the hand that had unconsciously risen to her nose.

Another look around the room, and she had to acknowledge that the man factor in this place scored high on desirability.

She spotted a couple of people who had appeared on *Homme*'s party pages; none that she had been introduced to.

That was okay; when she was on her game, she was good at parties. Even better when she didn't know anybody. She could be as outrageous or indifferent as she wanted.

Her friend said something. By the time Sitara turned her head around to ask her to repeat herself, Maya was no longer there. The bar, she therefore decided, was the most logical place to go to.

There was no Maya but there was Advait. After Advait, there was Binoy, then Cyrus. An hour and a half later, Sitara was tempted to make an announcement for a man with a name starting with D to make his way by her side.

She looked around. Nobody seemed to be making a beeline for her. Fine, this would be a good time to see whether she was right about the pool.

She was. It was on the level above.

Sitara stood in a secluded corner of the terrace enjoying the fresh air. And tried to ignore the rustling of cloth and the heavy breathing from the other occupants of the same secluded corner.

'Hello Sitara,' said a voice from behind her, causing her to jump a mile. There was a pause in the heavy breathing in the yonder darkness.

Sitara turned around, and for a moment – enough time to give her heart a giant-wheel sort of flying sensation – thought it was Nasser. Then she caught sight of the beard.

'Naeem!' Sitara hugged him, thankful that it hadn't

been his brother. It gave her time to work on being cool and polite and strangerly because she had no doubt that if Naeem was here, Nasser would be around, too. 'What are you doing here? Do you know Lokesh?' Maybe he could throw some light on the mysterious party thrower.

Naeem muttered something under his breath.

'Whose reputation?' Sitara asked.

'Nothing. Yes, we know Lokesh. We were in the same school. Nasser used to stop him from being beaten up once in a while.'

'Oh no. Why? And didn't Nasser get beaten up?'

'Poor Lokesh was new money. And Nasser was always in fights but he didn't lose too much.'

'Oh well, don't really care about that. Aren't you afraid you'll reveal the big black sheep secret? And what about Turkey?'

'What big secret will anybody learn from me? I decided to put Turkey on hold. I hope I haven't let myself and this proud, ancient nation down desperately?' Naeem said, a slight edge to his voice.

'Getting it a lot, huh?'

'Surprisingly, yes. A midlife crisis that at least follows a planned trajectory seems to be more acceptable than one in which I ricochet hither and thither.'

'Hither and thither.' Sitara couldn't contain the disbelief in her voice. 'Did you actually use that in a sentence? Say the words aloud?'

'I can't help it if my vocabulary is wider than yours, young Sitara,' Naeem said loftily.

Sitara snorted.

'Why are you moaning?'

'I'm not the one moaning, you are,' Sitara said.

'Not like that, more like...,' he paused trying to think of the right words. A moan, unmistakable in the activity that had led to its origin, punctuated the silence. 'That.'

'Oh,' Sitara said in a small voice, trying hard to swallow the laughter. A snort escaped her.

'Are you laughing?' Naeem's voice was strained.

Sitara shook her head. Another snort escaped her.

Naeem's shoulders began to shake.

There was a tense silence from the corner as everybody waited for the next move. 'Oh, for god's sake, can the two of you go somewhere else and laugh?' an exasperated voice rang out from the darkness. 'You're interrupting us.'

Nasser and Shiv found them at the far end of the terrace, propping each other up as they laughed.

The pleasure Nasser felt at seeing Sitara again was no surprise. The need to bury his fist into his brother's face definitely wasn't either. Hadn't he felt the need a week ago? But another feeling out there was a hugely unwelcome surprise; it tasted like insecurity. Was Sitara better suited to Naeem than to him? They were both intellectual types, they liked reading, they knew their art, and were passionate about music. Their lives were similar. They had bonded from the beginning.

She had never laughed like that with him.

The urge to hit his brother was overwhelming.

'What's so funny?' Shiv asked; Nasser almost hugged him for providing a distraction.

Naeem and Sitara choked out what they probably thought was an explanation. Their audience couldn't make head or tail of it. Shiv sent Nasser an amused look, and surprised a completely unamused Nasser as he gazed intently at the couple in front of him.

'Oh god, I can't laugh anymore,' Sitara said. 'It hurts.'

'Are you moaning?' Naeem said.

'Oh don't,' Sitara pleaded. She took a deep breath and visibly pulled herself together. Naeem wiped his tears, and sputtered to a stop. They told the story again.

'Okay, it's not very funny when you hear it, but it really was funny. Anyway, Sitara, have you met Shiv?' Naeem made the introductions in an attempt at normalcy.

Sitara gave Shiv a bright smile, intensely conscious of the man standing silently at his side. 'The food Nazi,' Sitara identified. There was a choked sound from his left. Sitara's eyes didn't waver from Shiv's as she explained. 'Naeem told me about the removal of all the MTR packets from Nasser's suitcase.'

'That's not the way I would introduce myself,' Shiv turned on the charm. 'Especially to a beautiful woman.'

'But I'm sure Shalini would agree with that description,' Nasser said. 'Shalini is the future Mrs Thakru,' he explained to Sitara, with all the subtlety of a sledge-hammer, ignoring the raised eyebrow from his brother.

'Oh.' Sitara was forced to look at Nasser and discovered that her body was now performing stomach levitations. 'You look good for a man who's been in a fight,' she said, as much in an effort to put her stomach back in its place as him.

'Rumours,' Nasser dismissed. 'You know how the media is.'

'Full of liars I gather.' Sitara was quick to take offence. Anything to get away from him because, despite all that prepping to be polite and strangerly, she realized she was nowhere near ready. 'I'll take my lying self off then.'

Nasser grabbed her by her shoulders as she made to pass him by. 'That's not what I meant and you know it.'

'Whatever. Fine. I'm heading to the bar.' Sitara didn't want to escalate matters; she just wanted to get away, except that Nasser still hadn't released his hold on her.

Nasser looked down at the woman in his arms – who was trying to get away – and jerked his head at his openly staring brother and friend indicating they should shove off. They ignored him. Sitara made another effort to free herself, and Nasser turned to deal with more important matters.

He chose his words carefully. 'I meant that a large part of the news media likes to sensationalize events. They'll take one speck of gossip and turn it into primetime news. And Bollywood is more likely to get that sort of treatment than anybody else.'

'You mean the truth is that your nose is actually puffy because of the hot air you're emitting and not from being hit? Damn, the media really screwed up that story!' Sitara shot back, wrenching herself free.

'Are you trying to pick a fight with me?' Nasser caught her again.

'Of course not! What gave you that idea? Ooh, could it be that you have mocked my profession at every turn, and have now descended to calling us all liars? No, surely I couldn't take offence at that. Will you please let me go?'

'No. And I'm sorry if I have mocked you. I think you're a great writer with an excellent instinct for stories. But that's not true of everybody in your profession. And–'

'Be still, my beating heart,' Sitara jeered. 'How will I absorb this statement about my career? Especially when it comes from the man who didn't know my name a month ago?'

When Nasser didn't answer, Sitara wrenched herself away. 'Lovely meeting you again. And goodbye.'

Sitara stalked back inside, straight to the bar. Unfortunately by the time her vodka reached her, her fury had turned to depression, and she couldn't think of any place she wanted to be more than her bed. She was just taking out her cell phone to message Maya, when a familiar voice spoke. 'People are so unreasonable, aren't they?' Naeem said. He continued, undeterred by the lack of response from Sitara. 'Look at Nasser, giving his driver half a day to round up every issue of *Homme* from the past year. Wonder what he wanted with them,' he said innocently.

'I don't care–'

'Good. You can accompany me to dinner because it's really boring to stand here nursing a lime juice, and we can talk about other fun things.'

Sitara hesitated. 'I was just going home–'

'Don't worry. Last time I looked, Nasser had taken root at the far side of the pool. I don't think he's moving for a while.'

The only thing that proved blood was thicker than friendship, Sitara fumed, was when the first person she saw in the dining area was Nasser.

'Oops!' Naeem didn't even work at his remorse. 'He's a banyan tree. I'll just...get us some plates.'

'No. Wait,' Sitara tried to grab at his sleeve but he had already slipped away. Sitara turned back fatalistically and sure enough Nasser had come to stand by her.

'I'm sorry,' he said, his tone more formal than she had ever heard. 'We seem to have got off to a bad start. Can we try again?'

Sitara assented, more because she couldn't come up with a good way to say no.

'Congratulations,' he continued.

'Thanks.' She knew she was going to regret this. 'But what for?'

'Your engagement.'

'I'm not engaged.'

'Oh yes, I remember. You're skipping straight to the wedding.'

'I'm not–' what was the use '–Thanks. And congratulations to you too.'

'For?'

'You and Richa. Back together. Engaged?'

'We're not.'

'What a coincidence,' Sitara said brightly. 'Neither of us is engaged.'

Naeem and Shiv walked into a deathly silence. Looks were exchanged.

'Sitara! Where have you been? I've been looking everywhere for you.' Maya was back, and she had an arm attached to her waist, an arm that belonged to the most nondescript man Sitara had ever seen. He was thin and weedy, with designer stubble, and desperately designer jeans. 'And this is Lokesh.' Sitara could understand why Maya had no memory of him.

'Lokesh, meet my best friend.' Maya gave Sitara an expectant look. The three men were also giving Sitara expectant looks.

Sitara resigned herself to being relegated to the background for what remained of the night as she made the introductions.

Only it didn't quite happen like that. Sure Nasser did his rat-abandoning-ship routine and hung on to Maya's every word for the rest of their time there, but Shiv, it seemed, had taken a shine to Sitara and spent the evening glued to her side – though the conversation was between Nasser and Shiv as they took digs at each other, with Naeem adding to the fire, choosing his side at random. Lokesh stuck to Maya's side doggedly, though it was obvious she forgot about him every time he stopped talking.

At about 12.30 a.m., there was a stir indicating the arrival of 'somebody'. Two familiar figures walked toward them.

Richa and Anurag were the latest guests.

Nasser muttered something unrepeatable under his breath. Having put off dealing with Richa all day, it was just a little unfair to meet her at a party.

'Let her come to you,' Shiv advised him in a low voice.

Nasser glared at him.

'You forget to relay details,' Shiv said. 'It's just easier if we listen in.'

Nasser didn't dignify that with a reply. Anurag left Richa's side, presumably to get a drink from the bar, and flirt with a tall leggy babe who had taken over as bartender. Nasser made his way towards his former fiancée. He was pretty certain it wasn't his imagination that a hush had fallen over the room. He kissed her cheeks from force of habit and stepped back.

'You look beautiful. As usual.' It was true. She did. Even if it was touched up and erased of everything that had lent her character, with perfect lips, a nose that showed the art of reconstruction, plump cheeks and an unlined brow.

'Thank you,' she mocked. 'That means a great deal to me.'

Nasser couldn't blame her; after all, the end of their relationship had been rung in over her obsession with her appearance – his inability to see the need for so much cosmetic work and her impatience with his 'last-century views' as she'd called them. 'All the actors are doing it, not just the actresses,' she'd railed at him.

'And you can see how difficult it is for them to act after that,' Nasser had shot back.

'The public can't see the difference. Or at least they can see that their heroes and heroines aren't getting old. They go back to watch them.'

'No! They go and watch the movie,' Nasser had tried to explain, but he could see she wasn't listening. No use thinking about that now. 'Shall we go out onto the terrace? It's a little bit more private.'

'And ruin our great reconciliation for the audience? No, I don't think so,' Richa replied, smiling at him.

Nasser's gaze drifted to the bar where Anurag was unabashedly flirting with the bartender. 'Anurag really likes the ladies, doesn't he? It's hard to picture him married. Or faithful.'

'While you will soon be married to the fatty, sorry, I meant journalist.' Richa smiled at him, though her fingers had tightened around her clutch.

'I hope so!' Nasser agreed fervently. 'I know you set it up but I really must thank you for interfering. I would never have found Sitara otherwise. She's...maddening and funny and real and makes me so furious, but she's perfect for me,' he finished. Richa looked faintly nauseated. His job was done. Almost.

'I would thank you for the spin you put on last night if I didn't know it was all about saving your skin, in this case the Pepsi deal. But if you want it, and I haven't said yes yet, then you need to stay far, far away from anything in my life. I'm sure we understand each other.' He didn't kiss her goodbye.

Nasser walked back with a feeling of satisfaction. It didn't last very long when he had to watch Shiv flirt even more outrageously with Sitara.

Then Anurag drifted in – Richa following determinedly in his wake – and greeted Sitara with unwonted enthusiasm. His eyes widened when he saw Maya – Nasser could see that it cost him – but for some inexplicable reason he kept his attention focused on Sitara.

The night became surreal after that. Sitara thought that the only one having fun was probably Naeem. Which fairly summarized that what followed was not normal.

Richa attached herself to Naeem, then finding him unsatisfactory, made a play for Nasser. Maya took that as a challenge to her womanly wiles and a bit of competition ensued.

But they weren't the only ones. Anurag, in a flamboyant gesture, swept a very surprised Sitara into his arms; Shiv tried to slip her away. A slight tug-of-war ensued. With a sound of disgust Nasser stepped in and freed her from both. Lokesh immediately tried to take Maya away, and Naeem Richa.

Neither was successful.

Shiv and Anurag had descended into veiled hostility, both trying to get Sitara's attention.

'Can you stop encouraging them?' Nasser's voice was low and angry.

'I am not doing anything to encourage them.'

'No? Just look at them.'

They were arguing about cricket.

Sitara pointed that out to Nasser.

'They are trying to impress you. Just one more way to show off to you.'

'With cricket?' She would never understand men.

'You are the one who brought up Sachin,' Nasser accused.

'Yeah. Because I was going to say that despite interviewing him I don't get cricket,' Sitara protested.

'Obviously you weren't quick enough. Cricket is even worse than politics and religion. They are going to start hitting each other any minute now.'

'Could somebody get me a drink?' Sitara said in desperation, just needing them to be gone. 'A rum and coke.'

'I will get it,' Shiv said.

'Excellent,' Anurag agreed. 'I will entertain this

beautiful woman till you return.' They glared at each other.

Sitara could see heads turning at his loud delivery.

'Oh excellent. My second fight this week,' Nasser muttered.

'Rumoured fight,' Sitara murmured. More loudly: 'That's so sweet of you, Shiv. I'm going to be *very* grateful,' Sitara said, and was beyond relieved when that spurred Anurag to finally make a move.

'Anurag,' Richa said sweetly. 'Are you leaving me here all alone?'

'Just for a moment, Richa. Hang on.'

Sitara unconsciously moved closer to Nasser. She didn't like the way Richa was looking at her. An arm slid around her waist and pulled her close to him. 'She's dangerous,' Nasser kept his voice low, but his eyes were amused. 'Don't worry, I'll protect you.'

Their eyes locked and Sitara had a world-fading-away moment.

Maya broke it. 'Nasser, could you drop us home please?'

Sitara loved Maya like a sister but she was really going to have to rip her heart out.

'I told you I'll do it.' The players left behind turned surprised eyes to the man who had drifted out of their consciousness with such ease.

'But Sitara–' Maya began.

'I'll drop her home,' Nasser said. 'You go on. No. In fact, we will go on. Naeem, you can get a ride home with Shiv. Richa, please tell Anurag I'm sorry I couldn't say bye to him. Come on.' Nasser put his hand on Sitara's elbow and propelled her out of the party.

Out of the corner of her eyes, Sitara thought she saw Shiv and Naeem exchange a high five. And was Maya smiling?

Sitara wondered whether she could pass off the silence as comfortable. She studied it for a few more minutes to make her decision. Ten minutes into the ride she was forced to concede that calling it comfortable would be akin to calling the Commonwealth Games organized.

But Nasser wasn't making the slightest effort at a conversation, she thought resentfully, so why should she? She counted off another 120 seconds before she reached breaking point. She couldn't take it any longer. She had made polite conversation with bigger idiots than him; she would just talk about the weather.

'So you seemed to be having a good time with Maya?'

Sitara examined that dispassionately. It didn't seem to have anything to do with the weather. Though it did make the atmosphere in the car a little chilly.

'Yes. She's lovely. Not only beautiful, but very warm, very smart, very easy to talk to, very...'

'Yes, she is,' Sitara cut in. Damn it. She loved her friend, but did every man need to love her equally, if not more? 'You're lucky to have Shiv too. I liked him very much.'

'Did you?' Nasser's voice took the temperature a few degrees lower.

'Yes, he's very passionate about what he does, isn't he?'

Nasser didn't hear anything after passionate. His hands tightened on the wheel. 'Yes, he's intense about food,' he said shortly. 'Even forgets about Shalini when he gets going. Shalini is–'

'Yes, I remember,' Sitara cut him short. 'The woman he's going to marry. I got the point the first time. He's taken.'

'Really? Didn't seem like that back there,' Nasser said.

A sudden pounding in her head indicated to Sitara that her blood pressure was hitting the high hundreds. She had barely talked to Shiv and Nasser was treating her like some Mata Hari. 'You mean all those sparks flying?' Sitara watched his hands tighten on the wheel. 'Those were between you and him. Is there something you're keeping secret from the world?' As soon as she said it, Sitara realized that was the most likely explanation. Of course, he was gay. It explained everything. The broken engagement, the Pepsi-throwing from Richa, even the fact that he hadn't once attempted to kiss her. 'Oh my god, you are gay.'

'*What?*' Nasser looked at Sitara incredulously. And he looked again when he realized she actually believed it. 'I am not gay!'

'Sure. Whatever. I won't say anything.' Sitara looked out the window bitterly. Her choice in men really was spectacular.

'I. Am. Not. Gay.' Nasser bit out the words.

Sitara shrugged. 'Of course.'

There was a muttered curse and the next thing Sitara knew they had taken a turn into a side street.

"What? This is not–'

Her protests were cut off as Nasser turned her to face him and very firmly kissed her. And again. And again.

Sitara gulped when they broke apart.

'And just so we're very clear about things – that's not the stick shift; I am glad to see you,' Nasser said wickedly.

Sitara could only be glad it was dark, because she could feel herself blushing.

'Speechless?' Nasser laughed. 'I've finally discovered the secret to shutting you up.' He was disgustingly cheerful as he started the car and drove back to the main road.

'Are you ever going to talk again?' he asked, when the silence had continued for a while.

'Yes,' Sitara said, then groped for something to say. Her brain processes seemed to have blitzed. 'It's a very pleasant night,' she managed finally.

Nasser laughed. 'Isn't it?' he sounded unbearably self-satisfied. 'And going to get better when we reach your place.'

'No! I mean–' Sitara trailed off, finding no way to explain her vehemence.

'No?' Nasser's brows drew together.

'I mean, it's too soon.' Sitara tried again, hoping he would let it drop.

'Oh.' Nasser sounded anything but satisfied with her explanation. 'When will be the right time?' he asked.

'I don't know,' Sitara said, starting to get irritated. 'But after we've seen each other for more than three days.'

'Five,' Nasser corrected. 'We met yesterday too.'

'Five. Huge difference,' Sitara snapped.

Nasser didn't reply immediately. 'How many days?' he asked finally. 'What number do you consider appropriate we–'

'I don't know! However long you waited with Richa.'

'That would be four days less.' Nasser said.

'You made out on the first day?'

'Yes. First couple of hours, if I remember.'

Sitara gave him a fulminating look. 'What's the longest you've waited?'

'Hmm. Yes, I think this would qualify.'

'Oh my god!' Sitara lapsed into silence.

'So if you could give me a ballpark figure?'

'I can't,' Sitara said tartly. 'You'll just have to wait. That is, if you want to.'

'What do you want to do till we wait?' Nasser asked, almost idly. 'Go out for dinner? A movie?'

The impossibility of the situation crashed in on Sitara. She couldn't go for a movie or dinner with Nasser Khan! He would be mobbed. She would be written about. Even more than right now. They were never going to have a 'normal' relationship.

'Yes. It's a little difficult, isn't it? That's why we don't date muggles, civilians, whatever you call them.' Nasser said. 'So how do you want our relationship to play out?'

'We don't have a relationship,' Sitara denied automatically.

'You want another demonstration?' Nasser asked, signalling for the next side street.

'No! That's just... Just drive me home.'

'Are you sure? Spoilsport.' Nasser switched off the indicator. 'So, that's just what? Lust?'

'Yes. No. I don't know.' Damn it, why should she be on the defensive? 'And don't push me. You aren't going to talk me into bed.'

'Talk? No wonder you're hesitating. Talk.' He snorted derisively. 'I'm more into action, actually. You may enjoy this new way of doing things,' he added persuasively.

'No.'

'I had a feeling you'd say that,' Nasser sighed. 'So now that you've shot down every one of my suggestions, how are we taking this forward again?'

'I don't know,' Sitara was starting to feel harassed.

'And you don't know when you'll figure it out?'

'Yes.'

'Right. Here we are,' Nasser nosed the car into a parking spot on the street. He turned to face her. 'A much pleasanter ride than the last time I dropped you home. Puke free. Though the end was memorable. You felt good in my arms. Shall I carry you up again?'

'Thank y–' Sitara registered his words in the middle of her polite good night speech. 'No!'

'Are you sure?'

'Yes.'

'Shall I come up so we can discuss it?'

'No.'

'You might...'

Sitara lost her temper. 'Do you understand the word no? N.O. Read my lips. Stop harassing me! I'll let you know when I'm good and ready. I'm not going to join the legion of your groupies. If you're so desperate go–'

Sitara pushed the door open and scrambled out of the car.

'You know why you're yelling, don't you?' Nasser called out to her. 'You're frustrated.'

Sitara slammed the door in his face.

Nasser let himself into his apartment and found that his brother and friend had made themselves at home.

'What are you two doing here?' he demanded irritably.

'The question is: What are *you* doing here?' Naeem asked. 'You've left the fair Sitara rather early.'

'Yes,' Nasser said shortly, walking away. The bedroom door slammed behind him.

Shiv took a long swallow of his whisky and sighed. 'All that flirting for nothing.'

Naeem looked at him pityingly. 'Even at my most loser self, I've never seen anything so pathetic.' He put down his cup of tea and stood up.

'You're right. That was pretty bad,' Shiv reflected, making his way toward the door. 'But still, sustained flirting takes a lot out of a man.'

Naeem shook his head at him. 'Pathetic. Anyway, what now?'

Nasser's door was flung open, and he came striding out. He came to a halt in front of them. 'And just in case I haven't made things clear – Sitara's out of bounds for you two. *You* stick with Shalini,' he told Shiv, 'and you, I don't know, find a backpacker!'

'Are you warning us off?' Shiv gave a disbelieving laugh.

'Yes. Totally. Was I clear? Good. Good night.'

They watched him disappear back into his room; the door shut with a bang. Naeem put his hand out and Shiv high-fived it.

'Our emotionally stunted Nasser is growing up,' Shiv said, emotionally. 'This is a big day. *Huge*!'

'Yes. I think so too. How long do you think she'll hold him off?' Naeem asked. 'I give it forty-eight hours.'

'Thousand bucks says twenty,' Shiv replied.

'Twenty. No way. You're on. I like easy money.'

13

Sitara opened her eyes and watched the pale sunlight illuminate her room. She looked at her mobile and sighed. It was 6 a.m. She shut her eyes and willed herself back to sleep. She'd never woken up so early in her life. Not when she only had to get to office by noon.

Thirty minutes later, she gave up. She wasn't going back to sleep. There were too many thoughts flooding her mind, most of which circled around a certain ratfink actor and what she was going to do with him. About! About him, she corrected herself.

At 7 she reluctantly got out of bed. Her sleep might have evaporated but her appetite remained healthy. Her stomach was demanding sustenance. It was so unfair. To wake up early and want to eat.

Her thoughts were bitter as she brushed her teeth, ate a slice of leftover pizza and made herself coffee.

She felt like a Nescafe advert as she stood in her three-foot balcony and watched a world of early risers get some exercise in the park beside the sea. Who would have thought there were so many of them?

She read all the papers – the supplements were full

of the Nasser–Richa reunion coming so quickly on the heels of his quarrel over her -- had another coffee, and yet it was only 9.30. Did time always pass so slowly in the mornings?

Her thoughts weren't getting her anywhere either – relationship with Nasser or no relationship with Nasser? She could come up with a million things against the idea, and not one for it. Unless you counted sex, Sitara thought, pausing in the act of burrowing through her cupboard and considered that again. She reluctantly discarded it for the nth time; sure it could be great, it would have been great in Italy, but right now, here, it just wasn't worth all the trouble.

Picking out clothes at random – a black maxi dress and bolero – Sitara kohled her eyes and wafted into the office looking like Morticia Addams with a bad perm at an unearthly 10.20 a.m.

Her appearance so startled Prabhakar that he bobbled a cup of coffee. Conversation in the office ground to halt for a moment but it wasn't long before it was replaced by smart-ass remarks.

The grooming editor sent her a mail with the number of a psychiatrist – 'He's really good, and Prozac works wonders.'

Debashish walked in with the publisher '...really must do something about her, reputation of the magazine, her lateness – Sitara! You're in office?'

'Yes,' she said, without looking up. She gave a sigh of resignation when she sensed his presence hadn't abated. 'Did you want something? Hello Anil.'

'How come you're in the office so early?' Debashish demanded.

'Office timings, no?' Her colleagues later told her she had sounded like this was the time she always came in.

Debashish gnashed his teeth.

'My daughter can't wake up early,' Anil said. 'When she was in school she was caught bribing the watchman to let her in late.' He shook his head indulgently, unable to disguise his pride at his daughter's cleverness.

'I wish I had thought of that,' Sitara was genuinely envious of the girl. 'Did you pick up those Rainas?'

'Yes. Excellent advice. The price for his works is already shooting up,' he smiled benevolently at her.

Debashish who hated to be left out of any conversation with the publisher, and more obviously hated that Sitara had any sort of relationship with his boss, interjected with a jocular, 'I didn't know Sitara was advising you on art?'

'Oh, yes. Sandeep did such a good job with my wardrobe that I thought I'd turn to all your other experts. You've chosen well,' he told Debashish. He saw the look on Debashish's face and turned back to Sitara. 'Oh. Debashish tells me you are having a...you and Nasser Khan...umm–'

'Yes,' Sitara said dangerously, daring him to continue.

'Debashish seems to think it's reflecting badly on the magazine,' he said, almost apologetically. 'Try not to be so public. Yes. I think that would be best. Okay?' He flashed a smile at her and turned to Debashish, obviously feeling he had discharged his duty.

'What?' Debashish exclaimed. 'What about–'

'Lina and Hyder are waiting,' Anil cut in, gesturing towards the conference room. 'Let's go discuss marketing and advertising.' He said something to Debashish in a low voice; Sitara couldn't hear it, but it earned her a calculating look from Debashish. He looked like his candy had been snatched away, but nodded and walked away.

Scoring victories over your boss should be recommended as a cure for the blues, Sitara thought. The look on Debashish's face when he had realized that Anil wasn't going to say anything to her... She played it on loop for a while, a warm fuzzy feeling filling her up. She would love to know what Anil had said. She smiled widely at Prabhakar, shocking him for the second time that morning and causing him to seriously consider going home early.

Sitara went in search of Sandeep to do some gloating, but he wasn't in – why was everybody so late? Martin was talking to a photographer, and everybody else seemed to be busy. She went back to her computer feeling dissatisfied and caught sight of herself in the monitor. She looked in distaste at her all-black ensemble. What had she been thinking?

Oh.

Nasser.

She sank in front of her computer.

Harsh was still incommunicado. And Nasser seemed to have landed himself in a fine mess without her, Anjali thought grimly as she paced in front of the TV.

Was it really an anger management issue if the two most important men in your life deserved to have their heads banged against the wall? Hard. Often.

She tried Harsh's number again. It was still switched off. Was this the way it was going to continue till the wedding?

Was there going to be a wedding? For the hundredth time Anjali considered whether she should send Harsh a text asking him that question. For the hundredth time she dissuaded herself with the same argument; she wasn't going to give him any ideas.

Anjali stopped her pacing. She didn't know what she was going to do but she couldn't live in suspense for the next ten days.

Richa kept losing her focus during yoga, thanks to the party last night. Thank god her forehead was Botoxed; the urge to frown was overwhelming.

Last night had been a disaster. And all because of that fat girl.

She, Richa Bali, last year's most googled person on earth, had been completely ignored.

She could have borne it better if the men were clustered around the other girl – there was a possibility she might be considered attractive – but the fat one? No, no, a thousand times no.

No. There was a reason it was so unbelievable, because it wasn't true.

Nasser and Anurag had been proving a point; there was no chance the men had found that girl attractive over her.

Nasser's actions were explained away easily – she had been trying to get his goat and he had decided to pay her back. Anurag, though, was more worrying.

She had been so careful with him, keeping him at a distance, making sure he didn't feel trapped. Then why the flirting? Had he got a whiff of her intentions? Or had she been too careful – was this his way of finding out whether she cared for him at all? Had he been trying to make her jealous?

She would have to give her next move some serious thought. She sat down for her half-an-hour of meditation.

'Anjali! You're back! You're okay?' Nasser stared blearily at his manager, automatically accepting the mint she gave him. She'd woken him up again, this time without the meltdown thankfully.

'Don't ask stupid questions,' she snapped, pushing past him into the house. 'Where's your staff? How come you're opening doors?'

Nasser ran a hand over his eyes. Had he forgotten Anjali's special charm or was this not normal? 'I'm supposed to be on holiday. I don't want to deal with a bunch of people,' he answered, as normally as he could when suffering from severe sleep deprivation. He wasn't going to have a very coherent conversation without some coffee. He told Anjali as much.

'Brush your teeth first,' she said. 'And make it quick.'

Nasser set his teeth. She really was insufferable. He turned to tell her so but stopped short at the sight of her puffy eyes. Had she been crying? His mind boggled. He walked away without saying a word.

Nasser took his second life-giving sip of coffee and felt almost human. He put a hand at the small of Anjali's back and guided her towards the breakfast nook – a semi-enclosed space just off the kitchen – and returned to get the coffees, the bread box he'd started stocking since his return, and a couple of plates.

'Right,' he said, plonking the lot down on the table, and himself into the chair beside it. 'What's happened?'

It was like a dam bursting open. Half an hour, a lot of incoherence and sarcasm later, Nasser gathered that Harsh had not called since the day he had seen her return crying from Nasser's house. He was refusing to take her calls either. He didn't answer her texts. She had tried to see him but he had got the servant to say he wasn't there. He had been cold when she had tried to see him and had removed himself within minutes. She didn't know why he was so mad, and she didn't know whether the wedding was on or not. There were only a couple of days to go and she was a nervous wreck. She was also very angry. And upset.

And she was looking at Nasser to provide a solution because in some twisted way she laid the blame for the entire fiasco at his door.

Women!

'I'm not really to blame for Harsh's jealousy or subsequent violent behaviour,' he pointed out, crumbling his croissant with a little too much force.

'I don't care. I don't know what to do. My parents don't know what to do. His parents don't either. You have to fix it.' She looked distastefully at the croissant he had served her. 'It's full of butter and flour, Nasser. I'm not going to eat that before my wedding. Not while there's still a chance it's happening.'

Nasser took it off her plate and dropped it into his. 'You're a pain when you're worried, you know. Fine. I suppose I can't ignore a cry for help.' He knew he sounded hopeful, but a man had to try.

'No, you can't,' Anjali said predictably.

'Fine. So to recap: he saw you the morning of your meltdown, beat me up that evening, and hasn't spoken to you for the past two days. And he's refusing to meet you?'

'That's what I just said,' Anjali said, but her tone was hopeful.

'Any idea what you said when he saw you after the meltdown?'

Anjali shook her head.

'And to get to the bottom of his behaviour you have to corner him, and he's refusing to be cornered?' Nasser concluded. He rubbed his nose unconsciously. Was it his imagination or was it starting to hurt again?

A solution had popped into his head, but since it involved his presence within a few feet of Harsh, Nasser was rather keen to come up with other ideas. He didn't relish the idea of being used as a punching bag again and didn't think he could go around a man who was going to be married in a week's time.

There was the sound of a door being unlocked and Naeem walked into his apartment. He stilled when he caught sight of Anjali and Nasser through the living room doors and gave his brother a disapproving look.

'Is there a reason you are here? And who gave you the keys to my apartment?' Nasser demanded, as Naeem walked within earshot.

'I'm here to get some tea,' Naeem said, walking purposefully towards the kettle, filling it up and turning it on. 'And Abba gave me the keys. Hi, Anjali. Is something going on between you two that I should know about?'

'Why can't you drink tea downstairs?' Nasser said automatically, ignoring the rest of his questions.

'Because, brother dear, Abba is under the impression that the only brew worthy to touch my lips is the one he makes with his very own hands. And I am not strong enough to survive that. So Anjali, tell me your problem.'

Nasser cut in before Anjali had said more than two words. 'Let me. I have the short, succinct version.'

'Jealousy, plain and simple.' Naeem said at the end of the narration. 'But he hasn't called off the wedding, so I would deduce that he intends to go through with it.'

Anjali interrupted with a strongly worded reply to the effect that she could not marry in this fashion.

Nasser stayed silent, hoping that his brother would come up with a solution other than the one he had.

'We need to run him to ground first,' Naeem said thoughtfully, his gaze flicking over to Nasser, lingering uncomfortably long on his nose. 'Get him in a room with you so you can get him to listen to reason.' He thought about it for a while. 'There's nothing else we can do. We need a grand gesture.'

Nasser rubbed his nose again. His brother had come to the same conclusion as him. Damn, he supposed he owed Anjali. He would rather have shown his appreciation with an extravagant wedding gift.

'His office is in Nariman Point,' he told Naeem. 'Are you good friends with any of his friends?' he asked

Anjali. 'Yes. Excellent. I'll tell you what to do. He turned to Naeem. 'Are you coming too?'

'Wild horses couldn't keep me away,' Naeem said.

'Okay, let's go make a scene at another hotel then.'

Sitara's stomach did an early start on the hunger pangs, bringing home the fact that she had already spent more time in the office pre-lunch than she ever had in her working life. Martin had been called into a meeting with Anil – which meant he and Debashish were going to spend some time almost coming to blows in front of Anil – and Sitara didn't feel like socializing with any of her colleagues. A solitary lunch sounded like a good idea.

She had barely taken a step out of the lift downstairs when she was hailed by a vaguely familiar voice.

'Sitara! I'm so glad I caught you,' said a vaguely familiar man. She was still trying to put a name to him when he solved that problem. 'Girish, remember? We met at your aunt's place.'

'What are you doing here?' Sitara made minimal effort to hide her displeasure at his appearance. 'I thought my notoriety had ended all plans for the wedding?'

'Oh yes, that was very unfortunate. We would have been perfect,' he said sounding like he actually regretted it. 'But after all that publicity... I'm seeing somebody more suitable this evening.'

'Great,' Sitara said, starting to walk towards the taxi ranks. Girish fell in step beside her. 'Good for you. I'm sure it'll work out. Best of luck. Now, I'm heading off for lunch, so...'

'I'll join you,' Girish said.

Sitara stopped abruptly. 'Huh? Why? What?'

'There's something I want to discuss with you,' he said confidingly.

Sitara had a bad feeling. 'It'll have to wait. I'm meeting somebody for lunch and I'm running late.'

'I'll talk with you in the taxi then,' Girish said determinedly.

'I'm not taking a taxi. I'm... My lunch is just down the road. At the Oberoi. I'm walking. Very fast,' Sitara added, suiting words to action, already knowing what was going to follow. She had a feeling she would have to accost some poor lone diner just to get away from Girish.

'I'll walk with you,' he said predictably.

Sitara increased her pace, praying for some divine intervention before her poor couch-potato body died of the unexpected exercise. Or the violence she unleashed when she stomped this man into the ground.

'So what I wanted to talk to you about – I don't want to beat about the bush – I mean, we're consenting adults, you're a woman of the world...'

It was almost lunchtime when they neared the Oberoi. Nasser looked nervous, Naeem thought. Who could blame him? It couldn't be pleasant to be at the receiving end of somebody's fist. And to knowingly put yourself there again, that took courage.

His brother wasn't too bad, really. A bit thick about some things, but love supposedly did that to everybody. Or so he had told his parents this morning.

They'd caught him as he was returning from Nasser's apartment and, surprisingly, his mother had wanted to know whether Nasser was back with Richa. 'Surely he can't be after I threw him that party.' She was clearly worried about that.

He had reassured both of them that Richa and Nasser were history; his brother had eyes only for Sitara. He had then spent the next half-an-hour answering questions about Sitara. It hadn't been satisfactory for anybody.

'Bring her home for dinner,' his father had commanded him, and Naeem had promised them he would.

The closer they got to the Oberoi, the more silent things got in the car. He supposed he should be doing something about it. 'Don't worry, I'll get the ice organized immediately,' he reassured his brother, who didn't seem to appear too impressed with his planning.

'I still don't see why you've come along,' Nasser said disagreeably. 'You aren't doing anything.'

'Moral support,' Naeem said. He would have other compelling arguments but his interest was diverted. Suddenly, he barked at the driver, 'Stop the car.' The poor fellow followed instructions with enough alacrity to cause a lot of rude honking behind them. 'I'll be with you in ten,' he called out behind him, ignoring his brother's yelling.

'Sitara! Sitara!' It took her a moment to realize that it wasn't her imagination; somebody was actually calling her.

She could have kissed Naeem for his timing. She hugged him fiercely.

'Whoa. What!' Naeem reared back in surprise.

'Oh, I'm so glad I'm not late,' Sitara launched into speech. 'I was hoping I wasn't going to keep you waiting for lunch. Now we can walk to the hotel together.'

Sitara could see Naeem was about to ask her what she was on and stepped on his foot hard to divert him. It seemed to do the trick, and she turned to the slime at her side. 'Girish, I don't think we can speak now. I have to go. Good bye.' She grabbed the arm of the still-hopping Naeem and towed him along.

'My proposition won't take very long,' Girish said, walking behind her. 'Your friend only has to wait for a couple of minutes.'

'Can't,' Sitara said briefly, increasing her pace again. The hotel entrance was in sight. Three minutes to get to the other side. She didn't know if she was going to make it.

'Sir. Hello.' Undeterred, Girish tapped Naeem's shoulder. 'My name is Girish Murthy. I need to talk to Sitara for a few minutes. Can you step aside for that time?'

Naeem opened his mouth to answer, and Sitara moved her foot in his direction again, causing him to skip aside nimbly.

'No, he can't,' Sitara said, abandoning all attempts at evasion. 'Go away. I don't want to hear your proposition. I don't want to talk to you. I don't want anything to do with you. If you follow me anymore, my friend is going to beat you up!'

Naeem almost looked around to see which friend before he realized Sitara was speaking about him. He tried to look suitably intimidating. Girish looked at him, sizing him up.

Sitara tugged at his arm to get him walking again. They were at the entrance.

'Are you sure he'll come?' Anjali asked Nasser, probably for the twentieth time.

'Definitely. Two hundred per cent,' he replied, as he had before. He'd been making it interesting by giving it a different inflection every time. 'If I got a call telling me that somebody was yelling at S...the woman I love, believe me I'd come running. If only to pound that person to dust.' He shook his head in amusement. 'Nobody gets to yell at her but me.'

'Sitara, the woman you love?' Anjali was quick to pick up on his slip. 'Are you sure you love her? Because your fans will be very upset. They won't understand why you picked a nobody who looks like nothing.'

'My fans can go... And Sitara is–' Nasser caught himself from defending Sitara's looks. 'Who said anything about love? I'm not in love. And I wouldn't pick somebody because my *fans* approved of them,' he said forcefully.

'Damn! I owe your mom five hundred bucks. She said you were in love with Sitara.'

'Excuse me,' Nasser's voice was cold. 'Did you bet about me with my mother?'

'I think she was just trying to cheer me up,' Anjali said. 'You should keep a lookout – he should be here any minute now.'

In the lobby, Naeem collided with a man in a hurry, who rushed on without apologizing.

'Hey,' Sitara said loudly.

'Hi,' said an annoyingly familiar voice from behind them. Girish had followed them in.

'My god!' This was it. Sitara had come to the end of her patience. She turned round to finish this once and for all. Naeem tugged at her arm.

'Not now,' he said urgently. 'We have somewhere more important to be.' He dragged her forward to one of the more private corners of the hotel.

'He's coming,' Anjali said. 'You can start now.'

'Yes,' Nasser said glumly. 'Take out the hanky. And remember this is all fake,' he warned her before launching into his role du jour. His voice rose, and he told her exactly how incompetent she was, how stupid, how incapable of following the simplest orders.

Anjali sniffed at the hanky, the onion juice setting her eyes tearing.

A peripheral movement warned him that Harsh was coming into range and he tamped down the urge to put a sofa between them. It was probably the hardest thing he had ever done in his life.

He moved his rant into more personal territory. How she had no brains and no beauty, and no wonder Harsh was getting cold feet about marrying her. In fact he very much doubted that Harsh would marry her. He heard a bellow, and turned to watch a furious Harsh rush at him.

He ducked behind the sofa. Some gestures were only foolish, not brave, and standing about waiting to be hit definitely fell in the former category.

He was concentrating so hard on Harsh that he didn't see the smaller figure run to him, till something swung into his side.

Harsh stopped bewildered, wanting to beat Nasser to pulp, but the girl already had that bit covered. He heard someone sniffle behind him, and turned to see his fiancée's red-rimmed eyes.

'How can you love that bastard?' he asked bitterly. 'How?'

'Love Nasser? You must be mad!' Anjali exclaimed, forgetting that she was supposed to be woebegone. 'Is that the reason for your mad behaviour? I could hit you.'

'If that's how you feel,' Harsh said, stiffly, making to move away.

Anjali lifted the hanky to her nose and tears trickled down, staying Harsh satisfactorily.

'I love you!' Anjali exclaimed. 'That's why I am marrying you. Nasser's just my employer. Is that what you think? Is that why you've been staying away from me?'

Harsh looked at the teary-eyed Anjali. 'You love me?' he asked doubtfully. 'But ever since I asked you to marry me, you began spending all your time thinking about him and talking about him. You were so upset with him that day. I've never seen you like that. And even when he was on holiday you kept on about him... And then I hit him.'

'You're right. But I have been upset because I wanted the perfect wedding. I've been obsessing about it, and I didn't want you to know...more than you did,' Anjali said. 'The other day...all the stress, the wedding arrangements, the wedding planner, your diet, it just came together.'

Harsh looked at her for a long moment before nodding his head. 'That sounds like you.'

'You believe me then?'

'Yes.' Harsh shook his head. 'All of this was over a stupid wedding?'

'I know. It's stupid,' Anjali wrapped her arms around him. She tipped her head back. 'Were you really worried I would be upset you hit him?'

Harsh shrugged. 'I thought it might be a factor. But what about today?'

Anjali waved the onion-scented hanky in his face. She jerked her head towards Nasser. 'He's not bad really. We couldn't think of any other way to speak to you.'

'You set this up with my friend?'

'Yes,' Anjali admitted. 'I also booked a room here. I was feeling optimistic.'

'You did?' Harsh said distractedly. Then the words sank in. '*You did!*'

'Uh huh,' Anjali smiled at him.

'What the...?' And there was Sitara getting ready to hit him again with her bag. He deflected the blow and turned to his brother for some help or enlightenment and saw Naeem doubled over with laughter. His inattention cost him dearly as Sitara took the opportunity to land a kick on his shins.

'Stop it Sitara!' he told the woman in his arms. The words had little effect and he spent the next few moments concentrating on subduing Sitara without hurting her.

'I knew it!' a strange voice exclaimed with a strange amount of conviction.

Nasser had no idea who the person was, but could only be thankful that it had stopped Sitara wanting to take the skin off his shins.

'Why are you still here?' she gritted.

'Who are you?' Nasser asked the stranger.

'Her fiancé,' said the man with a strong American accent.

'He is not!' Sitara exclaimed, trying to free herself.

Nasser hung on to her. 'Another one?' he said disbelievingly.

'No! He is not–' Sitara was outraged.

'We just broke it off. But this is exactly what I wanted to speak to you about,' Girish said.

'If you make another sleazy proposal,' Sitara threatened, her voice dire.

'Oh come on, I knew you were a wild one when I met you,' Girish leered at her. 'And look at you, you obviously like a bit of role playing and force. And if you're with him... I mean, I just want to be part of it till my wedding. And whenever I visit.'

Nasser looked at him in amazement. 'Did you just say what I think you did?' He shoved Sitara into Naeem's arms. 'Don't let her get away,' he ordered, before stepping forward and landing a beautiful right hook that laid Girish flat on the floor with a bleeding nose.

'Right. Make yourself useful. Take care of him,' he told Naeem, taking Sitara back from his brother's hold. He towed her to where Anjali stood with Harsh. 'Give me your room keys,' Nasser said as he drew level with them. 'You can go sort out your life in his office. Or book another room. I need some privacy.'

Anjali handed over the keys meekly to him and he half-dragged, half-lifted, a furious Sitara towards the lifts.

'You gave him the keys?' Harsh exclaimed.

'His need was greater than ours,' Anjali mollified. 'We have time to book another one.'

'Who was that anyway?'

'The woman he's going to marry.'

14

Nasser shut the door behind him and looked grimly at the woman who was facing off with him. The woman whose mission in life just a short while ago had been to beat him to pulp with her handbag. She looked back coldly. There was a twitch in the hand holding the bag.

'Don't try it,' he warned her. 'I've had just about enough of being beaten up.'

'And I've had enough of being towed around like a sack of potatoes,' Sitara flung back. 'What will you do anyway?' she goaded him. 'Attack me? That's all you can do, isn't it, attack women, and anybody who's weaker than yourself.'

'I realize what you're doing,' Nasser said in a seeming non sequitur. 'The question is, do you?'

'Is this your pathetic way of not answering a sticky question?' Sitara retorted.

'I'll answer your question when you actually want to hear the answer. Right now, you're too frustrated,' he said deliberately. 'That's fine. So am I. Let's do something about that.' Nasser suppressed a smile as he watched Sitara retreat to the far side of the room. 'Do you want some tea?' He watched her weigh the pros and cons of the offer and wasn't surprised when she acquiesced.

'Actually, I'm here on my lunch break,' she said as casually as she could. 'I need to be getting back to work soon.'

'Hmm. Then you should let them know you'll be back late,' Nasser informed her as he switched on the kettle.

Sitara decided to go on the offensive. 'I told you last night I'd let you know when I was ready. I haven't told you yet.'

'I realized I was being unfair. You're not evolutionarily equipped to make that decision – as an Indian woman, you've been reared to let the man make the move. I can't expect you to change decades of training. Want some chips?'

Sitara looked at him open-mouthed. 'What utter rubbish!'

'I was trying to make it easier for you,' Nasser said easily. 'Do you want sugar? No? Okay. Here you go.' He handed her the cup of tea, sat down on the chair across from her and opened a bag of chips. 'Want some? I'm quite hungry,' he said chattily. 'Anjali landed up at the crack of dawn and woke me up. And by the time we fine-tuned our plot to reunite her with Harsh – without a fist in my face – I've only eaten a croissant.' He popped a handful of into his mouth.

'Is this what passes for seduction in your circles?' Sitara said distastefully.

'No, I'm just trying to put you at ease. You've had an intense half hour,' he said. 'Not working? Want to get to brass tacks?'

Sitara shook her head in disbelief. 'Do you think you're cute? Or funny?' She stood up abruptly. 'You're not. And I'm leaving.'

She had only taken a couple of steps when he caught her. His grip wasn't hard, but Sitara was certain that she wouldn't be able to get away. She looked at where his hand held hers and then looked at him, letting him know what a cockroach she thought he was.

He had the gall to laugh. 'Is that what you call a killing look?' he asked. When she tugged at her arm he pulled her down so she landed on his lap. He gave in to temptation and ran a hand through her hair. It was as soft as it looked. 'Did you get any sleep last night? Because I found it impossible to get any.'

'Can't say I had any trouble.' Sitara pushed his hand away from her hair. 'Stop that.'

'No.' Nasser wrapped a strand around his finger. 'You know, I've never seen you in black. I wonder what you were thinking when you chose this? Didn't you say you were anti-black?'

'I'm not anti anything. I'm pro-choice.' Sitara tried to slide off his lap again. Her efforts were as successful as before.

'Uh huh,' Nasser seemed more interested in playing with her hair, twisting it around his fingers, lightly massaging her scalp. 'So you've been juggling two fiancés and me?'

Sitara, who sagged against him slightly, twisted around to face him. 'I have not! I wasn't engaged to them – well, I was engaged to Karthik, but not now – and there's no one else!'

'Except for this odd physical self on whose lap you're sitting, I suppose there isn't.' Nasser's gaze dropped to her lips and Sitara disconcertedly found herself swaying closer. Before she could do anything she would regret, Sitara turned around so her back was to him. Nasser made a muffled sound – a laugh? – but his voice was normal when he spoke.

'So today's sleazeball – he was set up by your parents?'

He had started that thing with her hair again; Sitara was finding it very hard not to give in to the pleasure. 'Yes. He thought because I worked with a men's mag I'd be easy; propositioned me the first time we met. In the balcony of my aunt's house! Creep.' She straightened up as a thought struck her. 'That was the day you were assigned to me – my life has been like this ever since! It's just gone to pot.'

'Oh no, you don't! You're not going to win this life-gone-to-pot business with me. Yours has been a cakewalk, darling. Do you know how much physical injury I've had to face since you walked into mine?'

'Emotional trumps physical,' Sitara said, loftily.

'You try and take a punch to your nose then,' Nasser said. 'And have you ever been hit by a peach? Who knew it could hurt so much?' His voice still held a note of disbelief.

A laugh bubbled out.

'Are you laughing at my injuries?' Nasser demanded.

Sitara clamped a hand to her mouth, but couldn't seem to stop the laughter. 'It was funny,' she gasped.

'Was it?' Nasser asked politely. 'Let me give you something to really laugh about then.' Before she could react he had picked her up, deposited her on the bed and started tickling her.

'No, no! I'm ticklish.' Sitara tried to squirm away from him.

'That's so sad,' Nasser said, showing no remorse and not letting up a whit.

'Uncle, uncle, uncle,' Sitara cried out. 'I'm sorry I laughed. I really am. I'm sure it hurt.'

'That has to be the most insincere apology I've ever heard,' Nasser said, but he stopped.

Sitara looked at him and wondered muzzily when his face gotten so close to hers. God, he had beautiful eyes. How had she never noticed them before? And his mouth... Sitara watched it intently but it took a while to realize he was speaking.

'...actions speak louder than words. You can show me how sorry you are.'

Nasser looked at her expectantly.

Sitara didn't hesitate for a minute before leaning up and kissing him.

'You took advantage of me,' Sitara accused him, a while later. It was somewhat undermined by the fact that she was sprawled across him, naked, in a rather contented fashion.

'I personally thought it was the other way round. Maybe we should try it again to see who's to blame,' Nasser suggested, the words causing his chest to rumble under her ear.

Sitara was giving it serious consideration when her phone rang.

'Ignore it,' Nasser commanded. 'Better still, turn it off.'

'I can't do that. It might be somebody from – Oh crap! I have to get back to work,' Sitara said scrambling out of bed and looking for her clothing. 'Can you see my–' Sitara dived under the bed to see whether anything had fallen there.

'You're serious? You're really planning to go back to work?' Nasser pushed himself to a sitting position and watching her.

'I have to. I have a couple of pages to release,' Sitara said, finally in possession of all the bits and pieces of her clothing. She clutched them in front of her and watched him uncertainly.

'Then I guess the least I can do is conserve some water with you.' He slid off the bed and stood next to her, and gestured toward the bathroom.

Sitara started walking towards the shower. 'You don't mind?' she asked, and realized that Nasser wasn't at her side. She turned and caught him staring at her butt.

Her lips twitched, but she added a little extra roll to her hips as she walked into the bath.

'You're a wicked woman,' Nasser said following her in and turning on the shower. 'And I approve.'

Nasser watched Sitara gather her bag and give the room a last look to check she'd got everything. 'My mother has invited you for dinner tonight.'

'What?' Sitara laughed nervously, her eyes skittering up to his face. Where the hell had this come from? He was going to take her to meet his mother? Already? 'Why?'

'Because Naeem has been talking so much about you.'

Sitara tried to see the good side of this. 'Is this a large party?' she asked hopefully.

'Not that I know. Just all of us.'

How to phrase this tactfully? 'Umm... It's not because of us or anything like that is it?'

'And if it were?' Nasser was looking at her intently.

Sitara tried a laugh. It didn't come off very well. 'I mean, there was no "us" till about a few hours ago... Meeting the family would be rushing things...I mean, they might think things were more serious...'

'So basically you're saying that at the moment you're just using me for sex and you don't want anybody to get the impression that it is or could be deeper?' Nasser said.

Was he upset about it? But what else could he be thinking? 'I wouldn't have put it like that, but, uh, yes.'

'So how do you see things going from now on? Us. Relationship. Meeting.' he elaborated, when she looked at him uncomprehendingly.

'Yes, I was thinking about that,' Sitara said. She ran a hand through her hair. 'Maybe we could keep it discreet for the moment. Low key.'

'Hmm. Okay, I think I understand what you mean.'

'Great. I knew you would,' Sitara said gratefully. 'So...will you apologize to your mother about tonight?'

'No,' Nasser smiled at her, all teeth. 'She asked for your number to invite you. I've given it to her. She'll call you in a bit and you can apologize yourself. Shall we go?'

'Go?' Sitara repeated stupidly, still grappling with what Nasser had just told her.

'I'll drop you to your office.'

He did just that.

And try as she could to dissuade him that there was no need for him to come up to her office, he did exactly that, pushing her reluctant form forward and through the door, bringing all conversation on that floor to a halt.

'My mother will call you shortly,' he announced in a lovely carrying voice, just before he dropped her a kiss, said bye to the rest of the team and departed.

Sitara sank into her chair and buried her head in her hands.

He got that from his mother, Sitara concluded shortly after. The woman had warmly, graciously bulldozed her into coming for dinner.

Sitara spent the rest of the day alternating between answering questions about Nasser and trying to figure out what Debashish would do next.

'I think you've confused him,' Martin said. 'Sneaking around and having an affair is very different from boyfriend coming to the office and mother inviting you to dinner. Can you imagine the press *Homme* would get if you married Nasser?'

'I am not marrying him,' Sitara exclaimed.

'Why?' Martin asked. 'Because he's Muslim? Would your parents freak?'

'My parents. That's a joke. They're dying for me to marry him. Or anybody. As long as I marry a man they're happy.'

'Then what's your problem?' Martin was confused. 'He's tall, dark, handsome, rich, smart, funny, obviously likes you, straight?' Martin raised a brow at Sitara. She nodded. 'Straight, good in the sack? Yes. Then what's the problem?'

'We're not in the marrying stage because I hardly know him,' she said.

'His mother is calling you home for dinner. This man's serious,' Martin said.

'But he's a film star,' Sitara almost wailed. 'He's not supposed to be serious. And even if he's serious, he won't stay serious long. I can't have a long-term relationship with him.'

'Yes. You're right,' Martin agreed. 'Except he seems set on having a serious relationship with you.'

Maya said the same thing to her when she called to inform Sitara that she wouldn't be meeting her for dinner. 'I'm going out with Lokesh. He's really...he's great,' Maya said, sounding not at all like herself.

'When you remember him,' Sitara muttered.

'Don't be mean,' Maya snapped. 'You don't know him. And don't be a baby, go meet his parents. What's the worst that can happen? You've already been written about in the papers – at least with his parents in the picture it won't be a sleazy affair.'

'Yeah, but I don't even know if this is going to be a relationship. I don't want to meet his parents so soon.'

'As your best and oldest friend who has been witness to your non-existent love life, it's my duty to tell you that you're fooling yourself. You're already in a relationship with him, you might already love him–'

'I do not,' Sitara protested.

'Yes, you do. You don't indulge in casual sex. Further, you had two perfectly good Tam-Bram men ready to marry you, and you chose this non-relationship film star over both. So again, do not fool yourself.'

'Fine,' Sitara admitted defensively. 'I might be interested in him. But what if I admit to being his girlfriend and nothing happens? I'll be a tainted woman and nobody will marry me.'

'Since they aren't exactly lining up to marry you, I don't think your prospects will be much affected. And in my experience, having dated a movie star will only add to your appeal. You know like, "she's the one who dated so and so, I wonder what he saw in her? Maybe I should have a go." The men will be lining up for you darling. And at worst, you can marry Nasser, divorce him and take all his money.'

'You're disgusting,' Sitara laughed.

By the time the clock struck 6 p.m., Sitara had decided that she would text Nasser's mom to tell her she was feeling far too sick to come. She was typing it as she swiped her card to sign out. She almost leapt out of her skin when a voice hailed her. 'Hello Sitara. Is that a text to my mother saying you're too sick to come for dinner?'

Sitara sidestepped the question with another one. 'What are you doing here?'

'I'm here to see that you don't back out,' Naeem answered cheerfully.

'This is ridiculous,' she exclaimed. 'I've said I'll come to dinner. Now go away. I'll be there.'

'Exactly what I told Shiv,' Naeem said warmly. 'But seeing that he's bet me a thousand you won't, I decided it would be best to help you in the right direction. Can I see that text?'

'No. And you're betting on me?'

'Old family tradition. Usually we bet on what Nasser will do, but...betting on you is the same as betting on him, so it's all good. You should delete that text. It might get sent by mistake, you know.'

'Leave my phone alone.' Sitara saved it as a draft and slipped the phone into her bag. 'And I am going home to change. You can go wherever you want.' Sitara got into the lift.

Naeem followed. 'Tsk tsk. That's not a gracious invitation. But I'll take you up on it anyway. You live in Colaba, don't you?'

'Is this you after the midlife crisis or were you always so annoying?'

'I like to think of it as a special gift I have honed to perfection over the years, to which I am allowing full reign in this period when my life and all it stands for is in turmoil.' He burst out laughing when he had finished. 'You look just like my undergrad students. Dazed and confused.'

'If you spoke like that, it's a wonder they ever grew out of it,' Sitara said feelingly. 'You've probably scarred them for life.'

'Many of them have thanked me in writing about what a life-changing experience it was to study under me. Wait up. Let me call the driver.'

'Yeah, they probably opted out of your course and couldn't restrain their happiness at it.' Sitara got into the car. 'Look Naeem, seriously, I'm not up to going out today. I've had a very emotional day, and it's all too soon.'

Naeem serioused up. 'Damn it. There goes my thousand. I'd better call and tell Amma before she kills the fatted calf; she couldn't wait to meet the woman who walloped Nasser.'

'You told her that?' Sitara gasped.

'Of course. Amma loved it. She's always telling us that she spared the rod and spoiled the children. Obviously she's wrong about me because I'm perfection, but Nasser could have done with some strong discipline.' He looked at Sitara, inviting her to enjoy the joke, and found her looking seriously worried.

'What's up? What did I say? Are you actually worried about beating up Amma's favourite son? Don't worry, that's me, so you can do whatever you want to Nasser. I gather you already did some of that in the hotel room today,' he added slyly.

Sitara fought to control the blush, but was pretty sure she failed. She thought she heard him say 'Eat my dust, Shiv' but when she looked at him he looked back questioningly.

'It's not funny,' she told him.

'It is. Do you know who's responsible for our betting addiction? Amma. She's got a great sense of the ridiculous, that's why she had been following your relationship so closely. She says she hasn't had so much fun since she married my dad.'

'I'm never going to be able to face her now,' Sitara said despairingly. 'And Nasser and I don't have a relationship. Why is everybody jumping to conclusions here?'

Naeem swallowed several wise-ass remarks that sprang to mind. He decided a change of subject would be the wisest course. 'Sure,' he said soothingly. 'Fine, forget dinner. Let's get some tea. Shall I get us something to eat for tea – you are going to give me some tea, aren't you? I promise to leave after that.'

'I've got some crackers. I think.'

Naeem shuddered. 'Please. I would backpack if I wanted crackers. Isn't there some place we could pick something up? Something good?'

'That was a good idea,' Sitara told Naeem, after they had washed down danishes, rolls and pastries with a couple of cups of tea. Naeem had kept her laughing with the horror stories of the tea his dad was determinedly serving him and then had segued into the tale of how his confirmed bachelor-father, all of thirty-nine, had married his mother, almost cradle-snatched, at twenty, one week after they'd met.

Sitara had countered with tales of her Facebook-savvy parents who had driven her off social media, and her mother who routinely sent both her children to make coffee at the first sign of intimacy while watching movies at home.

Her phone rang as they were laughing about it. Sitara looked at the screen for a moment before answering it. 'Mukul? Hey, what's up?'

'Hello Sitara. I hope I have not disturbed you.' Mukul said it so meaningfully Sitara rolled her eyes. 'I was just talking with Anil,' – Sitara waited for the pause for people to absorb that he and Anil were very close, and it came like clockwork – 'and it seems he heard about Nasser Khan's visit to the office and your relationship with him. You know, his mother calling you. He wants you to ask Nasser if he will come for *Homme*'s awards. We can give him a really good award if he confirms.'

'Excuse me?' Sitara was having trouble believing her ears.

'You know how these stars are,' Mukul continued, untroubled by nuances of tone. 'Nobody wants to confirm their attendance till everybody else has, and sometimes not even then. Even to me.' It was obviously a sore point. 'Anil thought since you had a closer relationship with Nasser Khan you could ask him.'

'And if he can't confirm?' Sitara wanted to see how far they would go.

'Nothing. He just wants you to try,' Mukul seemed to finally pick up a hint of danger. 'He just wants you to ask Nasser because he's more accessible to you. Otherwise I'd ask him.'

Sitara wasn't mollified. 'I'll let you know,' she said shortly and hung up. She put the phone back in her bag, but her good mood had evaporated. 'I'm sorry. I need to go,' she told Naeem. 'I'm just... I need to go.'

'Sure,' Naeem said. 'I'll take you home.' He overruled her protests, and Sitara let it go. It was too small a matter to fight over. Her phone rang as she got in. It was her mother.

Sitara tried to tell Amma she was on her way home, and would call when she reached, but her mother wasn't having any of it. She had already launched into a tirade against ungrateful daughters who ran away from their last suitors while running into the arms of men they had made no sounds about marrying; Girish's mother had called about the grievous bodily harm done to her son.

Sitara switched to Tamil to set her mother right, which resulted in a frank and frankly infuriating conversation. Her mother wanted to know whether Nasser had proposed. 'Of course not,' Sitara expostulated.

'Is he going to?'

'I don't know,' Sitara almost yelled. 'And I don't know if I'd marry him even if he did.'

That led to a fifteen minute rant about losing her reputation by hanging around loose Bollywood characters.

'You give up your job and come home right now,' her mother commanded at the end of it.

It was Sitara's turn to rant, a familiar one in which the highpoints were: 'I'm thirty', 'I'm an adult' and 'I will do what I want'.

'Not till you are married,' her mother told her, which led to both sides yelling at each other not caring that the other person wasn't too busy shouting to listen.

Both parties hung up furiously.

Sitara took a couple of deep breaths before she trusted herself to speak. Naeem was tactfully looking out of the window. 'I'm sorry,' she began.

Naeem interrupted her. 'Don't worry about it. At least you weren't coming to blows.'

Sitara managed a smile. 'It's taking a long time,' she said, looking for a safe topic.

Naeem made some noncommittal noise.

She looked out of the window. 'Are you kidnapping me?' she demanded, her voice rising with each word.

The look on his face was answer enough.

'Turn the car around right away,' Sitara ordered, beyond furious. 'Just stop it. I'll take a taxi home.'

'See, it seemed a good idea when I started,' Naeem told her apologetically. 'I didn't count on your fight with your mother. But we're nearly there. Five minutes. We made good time.'

'Stop. The. Car.'

'Just come up to the apartment,' Naeem pleaded. 'This bet with Shiv...he's unbearable when he wins. And he won twice yesterday.'

Sitara told him succinctly what he could do with his bet. 'Stop the car now or I'm going to scream.'

'...you don't have to stay for dinner. You step into the apartment and I win the bet. We–'

Sitara screamed.

The driver almost crashed into the car ahead.

Naeem would later describe her voice as being astonishingly powerful, and with a piercing quality that echoed in one's skull long after she had stopped. It echoed in the car, too, long after she had stopped.

'Are you telling him to turn around?' Sitara asked politely.

The driver wiped his sweaty hands on his pants and said a quick prayer that Naeem would ask them to turn around.

Naeem was feeling quite shaky himself, but he could see their building looming ahead. 'We...'

Sitara screamed again. She seemed to be able to hold it for surprisingly longer this time.

The driver's hands were quivering as he guided the car into the building, a wild look about his eyes.

Nasser must have had some early warning system – or maybe he heard her – because he was opening the door for Sitara as soon as the car came to a halt, drawing her into a quick kiss of welcome.

Naeem almost collapsed with relief.

'I'm so glad you came,' Nasser gave her a million-watt smile. 'I've missed you.'

Sitara tried hard to remain unmoved, but she could feel herself softening. For all she knew, he didn't even know about the kidnapping.

Or maybe she was delusional.

'I really am happy you're here. I didn't think you would come,' Nasser repeated, radiating such sincerity that Sitara believed him. She weakly allowed him to lead into the lift. He didn't even wait for the doors to close before he was kissing her again.

Somebody cleared their throat behind them and they jumped apart. They had reached their floor without noticing; the lift doors were open and a woman stood waiting for them to exit.

'Hello Kapoor aunty, we were uh...'

Sitara watched interestedly as Nasser's ears went red in the face of the matronly disapproval emanating from the woman in front of him.

'Getting out,' he completed, almost dragging Sitara from the lift.

'She's evil. She's always catching me with someone in the lift,' he muttered, watching the lift doors close.

'Making out?' Sitara clarified, enjoying his discomfiture to no small degree.

'Yes.'

'And you're worried she'll think you're a slut or she'll be disappointed by your lack of imagination?'

'Very funny,' he said, still looking disturbed.

'You can't really be worried about her,' Sitara exclaimed.

'No,' he said reluctantly. 'It's just that she's always complaining to my father. About how I'm a bad influence.'

Sitara almost laughed out loud. Then she remembered how she'd been brought into this situation. 'You are a bad influence,' she said sternly and building up steam, 'and you're training your brother to follow in your lying, cheating, kidnapping footsteps.'

It only served to lift Nasser's mood. 'I'd forgotten. I'll have to thank him for that. I'm sure it was no easy task. He was looking a little shaken back there. What did you do to him?'

'I screamed,' Sitara said.

The first thing that struck her was the number of people there. Either his entire family had turned up to meet her or this was a...party.

'You really are a lying scum.' Sitara said contemplatively. 'Worse than your brother.'

'Blood will tell,' he grinned at her.

'This is a party.'

'Uh huh.'

'I asked you if it was. And you said it wasn't.'

'I was going to tell you I was kidding,' Nasser said warily, 'but then, I got distracted. Are you going to scream now? My dad's got a heart condition.'

'I wouldn't want to be that predictable. I'll just let you worry about what I might do rest of the evening.' Sitara bestowed a blinding smiled at the man approaching. 'Hello Shiv.'

Shiv greeted Sitara with a hug and pulled her to his side. 'Now that I'm free, you can go do something else,' Shiv told Nasser. 'I'll take care of Sitara now. You can carry on dude.'

'Go get your own woman.' Nasser pulled Sitara away and wrapped a possessive arm around her waist. 'This one's mine.'

'Declarations of love already,' said the most exquisite woman Sitara had ever seen. This was what they called elegant. 'Hello, you must be Sitara. I'm Ayesha. I'm so glad you could make it.'

This was the mother, Sitara realized. The betting lady. And her son was dating Sitara. Old insecurities ambushed her; her mood, which had briefly shown signs of becoming better, dipped to new lows. She barely managed to greet her normally. She could feel Nasser's surprised look; she refused to meet his eyes.

'Didn't Naeem pick you up?' Ayesha said, looking around for her other son.

'Well, he certainly brought me,' Sitara said before she could stop herself.

Ayesha looked at her quizzically. Then at Shiv and Nasser. Neither quite met her eyes.

She shook her head in disappointment. 'I thought you had more finesse,' she told Nasser. 'And you,' she turned to Shiv, 'I'm very disappointed in you. And Naeem.'

Naeem, who had finally calmed his nerves enough to walk in, found four pairs of eyes looking at him. 'I'll just come back in a bit,' he said doing an about face and walking out.

Ayesha swallowed a laugh. 'Come here Naeem. You've been betting on Sitara? You kidnapped her.'

'It was his idea,' Naeem said, throwing his brother to the wolves without compunction. 'And Shiv led me down the devil's path, Amma.'

'What! You...' Shiv exclaimed.

'Shouldn't kidnapping me and altering the course of the evening count as a foul?' Sitara said. 'Doesn't that null and void the bet?'

'Aren't you satisfied from trying to kill us? Must you make me lose the bet too?'

'Kill you?'

Everybody laughed at the story, but Sitara caught what looked like an assessing glance from Nasser's mom. Was she wondering what her son was doing with Sitara?

Nasser must have felt her tense up because he rubbed her back and drew her in closer.

'You okay?' he murmured in her ear.

'Uh huh,' Sitara said, trying to put some distance between the two. She darted a look at Nasser's mom and found her unabashedly watching them.

'Do you call this decent behaviour?' a voice boomed at them, causing Sitara to leap out of Nasser's embrace with the vim of newborn lamb.

The speaker resolved himself into an older man who had come up behind Ayesha. He was just a couple of inches taller than Sitara, which put him around five feet seven, or eight. He was not only the shortest man around; he was also the most nondescript, despite his crisp kurta pyjama, and head full of white hair.

Sitara had just decided he must be some sort of a distant, older relative when he continued: 'Leaving the patriarch of the house out of a family gathering?'

Three people around her snorted. Shiv grinned. Sitara swallowed. This was Nasser's father? She would never have guessed. For a start he was so much older than their mother. And...so nondescript. She looked at him again to see what had attracted Ayesha to him, and how he could be the father of these two seriously good-looking men, and couldn't come up with a clue.

'Did patriarch come up in your crossword today?' Nasser asked cheekily, drawing her flush against him, and holding her there firmly.

'Don't be disrespectful,' Bashir admonished. He slid an arm around his wife. 'Your mother was too soft on you growing up,' he declared, a statement that was met with hoots of laughter.

'Says the man who had to be sent out of the room so that Amma could yell at us,' Nasser retorted.

Bashir ignored his son. 'Are you going to introduce me to this young lady or not?'

A grinning Nasser did the honours. Within moments Bashir had culled her away from the group, ostensibly to get her a drink.

His real reason, Sitara soon realized, was to find out

her life story. And he was good at it. Sitara found herself telling him where she had been to school, college, work, her parents, her sister, why she was doing her job and why she loved it, whether she could cook... It was at this point that Nasser stepped in.

'I'm going to take her away now, Abba. Go ask Shiv about the new chef they've got at the hotel. The one who likes him with a beard. Preferably when Shalini is not around.'

She allowed Nasser to manoeuvre her out to the balcony, which was blessedly empty. She leaned on the railing, focusing on the buildings towering above them as she tried to empty her mind.

'I didn't know you could sing,' Nasser said, reaching out to touch her hair.

Sitara was unmoving under his touch. 'You knew he would interrogate me?'

Nasser looked at her warily but his tone was light. 'Hard not to – it's his modus operandi. He was the best informed man in Bollywood at one time. Knew more than the yellow press.'

'And new chef? What about Shalini, the woman Shiv is going to marry?'

'If he hasn't popped the question in ten years, he's unlikely to do it now,' Nasser replied without a hint of remorse.

Sitara couldn't contain her indignation. 'And all that warning me off after the party?'

'Jealousy.'

He wasn't looking at her, and for a moment Sitara couldn't grasp that he had admitted it. 'Oh.'

'You were flirting with him all evening. I wanted to

rip him apart.' He finally looked at her, trying to gauge her reaction.

'Is that why you were flirting with Maya?' Sitara had one of those insides-melting sensations she associated with corny romances and strove to keep it out of her voice. She guiltily admitted that his admission was a bit of a turn-on.

'Yes. Were you jealous?'

'Of course not,' Sitara denied staunchly. 'She's my oldest friend, and I know she's gorgeous...'

'You were jealous,' Nasser said with extreme satisfaction in his voice.

'Wildly.' Sitara admitted. She grimaced. 'It wasn't nice.'

'No, it wasn't. I haven't ever felt like that. Not even with Richa.'

Sitara's sense of fair play asserted itself and she quashed it. He had brought up Richa; this wasn't a moment to waste. She couldn't lie to herself that she wasn't wildly curious about what had broken them up. 'Well, you were engaged to her, so there was no reason to be.'

Nasser laughed. 'Where do you come from? This is Bollywood, Sitara. There's always a reason to be jealous.' He shrugged. 'And after some time she wasn't the only one sleeping around.' He looked at her then, obviously waiting for her reaction.

What was she supposed to say to that? Sitara thought. Was she shocked? Hell, yes. Because she wanted the man she was in love with to be monogamous, to honour any relationship he had committed to. And...her brain caught up with what she had just admitted. In love with. How the hell could she be in love with him? She barely knew him. She'd known him, what, less than a week? That was hardly enough to be falling in love with anybody. Was it?

'Are you that shocked?' Nasser broke into her reverie.

'A bit,' Sitara marvelled at her understatement. 'I guess I expected you to honour your commitments.' She hesitated, wondering whether she should mince her words. But she'd never done it before and she saw no reason to do it now. 'It makes me re-evaluate my impression of you. And whether I'm ready to take what we have any further.'

Pride was a funny thing. It was useless and self-defeating, but one always gave in to it. Nasser could see that what he was going to do wasn't going to get him anywhere – in fact, it was going to be hugely backward – and yet he knew he would do it. He hadn't expected her to swallow his cheating without explanations, and he had been fully planning on giving a few; only now he found himself piqued that Sitara had immediately jumped to the worst conclusion. And she was using it as a crutch to not take their relationship further. Or even admit that they had one.

'You're really scared of this relationship, aren't you? Why is that?'

'Excuse me?' Sitara couldn't believe that he was blaming her. 'You just admitted that you cheated on your fiancée and you're blaming me for letting that affect me.'

'You can't even say the word, you know,' Nasser continued as though she hadn't said anything.

'What, relationship? I can,' Sitara said. 'It doesn't apply to us. We don't have one. All we have so far is a one-afternoon stand. And if you don't want to talk about your infidelity, just say so. Don't try and blame me for it.'

Suddenly he was sick of it. 'Yeah, you know what, fuck it. I don't want to talk about it. I don't want to talk about anything. I'm sorry we dragged you to the party – what can I say, the first flush of love.' Nasser laughed shortly. 'Won't bother you again.' He started to walk towards the door.

'Oh please. Do you have to talk like a bad Hindi movie? And walk away like some wronged heroine?' That stopped him in his tracks. Good. She wasn't done yet. 'Maybe sleeping around when you're engaged is so common in your world that it makes no difference to you, but you know what – I'm totally middle class and it makes a huge difference to me. And throwing that at me one minute and expecting me to accept it the next is completely unreasonable.'

Nasser turned back. 'I didn't tell you that lightly, Sitara. I'm well aware of your middle-classness. I expected you to ask me why. Instead, you use it as an escape route. To write me off. Write us off. So that you can retreat from any sort of commitment and remain self-righteous about it. What a win-win situation,' he said caustically.

'Self-righteous! Listen to yourself. So upset because I won't fall at your feet and kiss them because you've slid in the fact that you love me. Be honest. That's what's bothering you, isn't it? You think you can blow hot one moment and blow cold the next, and everybody will fall in line with your moods. You backed off in Italy without a reason, you admit to being in love with me today without a reason. Guess what, I need time to figure it out. So get over it.'

'Admit to being in love without reason – what are you on?' Nasser was incredulous. 'No wonder you haven't found anybody.' His voice went hard. 'Don't say things just because you have to. Make some sense.'

'Don't be so damn patronizing. You didn't give me a single reason to think you were in love with me, and now suddenly you are. You're treating me like some airhead who doesn't know what she wants. No, let me finish. I told you it was too early for a relationship and you got snippy about me using you for sex. I told you I didn't want to come and you kidnapped me. I tell you that your sleeping around bothers me and you tell me I am scared of a relationship. I have been telling you exactly what I feel all day. I've been upfront and honest and you're playing games with me. You fuck off. I don't need this in my life right now.'

'See, that's what I meant about being self-righteous. Everything you've told me today has only meant one thing – you don't want to take us any further. The truth is you don't have the guts to be in a relationship. You whinge about being single, but you don't have what it takes to make a commitment. That's why you haven't said yes to a single guy in the dozens you've seen.'

'I've known you all of less than a week,' Sitara bit out. 'Don't tell me about my commitment-phobia.'

'We've put in more mileage in our time together than a lot of people do over months. And you would have married any of your parentally approved men after one meeting. Don't give me this crap about our time together.' His voice was cutting.

'That's different,' Sitara snapped.

'Why? You know more about me than you know about any of them. Is it different because of our religions?'

'No. It's because of your profession,' Sitara threw at him. 'You're always going to have affairs, just like you admitted. I can't live with that. Don't give me that look. The film industry is not known for its fidelity or longevity in relationships.'

'And you dared to yell at me for writing off the media,' Nasser's voice was no longer cold. It was just indifferent. 'All relationships are a risk, Sitara. You have to be willing to take it.'

'Risks are only worth taking if there's a chance of success,' Sitara told him coldly.

'No,' Nasser shook his head. 'If you can always see the success, you're not risking enough. The bigger the chance for success, the bigger the risk. And you know, even if you fail, it's worth it. Because at least you will have tried. This safe, boring path you're on won't get you anything.'

'Life isn't your way or the highway, Nasser. I'll find my own path, thank you.'

'As you wish,' Nasser said. 'But you are right – my life's too short to waste on this.' He folded his arms and stopped in front of her. 'And look. No running away. You can tell me what you like.'

'Good,' Sitara said. She was trembling with anger. 'Don't waste your time on me then.'

'Fine.'

'Fine.'

'Ah ha, the lovebirds emerge,' Shiv exclaimed, looking up from his conversation with Naeem and Shalini. He saw their faces and fell silent.

'Sitara's going home now,' Nasser told Naeem, his voice cold. 'See to it, okay.' He walked up to one knot of people and immediately became its heart and soul, animated and funny, his laughter ringing out.

'I can get myself home,' Sitara's voice was equally cold. She walked to the door without looking back. She was aware of the whispered conversation behind her, and of somebody joining her as she waited for the lift but she ignored them. She kept her eyes trained straight ahead.

Naeem started to speak but received such an incinerating look that he shut up.

'I can get myself home,' Sitara repeated.

'I'll just see you downstairs,' Naeem said, his voice subdued.

Sitara shrugged and ignored him. They rode down in silence. The door opened on the lady she had met on the way up. She looked disappointed at seeing Naeem.

Sitara left Naeem making small talk with her and walked straight to the gate and hailed herself a taxi.

Naeem came running up and grabbed her arm. 'I'll drop you back.'

'Thanks, but I don't want to be near anybody called Khan right now,' Sitara said, shaking off his arm and climbing into the taxi. She told the driver where to go and shut her eyes blocking out Naeem's worried face as they pulled away.

15

When Sitara woke up the next day, she realized she couldn't bear to go to office. Or stay in Mumbai. She cooked up a family emergency, took a week's leave and went home.

Her parents took one look at her face and tactfully didn't bring up the subject of marriage at all. There was a lot of talk about the music and dance season, reviews and stories, performances to be analysed and dismissed to a new audience. Both were hard-core followers, and had very definite, and often, opposing views on whose had been the best performance.

Her sister had all but moved back home, only going back to her apartment to sleep. Cousins dropped in, uncles and aunts in tow. Sitara put in a good show as she regaled her family with stories of her own. Her mother brought up Nasser once, on a morning she found Sitara up far earlier than she had ever been. 'Are you and the actor still friends?'

'No,' Sitara's voice was flat. She successfully distracted her mother with news of her favourite singer's tour.

'Are you okay?' Nithya asked as she watched Sitara pack up to leave the next day.

'Yes,' Sitara said in a tone that didn't encourage any further talk.

Just in case her sister didn't take the hint, she remembered a pair of shoes she couldn't find and sent Nithya downstairs to look for them. It wasn't brought up again.

She found herself tearing up when it was time to leave, and she began bawling like a baby when she got home to her little flat in Colaba.

As she was listlessly signing into the office on Monday, Maya called and dropped a bomb.

'You're getting married to Lokesh? Lokesh the forgettable?' Sitara was frankly incredulous.

Maya wasn't amused. Sitara received a twenty-minute lecture on all his unique qualities that made him totally memorable. There was a ringing silence when she finished. 'Did I go overboard?' Maya asked ruefully.

'It was a bit extreme.' Sitara admitted.

'Sorry. It's just that...'

'You love him and are marrying him,' Sitara finished. She was having a hard time wrapping her brain around that.

'Yes.' Maya hesitated.

'Wow. Then uh... Congratulations.' Sitara winced at how fake she sounded.

'Thanks.'

There was an awkward silence. Oh, this wouldn't do, she couldn't be fake with her best friend. And this was Maya; she wouldn't be marrying unless she was convinced the guy was right for her. 'Maya, really, congratulations. I'm just surprised. But I'm thrilled for you.'

'Yeah, it's okay,' Maya laughed. 'It's all happening so fast. I'm a bit surprised myself.'

'But you're sure, right? It's been only a week.'

'I know. But how long does it take to know? I knew by our second date.' Maya's happiness was almost palpable.

'You've crossed over to the dark side,' Sitara exclaimed. 'And it's the best thing I've heard in a long time. Tell me everything.'

It emerged that the night of the party had been the big night for Maya. Lokesh had wowed her by being smart to genius levels, funny and confident and totally open in his liking for her.

'He told me he was determined to not let a second chance pass by without letting me know that he liked me,' Maya told her dreamily.

'But you didn't act like Lokesh was the one for you when I was there. You were...' Oh no, foot in mouth, Sitara realized.

'Flirting with Nasser?' Maya asked. 'Actually, he was flirting with me to make you jealous. Half the time he didn't even hear what I was saying, he was so busy listening to what you were telling Shiv and that other guy.'

'Oh.' Sitara tried to control the flash of pleasure at that revelation.

'Yeah. Anyway, then he swooped you away and I had to go back with Lokesh. We decided to have a cup of coffee when we reached the hotel, and we just stayed there talking all night.'

'Talking?' Sitara said disbelievingly.

'Yeah, I know. I sort of indicated that we could

move the action to my bedroom, but he declined,' Maya admitted.

'He did,' Sitara couldn't contain her amazement. 'Why?'

'He didn't say no or anything like that. He just moved the topic along. But I think he thought I wouldn't respect him the next day.' Maya's tone was frankly adoring.

'Hmm. That's true. Smart move.'

'Sitara, he's just super smart. I mean, we thought he looks kind of blah, but he is just so incredibly smart. And he's so intense. That's so sexy,' Maya added. 'And when you talk he's so focused on you, he's really interested in what you have to say even if he disagrees. He doesn't just think I'm sexy because of the way I look, but because of the way I think.'

Sitara could all but see Maya melting into a puddle of mush. 'I've never believed guys like that exist,' she said truthfully. 'You're lucky to have found one.'

'Yes, I'm feeling quite pleased about that,' Maya said, satisfaction radiating from her voice. 'Of course, he's lucky too, to have found me.'

Sitara laughed and congratulated her again, but she was even more depressed when she hung up. Her last single friend had bitten the dust.

By the time she got home she was over being depressed and had begun doing some soul searching. Had there been any truth in Nasser's accusations? Was she running scared?

She didn't know who had said soul searching was good, but they needed a sharp kick in the butt.

What was the point in knowing somebody else had figured out your fears when you couldn't do anything about it? Because the next step had to be hers and she didn't know if she was up to taking it.

She was still wrestling with the question the next afternoon as Anil and the events team droned on about the *Homme* awards – which were turning out to be a bit like the Commonwealth Games. Nobody could tell if they would happen and if everybody who was supposed to attend would attend. The venue they had booked months in advance had been shut down for structural repairs, the hotel had nothing else of the same size, and with a fortnight to go, the only other place of a similar size that was free was on the other side of town.

The celebrities, correction, Bollywood stars – her poor arts types had been fine coming to any location – now weren't sure that they would make it all the way across town, so the events team was still desperately scouting for another place.

There was a definite amount of stress in the air.

Still, Sitara didn't think that going over the same options and the same confirmations for the fiftieth time was at all helpful.

However, as she had long suspected, the goal of meetings was to waste time, and they were definitely doing that efficiently. She didn't mind actually, especially since Debashish was ignoring her existence. Martin thought whatever Anil had said to him had shut him up, but Sitara didn't think so. He wasn't going to give up on her in less than two months.

'So, do you think Nasser Khan will come for the awards?'

Sitara's eyes bugged out – had she conjured his name up by her thoughts? It took a moment for her to realize that Anil had posed the question and was looking at her hopefully for a response.

There was a stirring of interest around the table. Everybody was agog about the Sitara–Nasser relationship, but Sitara had refused to talk about it. But if Anil asked, she had to answer.

'Uh, I don't know,' Sitara replied, not meeting anybody's eyes. She waited tensely to see whether he would pursue the topic, but he seemed willing to let it drop.

'Why don't you call and ask?' Debashish piped up. 'All extra help would be appreciated, since Events can't confirm anybody.' Debashish certainly didn't let any grass grow under his feet; the Events team looked ready to spill his blood.

What could she say about that? Either she could tell them they had parted on terrible terms or she could make the call. Sitara chose the latter. 'Sure. I'll do that.'

Sitara spent the afternoon drumming up the courage to call him. She could just imagine his replies. None of them was likely to lead to a pleasant conversation.

As evening set in, Sitara wondered whether she could get away with telling them that he hadn't answered the phone.

Or she could just send him a message she supposed.

Could she be more cowardly? Disgusted with herself, Sitara dialled the number.

It rang.

He didn't pick it up.

It was quite anti-climactic.

The relief of not having to talk to him was soon replaced by the blues. The crash set in.

He hadn't picked up the phone. He was completely over her. He didn't even care to talk to her. She had blown her chance.

Or he could be busy shooting. According to the newspapers, he had started work on a new movie.

Was she clutching at straws? Sitara gave it a moment's thought and decided it was better than the alternative. She would just send him a message, Sitara decided, and then she would have done everything required of her.

She didn't care whether he replied or not.

Sitara opened an eye and reached for the phone. Seven a.m. And no messages or missed call.

She thought a couple of unrepeatable words, before willing herself back to sleep.

An hour later, she gave up the attempt. The flesh was willing but the mind insisted on running through all the reasons he hadn't replied.

Her eyes were gritty and when she looked at her reflection in the bathroom mirror she almost didn't recognize the wreck in front of her. She closed her eyes and breathed deeply. There was a new determination in her eyes when she opened them. If for nothing else, she had to sort out this thing with Nasser so that she could get her sleep back. She wasn't built to be a morning person. It left far too much of the day to fill up.

And the horror of that was that she was trying to fill it up by going to the office.

If he wasn't going to answer, then somebody else would have to.

Abba was making him dizzy and Nasser hadn't had enough sleep to cope with it at the moment. He'd been living it up for the past week at Anjali's wedding parties, and his body was telling him he was too old to do that anymore.

'Abba, why don't you sit down?' Nasser suggested.

It was lost on his parent who continued striding his circular route through Nasser's living room.

'Did he tell you anything before he left?' he demanded.

Nasser shut his eyes and let his head fall back on the sofa.

'What does he mean by finding himself?' Abba continued testily, not waiting for an answer. 'Why can't he eat, pray, love here?'

Nasser couldn't quite summon up the energy to roll his eyes. As his father's rant continued, he could feel sleep stealing over him...

'...what did you say?' He was pretty sure there had been something important in there.

'What? That your generation is a navel-gazing waste of time?' Bashir repeated.

'No. Something important.'

Bashir snorted. 'What is the use of being a star if you can't even get to bed at a decent hour?'

'Abba,' Nasser exclaimed exasperatedly.

'Zara is arriving tomorrow.'

Nasser looked unblinkingly at his father while he processed that bit of news. 'Why?' he said finally. It made no sense.

'Khurshid said she wants closure about the broken engagement.' And what he thought of that was writ large on his face. 'What is there to close when the engagement is broken? I don't understand your generation.'

For once Nasser was in complete agreement with his father.

'We need him back,' Bashir continued. 'We can hardly tell them that we have lost our son.'

'You haven't lost him. He's an adult now – he can go wherever he wants without telling us.'

'That is not my definition of an adult.' Bashir moved to stand in front of Nasser to tell him his definition of an adult. He'd just opened his mouth when the doorbell rang.

'Saved by the bell,' Nasser murmured under his breath.

'What did you say?'

'That must be Amma.'

On cue, Ayesha walked in. She was waving a chit of paper. 'Once you used to write me *shers*.' She looked at the offending object. 'Now I get "Come up quickly".'

'Hello Amma.'

'Hello *bete*. Yes?' she lifted a brow at her husband, waiting for her explanation.

'There are important things to discuss. You were asleep. I didn't want to wake you up with an SMS,' Bashir said defensively.

'You wrote poetry for Amma?' Nasser asked.

Bashir looked at him scornfully. 'Of course. We knew how to woo in our time. Not like you young people, waiting for women to fall in your lap.'

'I don't wait. They just do,' Nasser said with a straight face. He caught his mother sniff. 'You don't agree,' he asked her.

'No, I'm just thinking of the ones who fell into your lap,' she said. They obviously weren't pleasant thoughts.

'Yes,' Bashir reiterated. 'I think the only one who didn't was that Sitara girl. And look what happened.'

'What happened? Nothing happened,' Nasser said aggressively.

'Exactly my point,' Bashir said smugly. 'At the first sign of having to do some work you gave up and let her go.'

'I did not give up,' Nasser said hotly. 'I wanted the relationship and she ran away.'

'But relationships cannot begin in a wham-bam-thank-you-ma'am fashion. From what you've told me there wasn't the slightest hint of romance in the entire thing,' Ayesha interjected.

'Romance,' Nasser spat it out like it was something bad. 'We knew all the important things about each other.'

'She knows you and Naeem are twins?' Ayesha asked.

Nasser waved it away.

'That's not important?' Bashir was outraged.

'Or about Richa and the drugs,' Ayesha continued.

'I was just beginning to tell her when she gave up on us.'

'She gave up on you because you told her Richa was addicted?' A frown creased Ayesha's forehead.

'Sort of,' Nasser mumbled.

'Sort of?' Bashir asked.

'I told her that Richa was sleeping around while she was engaged to me. And so was I.' He was surprised at the amount of distaste he felt for that particular memory.

Ayesha sat down next to Nasser and rubbed his shoulder. When she was done, she spoke to him as though he were a backward child. 'How is it possible that I have raised you? Don't you know that testing another person like that is bound to lead to failure?'

Nasser could see Bashir shaking his head from the corner of his eye.

'Relationships take time,' Bashir added. 'How long did you know her?'

'Exactly how long you knew Amma before you married her,' Nasser retorted, stung.

'Ah,' Bashir said.

'*Ah*?'

'I knew I wanted to marry your mother the first time we met. So when we met the second day I told her everything,' Bashir said, 'so she could know exactly what she was getting into. She still led me a merry dance though.' He exchanged a look with his wife.

It had everything that Nasser had ever wanted for himself – humour, love, respect. 'So why did you write her letters?' he asked, wanting to take his mind off stuff he didn't have.

'It's known as romance. You don't seem to be familiar with the concept,' Bashir said.

'Yes, we wrote to each other till the internet came up,' Ayesha said. 'Now there are only notes saying come up quickly. What was that for?' Ayesha changed the subject hoping they had given their son enough to think about.

'Naeem. Zara is coming to meet him tomorrow. Khurshid called this morning.'

'Zara? Why?' Ayesha sounded as confused as Nasser had earlier.

Bashir rolled his eyes. 'You tell her,' he told Nasser.

'She wants closure, I believe.'

'Hmm. I can understand that,' Ayesha said, drawing incredulous stares from the two men. She moved one of the armchairs and sank back into it. 'What? You think you can wake up one day and tell the woman you are engaged to, "Sorry, I want to discover myself and live my life, so I don't want to marry you," and that's enough? And that too over the phone. I wouldn't be surprised if she wants to slap him first.'

She looked at both husband and son gaping at her and shook her head. 'Just because he is my son doesn't mean that I'm blind to his bad behaviour.'

'*Bad behaviour*?' Nasser burst out. 'It's more than that. I don't know what happened to lead him to this, but it has to be serious. And he's woken up and realized all he's ever done in life is physics and wants to see what else life offers him. You can't call that bad behaviour.'

'I can,' Ayesha said calmly. 'I know something bad must have happened, but wanting to experience life doesn't mean you have to break off your engagement.'

'It's a far more decent sight than sleeping with a

string of women and going back to your fiancée,' Nasser said bluntly.

'What? Life's experiences mean sleeping around?' Ayesha said acerbically. 'In which case he definitely deserves whatever Zara has in store for him.' She turned to Bashir. 'Was there anything else to discuss? Otherwise I'm off to work.'

'Yes. Zara. And no Naeem.' Bashir said.

'Have we been told to produce Naeem? Surely she can't just arrive and expect him to be waiting?' Ayesha asked.

'Khurshid said she had informed him she was coming.'

'He'll show up if she's written to him,' Ayesha said. It was eminently obvious that neither her husband nor son shared her faith. 'Or Nasser can pretend to be Naeem. What's the use of being a twin otherwise?'

The doorbell rang in the silence. Anjali walked in.

'Aren't you supposed to be on your honeymoon?' Nasser demanded

'We're leaving in the afternoon. Hello uncle. Hello aunty. Why aren't you answering your phone, Nasser?'

Nasser waited for his mother to finish hugging Anjali before he spoke. 'Hello to you too,' Nasser said. 'Whose phone haven't I answered?'

'Sitara Gopalasundaram's,' Anjali watched the effect of her announcement with satisfaction. Ayesha and Bashir became super-attentive.

'Oh, the awards night,' Nasser sounded bored.

'You know about it?' Anjali sounded deflated.

'Yes, she messaged me last night.'

'And you didn't call her back?' There was a definite note of accusation in her voice.

'I very rarely call back journalists,' Nasser said.

There was shocked silence at his words. It lasted just a moment. Bashir was the first to go. He threw up his hands. 'This is exactly what I mean,' he exclaimed. Anjali nodded vigorously, and opened her mouth to add something and closed it again – no doubt reminded of his help with Harsh, Nasser thought. Nasser's gaze flicked to his mother, who, though silent, looked worried. It was to her that he spoke. 'She called me in her role as a journalist,' he shrugged. 'There wasn't the slightest mention of anything personal in her message. So why should I give her any special treatment over hundreds of other journalists I know?'

It was like he'd set of a case of fireworks in his living room.

'...lazy son...generation...scared...' Bashir sparked off.

'...rude...hard...Richa...married...' Anjali threw at him.

They were both talking so furiously and loudly that he could only catch a stray word here and there. His attention was focused on his mother who hadn't said a word.

'What?' he asked her.

'I'm going to the office,' Ayesha said mildly.

'That's all you have to say?'

'What else?' She widened her eyes innocently. Nasser mistrusted it instantly.

'Oh, of course,' she exclaimed, 'you can pretend to be Naeem for Zara. I'm sure it will be great fun. Come down for dinner tonight, we can plan how you'll do it.'

Nasser looked at her like she'd come from Mars. 'Naeem. Zara What are you talking about? We were talking about me.'

Ayesha stopped in the middle of gently propelling Bashir towards the door. 'But don't you know what you are doing? You sounded like you did,' she sounded shocked. 'I wouldn't presume to tell my adult son what to do. I'm sure I raised you smart enough and determined enough to go after what makes you happy. Call and tell me if you are coming for dinner. We'll make the *shikhampur*. Bye Anjali.'

Anjali was grinning rather widely when Nasser finally looked at her again. His dark frown had no effect on her. 'Are you here for something besides telling me about Sitara's call?' he asked her coldly.

'Oh no,' she replied cheerfully. 'I'm only here for that. So are you going for the awards?'

'I'll think about it,' he said shortly.

Anjali waited a beat. 'Okay, so have you thought?' She looked at him expectantly.

Nasser considered throttling her. He opted for sarcasm. 'I'm afraid my brain doesn't work at the same lightning speed as yours. You'll have to give me more time.'

It was entirely wasted on Anjali. 'Okay. I'll put it down in your calendar. Are they giving you an award?'

'Don't presume things about me, Anjali. Not even my parents do and you are only my manager.'

His words certainly had the desired effect, wiping the smile from Anjali's face. She even looked a little hurt. Nasser refused to feel bad about it. He had only been stating the facts, he told himself.

'Yes. And as your manager I demand a little politeness,' Anjali told him coolly. She slipped her phone into her bag. 'I'll be waiting for your apology.'

Sitara thanked the waiter for the third time and assured him that she would be fine with a cup of coffee, and no, she didn't want anything more, and no, she didn't want anything to eat, and yes, she was sure the pastries were delicious but she was fine, really.

She held her breath watching him waver between asking her another question and leaving. She let out a huff of relief when he chose the latter. She plonked her bag on the floor and settled herself down in her corner of the hotel lobby, hoping the staff would let her be. It didn't seem like that was an option here.

They must have recently been told to be more attentive because everybody was sort of falling over themselves to serve her. She had already been met by five people.

She looked at her watch again and sighed. Her author was running late. She hoped it wasn't going to end up as late as the last time she had been in this hotel for an interview, when...oh...Nasser had run three hours late.

She'd been putting off thinking about him after the text she had received, but maybe this was the time she should.

She looked at the SMS for the tenth time since she had got it. When she'd repeated its contents to Anil, he had barely restrained herself from kissing her. Debashish had been satisfyingly unhappy.

But while it was great that Nasser was going to come to the awards night, why had he confirmed via Anjali? And what about the other part of the message? She read it again.

'N wnts 2 mt u @ hom asap. Wen r u free?'

What was that about?

She was simultaneously pissed that he'd ordered her to meet him in this fashion, and thrilled that this might mean another chance for them.

The roil of thoughts kept her occupied for another half hour, with a few breaks to assure the man that the coffee was excellent, and to assure his boss that yes, the coffee and the service were both very good, but she was sort of looking for some quiet.

At the end of that time, Sitara came to a couple of conclusions. First, there had to be something more personal to Nasser's invitation to his house. Secondly, she was never going to accept this hotel as a rendezvous for any other interview. This timing thing was getting out of hand. Her author had still not arrived. And lastly, was it her imagination or was an unaccountably large number of staff on duty near her?

'Sitara,' a voice greeted her warmly. It resolved into the face of somebody she would have preferred never to have seen. 'I thought it was you.'

'Aunty! I mean Mrs Khan,' Sitara got to her feet, hoping she had been able to disguise her horror, but she wasn't certain about it. 'Uh, how are you?' That sounded more normal considering that her mind was screaming.

Out of the hundreds of people she didn't want to meet at this point in time, Nasser's mother would definitely be in the top three. Wasn't it enough that she had a complicated non-relationship with Nasser without having to deal with a relationship with his mother? A woman who looked intimidatingly lovely and elegant. And here she was in her flea market skirt and tee. She had thought them cheery and bohemian, now they felt tacky and must make her look like a help.

'Aunty is fine. Or you can call me Ayesha,' Ayesha smiled. 'You look like somebody is keeping you waiting.'

'Uh yes, an author I'm supposed to be interviewing.' She would have a few things to say to him when he did turn up, Sitara thought vengefully. Unless he came in right now. That would be his only chance to redeem himself. She looked at her phone and then glanced towards the entrance to the lobby desperately. The author didn't oblige her.

Ayesha swallowed a laugh at Sitara's transparent desire to get away from her. She wondered how she would feel if she knew how word had spread like wildfire that the woman Nasser was going to marry was in the hotel, and how many people had managed to find an excuse to have a look at her. 'Are you being well-looked after?' she asked, and barely restrained a smile when Sitara winced.

'Very well aunty. Very assiduously.' Sitara ensured that she didn't make eye contact with anybody on the wait staff.

'Too assiduously?' Ayesha smiled. 'Shiv must have yelled at them recently.'

'Shiv? Oh, of course, he's the F&B manager here.' Thank god there was a rational explanation to this. 'And you work here too, don't you?'

'Yes, it seems I've been here a lifetime. But I don't mean to keep you standing. Please sit down.' Ayesha suited action to words too and sat herself down in the sofa next to Sitara.

Sitara watched her with dismay. Ayesha seemed to have settled in far too comfortably to leave quickly. Where was an author when you needed one? At all other times, they were just tumbling out of the woodwork. She glanced once again in the direction of the entrance and looked back to find Ayesha watching her, the expression uncannily like Nasser's and blurted out the first thing that came to mind. 'Nasser looks just like you; he has the exact same look when he's amused.' She cringed the moment the words were out of her mouth. She sounded like some mindless groupie.

Ayesha didn't seem to mind. She looked intrigued. 'I guess he must, mustn't he? It's just that he's so much his father's son in temperament that I don't see myself in him as much as I should.'

Sitara made a valiant effort to not be drawn into the conversation. Her next words showed that she couldn't rely too much on her valiant efforts. 'Really? I heard so much about you that I thought it was the opposite.'

'Does he talk about me? I always assumed Naeem did, not Nasser.' She looked at Sitara curiously.

Thinking back to her conversations with Nasser, she realized that what Ayesha had said was true. Nasser didn't talk very much about his mother. Or his family. Or about the people in his life. Even when he had been shooting off his mouth in those early interviews he had usually stuck to co-stars and movies. 'You're right,' she admitted. 'It was Naeem.'

'Yes. From the time he decided that his life would be lived in the public eye, Nasser has programmed himself to keep his friends and family out of it. And his way of doing that is to not talk about them at all. He's very protective that way. He's inherited that from his father.' Ayesha paused, before adding mischievously, 'It can be very infuriating.

'Oh yes,' Sitara said feelingly.

Ayesha laughed. 'Yes. It's very frustrating because you know he will go out of his way to help you. He's the sort of person you can count on to get things done. But it really puts a damper when you want to fight.'

Sitara was startled into involuntary laughter.

'No, no, it's not funny. My first few years of marriage were really very difficult because of that,' Ayesha continued earnestly. 'I had to keep holding back. It was such a strain. I felt horrible. Then I couldn't take it anymore and I just told Bashir that enough was enough. I recognize every one of your good points, including some you don't know yourself, but we were going to be a fighting household. We can just have great make-up sex. Our relationship was much better after that.'

Sitara goggled a bit at this revelation. Had Nasser's mother just blithely told her about make-up sex?

Ayesha continued unaware of how she might have scandalized her audience. 'Anyway, Nasser is very much like his father...'

Sitara was ambushed by a flashback of Nasser and her in another hotel bedroom and some very hot make-up sex. She was sure she had turned a bright red.

'...he takes a long time to trust somebody, but when he does, it can be a bit like opening the floodgates. It can be all or nothing. He doesn't always realize that other people trust differently, or open up slowly.'

Sitara looked at her with sudden comprehension, but Ayesha had already moved on. 'Have you heard from Naeem by any chance?'

'No,' Sitara said distractedly. 'No. Not since...the last I saw him was at your place. Why, what's happened to him?'

'Oh nothing. He has disappeared. The day after the party. To find himself, you know. At least finding yourself now is better than back in my day. Then it was all drugs and sex, now I believe it's yoga and ayurveda and vipassana and colonic cleansing.' She paused. 'Did I say it's more fun now?'

Sitara had to laugh. 'He's not carrying his cell phone?'

'No. But I see somebody making their way very purposefully towards you so I will make myself off. It was lovely to meet you again.'

Anurag had finally called her. Richa hadn't seen hide or hair of him for ten days – business trip, he said; lousy excuse – and he had finally called to tell her they had to talk. He was coming back to the country at night, so he wanted to know whether he could come over the next day.

Like she was going to tell him no.

But he might. Either he was going to propose to her or he was going to break it off. For once, Richa had absolutely no idea which. And she couldn't come up with a single scheme that would make him want to stay. She had even gone through her list of eligibles in case he broke it off.

There was nobody else. Or at least, there were, but she would have to break up their marriages first. She could do it, but it would take so much longer.

And the timing would suck. She had the Pepsi campaign. If she got married now, she could end her career in a blaze of glory.

Women! Nasser was sick of them. He slammed the phone down and walked moodily to the balcony for some fresh air. Well, air. The night skies looked appealing. Then he opened the door and a blast of humidity hit him, making him recoil into his air-conditioned living room. He shut the door hastily. Damn it. He couldn't even stand outside. He barely resisted the urge to kick the door out of frustration. He flung himself onto the sofa instead, a frown scrunching up his face as he considered the opposite sex and their concerted attack on his blood pressure.

His mother, Anjali, Zara, Sitara. Every one of them was behaving super-strangely. His mother who had spent all day insisting he impersonate Naeem for Zara. Like this was some movie from the 70s. She had even had his make-up man conjure a beard for him. 'Just in case Naeem doesn't make it in time for dinner,' she had told him.

Zara was going to arrive in the morning. For closure. She had mailed to let them know she would arrive for dinner at 7.30 p.m.; Abba was having conniptions.

If that wasn't enough to deal with, Anjali continued to give him the cold shoulder. It had been so long since he had genuinely pissed her off that he had forgotten she was one to hold grudges. She didn't believe in forgiving anybody without getting even. It was driving him nuts trying to figure out what she would do. He just wished she would get it over and done with.

And then there was Sitara.

Nasser was unable to sit still any more; he got up and paced about the room a bit. He had been waiting for her to contact him again; she hadn't. What sort of a journalist was she? He brooded about her a bit, phone in hand, as he battled himself about calling her. He put the phone away after a while, but it was becoming harder and harder to keep from speaking with her. He flung the phone away and walked into his bedroom, and slammed the door shut behind him.

16

Naeem had had a narrow escape. Nasser could see the realization writ large in his parents' eyes. At least his father's. His mother's had glazed over.

Zara was drop dead gorgeous. She was articulate. She was highly educated. She was also insufferable. She was rude, superior and patronizing. With not a smidge that could be mistaken for a sense of humour.

Nasser had never met her before. Naeem had taken one look at her photograph and her educational qualifications (a doctor), her opinion on alcohol and smoking (shock! horror!), a willingness to have children and said yes to the engagement.

Obviously Zara must not have spoken a single word during the engagement ceremony or he would have heard about it from his mother.

She had arrived at 7.25 p.m., discomfiting his father considerably, who frowned upon people arriving early for anything. And he had never had a dinner guest arrive before 8 in his entire life.

Abba had shrunk back into his room like a woman in purdah accidentally espied by a non-family member – which could have something to do with his still lounging around in a kurta pyjama – and had taken half an hour to emerge fully dressed.

In the meantime, Nasser and his mother had had the full impact of Zara unleashed upon them. She had addressed him as the actor-brother, laughed at Bollywood movies and how absurd they were – she didn't have time for frippery entertainment; she was too busy saving lives – and how she had had to appease her parents' fears about being married into a filmi household. But then she had seen Naeem and been reassured.

Nasser had quickly asked her about her flight and hotel, afraid of what his mother would do to her if she continued on the other subject. He might be sanguine about what people said about him, but his mother didn't take kindly to having the careers of half her family dissed.

Zara had marvellous breath control, because she hadn't even paused to draw in a breath before providing them with a wealth of detail about her flight (uncomfortable, long, full of crying babies and rude airhostesses, the food bad, the air turbulent) and her hotel (shabby pickup car, staff speaking with weird accents, noisy, bad view, food not authentic, terrible service). She had just finished when Abba walked out and greeted her. Zara clearly didn't think his father cut an impressive figure because she just about said hello before ignoring him and moved on to the next topic: 'Is Naeem going to join us soon?'

'We hope so,' his mother said with a complete lack of inflection. 'He told us he would be here tonight. But we'll just go on for dinner without him,' his mother declared, suiting action to words. An involuntary sound escaped his father, who had never in his life eaten dinner before 10. Ayesha ignored him. 'You must be used to early dinners,' she commented to Zara chattily.

Nasser followed suit, ignoring his father and rising to move for dinner. He could see how he had never realized that his mother didn't like Richa.

'Oh yes, I finish dinner by 6.30, but Dad warned me that I'd have to get used to late hours in India. I can see he was right.'

Nasser could hear some heavy breathing coming from his father's side of the room. He and Ayesha spoke simultaneously, stopped, looked at each other, both reluctant to repeat their filling-the-breach remark, when the bell rang.

There was a general sigh of relief that Naeem had arrived. Nasser took advantage of his youth and easier manoeuvrability by dashing off to answer the door. He wasn't slowed an iota by the reproach he saw in his mother's eyes.

'Oh hi. You are here.' Sitara rushed into speech. 'I didn't know if you would be because I just realized that I only knew your parents' apartment. And Anjali wasn't picking up her phone and you weren't picking up yours and I didn't feel like asking your guard...'

Nasser let the words wash over him. He had no idea what she was talking about. All he could think was that she was here. The kohl-lined eyes were a touch wary, and a little tired; the smile that always lingered around her mouth was missing, but the rest of her was as he remembered. The hair frizzing out madly, the same defiant bright outfit, the words spilling over themselves as they did when she was nervous.

Sitara trailed off. Nasser hadn't said a single word and was staring at her in the most discomfiting way.

'Who is it?' Ayesha appeared at Nasser's elbow, no doubt escaping before she murdered her other guest. 'Sitara!' She sent a questioning look at Nasser; Nasser shrugged infinitesimally.

It was over in the blink of an eye, but Sitara caught it. 'Didn't you know I was coming?' she demanded. 'Anjali told me you asked me to come...' As she watched, Nasser's face sort of froze, his eyes becoming shuttered. She backed away.

Ayesha reached out and grasped her arm firmly. 'How lovely to see you again, Sitara! We were just going to have dinner. I am so glad you arrived in time to join us.'

Sitara found her every protest ignored as Ayesha gently but inexorably manoeuvred her inside.

Fear could make people act very uncharacteristically, Nasser thought. His mother was holding on to Sitara as though she were the only thing between her and disaster. Like stabbing Zara with a fork. Which she probably would.

For his part, the flood of joy at thinking Sitara had come to sort things out had retreated with the realization that this was all part of Anjali's payback. Pride dictated that he continue to ignore her, but there was no place for pride when you had the guest from hell, and the person she was supposed to meet wasn't there.

'Sitara!' Bashir had spent enough time in one guest's company to realize just how difficult dinner would be. His joy at seeing another person was unalloyed. And it wasn't lost on him that the presence of a stranger at the table would keep things formal even when Naeem arrived.

Before she knew it, Sitara had been introduced to Zara, and seated for dinner. Right next to Nasser.

At least she wouldn't have to look at him, she consoled herself, but she couldn't help being intensely aware of him. She struggled to concentrate on what was being said. It was an uphill battle. Every time Zara opened her mouth, a little more of the spark was extinguished around the table. She summarized and solved India's problems at one go. America's took a little longer. She was in the nature of being an art connoisseur (as she told them) and when she discovered that Sitara was an arts editor, she had picked apart a bunch of artists (some of them Sitara's most revered) and told her about the few who were actually good (Sitara had dismissed a couple as poseurs; the rest were only slightly better).

'I believe the complete opposite. It will be interesting to have a dialogue on this,' Sitara said. She ignored the strangled sound from beside her. 'But you are one up on me – I still don't know what you do.'

In short order Sitara discovered that Zara was Dr Zara Ansari, an orthopaedic surgeon, and how she was the youngest doctor to have been selected to be part of some legend's team.

'Is he like *House*? I love the man,' Sitara said.

'Not at all,' Zara said coldly. '*House* is completely unprofessional. Nobody who behaves like that deserves to be a doctor. Shows like that should be banned from television. They completely give a wrong picture about medicine. I think movies and TV should stick to making shows like *Friends*. Do the fluff entertainment, all the mindless stuff; they can't be allowed to mess with the important aspects of our life.'

Sitara listened to her with growing astonishment. If she took her seriously she would have to annihilate her. 'I think you are preaching to the converted here,' she said instead. 'Nasser's a Bollywood superstar. He can give you lessons in mindlessness.' She couldn't resist looking up to check for Nasser's reaction.

Nasser met her eyes blandly. 'I've always found generalizations lazy thinking,' he said.

'I've come to the conclusion that you're right,' Sitara said.

His eyes sharpened. An eyebrow lifted. Sitara nodded.

Zara broke the moment with her opinion of the Indian media. Sitara looked at her, not hearing a word she said. A fork clattered to the floor breaking her reverie. It was hers, she realized, and dived after it.

And froze.

Nasser had bent down to pick up the fork too, and his face was a hair's breadth away from hers. She looked at him helplessly, feeling for the fork blindly. Something heated in his eyes, finding an echoing spark in her. Her gaze slid down to his lips. It took her a moment to realize that his were moving and that he was saying he had found the fork.

She hoped that being brown meant her face didn't show how flushed it was, but she had a feeling that it wasn't quite the case. She gratefully tuned into what Zara was saying.

'Did Naeem say when he would arrive tonight?'

'He said he would be here by dinner time, so another fifteen minutes,' Bashir said, meeting his wife's quelling look innocently.

'We hope so,' Ayesha said. 'But he could only get a short text across in all his travelling, that too from a stranger's phone.'

Zara's face scrunched up in distress. 'He's not carrying a mobile phone when he's travelling? He's been acting so strange since his accident.'

'Accident?' Ayesha's tone was sharp. Sitara could feel the family leap to attention. Everybody was focused on Zara.

'Yes. Last July. Or was it August?' She mulled it over a bit. There was a general reigning-in of impatience around the table. 'I think it was August. It was so hot. And he said he had never felt so cold.'

'What happened?' Ayesha asked. Sitara could only marvel at her control.

'He was on his way back from meeting me and there was a pile-up on the freeway. I don't remember what his car hit, but his car was completely crushed on the passenger side. He was trapped in there for an hour. They had to cut him out. But he was very lucky. He didn't have a scratch on him. And the gas tank didn't explode either,' she added as an afterthought. 'I believe it had started to leak, and they were afraid that the sparks from cutting him out would set it off. But he came out without a scratch.'

Sitara was horrified. She could only imagine what Naeem must have gone through in that hour of being stuck inside. She could see the impact of the news around the table. Bashir's face was drawn, there was a sheen in Ayesha's eyes, and she could all but feel the tension vibrating out of Nasser. His hand clenched the edge of his chair, and without thinking she covered it with hers. There was a moment of stillness and then he held her hand tightly.

'Anyway, that's when he started to act strange,' Zara said, completely impervious to the atmosphere around the table. She helped herself to the dessert. 'Saying how he could have died without having lived. And how he hadn't done so many things in life. I told him we could advance the wedding if he wanted.'

Sitara barely had time to be horrified at what that statement meant when the bell rang.

The cook opened the door. There was the murmur of voices and then a firm step and a tall, bald, clean-shaven man looking very travel-stained stood in front of them.

'Hello. I'm sorry I couldn't get here earlier,' he said, looking at Zara. 'I only got your message this morning and it was a long bus ride to the airport.'

'Naeem?' Zara sounded shocked.

She didn't like the new look, Sitara guessed.

'Yes, it's me,' he grimaced. He went over to hug his father, and found himself engulfed in a bear hug. 'I'm glad to be back.' His father released him, patted his back several times, and hugged him again. 'Abba, I wasn't gone that long,' Naeem laughed.

He caught a movement from the corner of his eye, and caught his mother surreptitiously wiping her eyes. He looked at Nasser, standing grimly separate, Sitara holding his hand.

'I guess you heard about the accident,' he said.

Nasser nodded.

'You're twins,' Zara said flatly.

'What?' Sitara couldn't contain the exclamation. 'Don't be silly. They look nothing alike. And anyway Naeem is younger.'

Zara looked at her with disdain. 'Just look at them. They look exactly like each other. This is what you were hiding under the beard,' she accused Naeem.

'You could say that,' Naeem shrugged.

'What! What are you saying? You're twins?' Sitara looked from one to the other. Yes, there was some family resemblance. But twins? 'Fraternal?'

'Identical,' Zara answered, her expression showing how demented she thought Sitara was.

'I can't see it,' Sitara said flatly. She looked questioningly at Nasser.

Nasser shot his parents a look. 'Yes,' he admitted. 'We're twins. Identical. Naeem's two minutes younger.'

'And you didn't think this was important enough to tell me when we were engaged?' Zara shot off at Naeem. 'What else didn't you tell me?'

'You didn't?' Surprisingly, it was Nasser who spoke.

Naeem shrugged.

'What are you asking him?' Sitara poked Nasser. 'Where was this grand revelation when you were telling me you loved me?'

'I was getting to it,' Nasser said. He looked like he was going to say some more but Zara's voice put an end to that. 'What else didn't you tell me? What's your real reason for breaking off the engagement? Do you have another woman stashed away somewhere?'

Sitara watched in fascination as the lot of Khans aligned themselves alongside Naeem.

'Zara, I *am* sorry for breaking off the engagement so abruptly. I wish I could offer you a more understandable reason than that I went off the deep end, but I just want to experience life. There really is nothing more. This is about me totally. You are beautiful, smart, qualified – only an idiot would let you go. Unfortunately, I am that idiot right now.'

Sitara looked at Naeem respectfully. His long-windedness wasn't such a bad thing after all.

'I don't believe you,' Zara said. 'I'm not the sort of woman people reject. Not unless they've been cheating on me.' She looked around the room wildly and her gaze stopped at Sitara. 'Is it her? Is she the one you left me for? Is that why she's here?'

Everybody was taken aback at the accusation. Sitara recovered first. 'What? *No!*'

'I don't believe you. Why are you here otherwise? It's obvious that this is a family occasion. A private family occasion. Who are you connected with? Why should you be here?'

Was it telling that she hadn't even thought of her in conjunction with Nasser? Sitara deliberately didn't look at Nasser. 'I'm with...'

'...me.' Nasser finished. He repeated it. 'She's with me.'

Sitara's eyes flew to Nasser's face. He looked at her challengingly. This was it then. If she wanted a relationship, this was her last chance. It took her no time at all. She looked at him steadily. 'I'm with Nasser,' she said and saw his eyes flare up with emotion.

'I don't believe you.' Zara said flatly. 'You are lying to cover up for Naeem.'

'Nobody is lying here,' Bashir began.

'They are,' Zara cut in indicating Nasser and Sitara. 'It's so obvious. Nasser's a film star. Just look at her. There's no way somebody like *him* would be interested in somebody like *her*.'

Nasser saw Sitara's eyes cloud over with doubt and couldn't believe it. How could Sitara be insecure about looks? Sitara of all people! He shook his head in disbelief.

'I don't see any other woman when Sitara's in the room,' Nasser said simply. It was impossible not to believe him. Sitara blinked her eyes rapidly and looked down at the table, shaken. Bashir wiped his eyes. Ayesha smiled proudly. Naeem looked at his brother consideringly. Even Zara seemed impressed by his sincerity.

'You look like you are done with dinner. Let me take you back to your hotel and answer your questions to your satisfaction,' Naeem told Zara.

Zara considered it for a moment and finally nodded in agreement. It must be the twin thing, because both brothers were out with their respective partners in five minutes flat.

Sitara's journey wasn't long. In two minutes she was upstairs in Nasser's flat. Feeling awkward, she devoted herself to looking around the flat. She knew it was ridiculous to feel so uncertain when she had declared her intentions, but she couldn't help herself.

'Like my house?' Nasser asked, his amusement at her intense scrutiny apparent.

'What? Oh, the flat. It's lovely.' Sitara winced at how unconvincing that sounded. She tried to make up for it in a rush of words. 'I mean, it looks impressive without that sense of being designer. It looks...I don't know...you.'

'That's because it is me,' Nasser said, and was finally rewarded by having Sitara looking at him. 'Amma refused to let me get an interior decorator to do it.'

'You did all this?' Sitara said. She looked around again. 'By yourself? It looks so good.'

Nasser's lips quirked at the implied insult. 'We discovered that I had some taste. And access to a vast number of magazines and books on interiors.'

'Wow.' Her tone suggested that she was still unconvinced. 'You never thought of getting in an interior decorator?'

'Caught me,' Nasser admitted. 'I secretly hired a decorator to do it when it was proving to be too much trouble, but Amma found out and guilted me so much, I had to let her go. It was fun at the end.'

He gestured toward a sofa. 'Why don't you sit down on my greige sofa, made in Lucknow, and kick your shoes off on my made-to-order Kashmiri carpet and we can get down to the more interesting stuff?' He took a step toward her and watched ruefully as she hastily made her way to the sofa and sat down.

It reminded him of that flash of uncertainty when Zara had made her comment. His father's words came back to him. Maybe it was time to follow in his old man's footsteps and woo Sitara.

He sat down on the sofa next to her. Sitara pressed back against the arm automatically. Nasser controlled a wicked urge to move forward. 'I'm glad you came tonight,' he said instead.

'Anjali...' Sitara began.

'...set it up. Yes, I figured.'

'Why?'

'I lost my temper. And Anjali doesn't believe in forgive and forget. She believes in getting even. Or teaching me a lesson. Whichever works for her. I guess she confirmed that I'd be at the awards too?'

'Yes,' Sitara looked at him uncertainly. 'Are you going to come now?'

'If she's confirmed I'll have to, I guess.' Nasser watched some of the tension drain out of her but there was still a watchful look in her eye, and he thought he knew what had put it there. 'I dated her in my teens,' Nasser said. 'And she's been my manager since I started. She's a friend. I've known her for a long time. We don't have your usual boss–employee relationship.'

'No,' Sitara said, carefully expressionless.

'You can say that again. She's very taken with you, you know. Gave me hell for breaking up with you. I guess this was her way of spreading the happiness now that she's married and basking in the honeymoon glow,' he ended casually.

'Oh.' Sitara looked at him consideringly. 'Are you congratulating yourself for telling me she's happily married? She told me already. And how you were never the man for her.'

Nasser grinned. 'Stealing my thunder? Don't you know that as an actor in mindless Bollywood pap, it's one of the few things I look forward to?'

Sitara was suddenly attacked by doubt. 'I was only kidding. It was only because Zara was so unbearable – what was Naeem thinking getting engaged to her? – and it was either fight with her or have some fun.'

'The one thing I've realized over the years is that most people, consciously or unconsciously, are ashamed to like Bollywood. They may watch it but they also look down upon it. Especially in the educated circles. I'm used to it.'

'That's not me,' Sitara denied vehemently. 'I may hate a movie or love it or think it's timepass, but it's about the movie, not the industry. I don't like a couple of yours, but I understand that there's a certain structure to a Bollywood movie and you work within that, and you do a damn good job, even if it's running around trees.'

'Thank you,' Nasser said meekly.

Sitara eyed him suspiciously. 'Nasser? Are you winding me up?' He looked at her, his eyes laughing. 'Oh. You...' Sitara moved forward to whack him, but Nasser caught her arms mid-swing, and used her momentum to topple her flat on the sofa.

Sitara was suddenly aware of their proximity, and that he still held her hands, leaving her pretty much at his mercy.

Nasser stopped laughing, and his face was so close now that she saw his pupils dilate. His eyelashes hid his expression as his gaze moved lower down her face to rest on her lips.

Sitara tilted her chin up, her eyes drifting shut and... nothing happened. Nasser cursed and let go of her hands and removed himself with some speed to the next sofa. Sitara sat up feeling foolish. And angry. 'What? It's time to blow cold now?'

He ran a hand over his face. 'I guess I deserved that. But no, I'm not blowing cold. I'm trying to do this normally.' He got up. 'You want some coffee. I make a mean cup.'

'Not really,' Sitara said unhelpfully.

'Fine. You just come and watch me make one then.' He caught her hand and pulled her off the sofa. When she dug in her heels, he swung her into his arms effortlessly and strode towards the kitchen.

'I'm not a fan of caveman tactics,' she told him, when she found her voice, quelling the little thrill that had shot through her. 'Don't be under the impression that this is hot or something.'

'And here I was, thinking you'd be a puddle of lust,' he mocked, parking her at a bar stool around the kitchen island.

Sitara looked at him coldly. It was wasted on his back as he switched on the machine and opened his freezer to get out the coffee. She watched as he filled water and dumped the beans into the coffee maker and pushed a cup in place.

He turned around finally. 'I had to do something with my hands,' he admitted ruefully, 'since the plan is to have a conversation with you.'

Damn the man for being so disarming. 'Oh,' was Sitara's brilliant reply.

'Yes.' He grabbed his cup, pulled a stool and sat down across from Sitara. 'Our...relationship has been either slow-mo or fast forward. There's been nothing normal about it. But we've got something special.'

Though it hadn't been a question, Sitara nodded. He caught the movement and smiled.

'Very special,' he repeated. 'I don't even know if you realize how much. Naeem and I *are* identical twins. Unlike most twins we haven't grown apart, not in looks anyway. Maybe that's why we *have* grown apart. Anyway, that's why he's had the beard and I've never worn one for a movie. That's why it's a big secret.' He shook his head. 'And that you can't see the resemblance, means you *see* me. You know what I mean?'

Sitara nodded. 'I guess. Sort of.'

Nasser reached for her hand and entwined his fingers with hers. 'You were right to say we rushed it earlier. I stand by what I said, when I said we know the important things about each other, but the little things make a lot of difference too. The normal things. I'd like to give that a try. Is that something you could live with?'

Sitara didn't have to think about it. 'Yes. Yes, yes, yes.'

Nasser hesitated only briefly before going to his parents' place. It was late, but he wasn't surprised to see both of them awake.

'Dropped Sitara home?' Bashir asked.

Nasser nodded. 'Naeem's not back?'

'Not yet,' Ayesha replied.

Nasser pulled up a chair and sat down.

'Did you sort things out with Sitara?' It was Bashir who asked.

'Some. We are going to take it slow.'

'Good.'

'Did you know?' Ayesha asked.

She didn't need to clarify. Nasser knew what she was talking about. 'No. I'd be the last person to.'

'I thought...you seemed closer now.' Ayesha said. His parents had never commented on his estrangement from Naeem. They'd tried in the early days to do something about it, but the twins had been antagonistic from the time they hit their teens and things had only gotten worse later. There'd even been an unspoken understanding that if Naeem came home on holiday, Nasser wouldn't be there.

Of course Naeem had stopped coming a while ago. His parents went usually.

'Yes. I think we have finished our feud. Or to be more specific I've got over my...jealousy–'

'Abandonment,' Ayesha corrected gently. 'You were so close, and then he found a passion you couldn't share–'

Nasser shifted uncomfortably. He didn't need these things said aloud.

'–and you never considered acting your genius–'

'It isn't,' Nasser cut in. 'Not the way Naeem–'

'*Exactly* the way Naeem has physics,' Ayesha said firmly. 'It seemed fitting that you were a left-brain–right-brain split.'

Nasser absorbed that. 'But to return to your question, we are basically still strangers.'

It was well past midnight – if you could still say that for 3 a.m. – when Naeem finally came home. Both Ayesha and Bashir had retired a couple of hours ago. Nasser didn't know why he was waiting up – but he'd been unable to stop his vigil. Naeem rolled his shoulders as though trying to work out the knots.

'All okay?' Nasser asked.

Naeem started. Nasser could see the tension in his frame. 'Didn't see you bro. Why're you sitting in the dark?'

'I don't know,' Nasser said. He switched on a lamp, and a pool of light appeared around Naeem. 'It seemed right earlier. So did it go okay with Zara?' Nasser asked again.

'Is this where we bond like brothers?' Naeem asked, stepping out of the light, and sinking into a sofa on the side. His head fell back tiredly and he closed his eyes.

'We could,' Nasser said. 'It wasn't so bad in Italy.'

'I didn't die in that crash, Nasser. Don't feel sorry for me.'

Nasser controlled his anger. This was familiar territory. They'd fought like this for decades. 'Why the hell should I feel sorry for you? You got a wake-up call, horrible as it was. You got a chance to rethink your life. I'd be sorrier for me. I would have cared if my brother died. I don't want that to happen.' He paused. 'Don't you think this new life of yours warrants a chance for us to be brothers again?

'I don't know,' Naeem said tiredly. 'I've lived alone for a long time. It's hard to do the family thing again.' He shrugged, and smiled tiredly at Nasser. 'I could give it a try I guess.'

Nasser acknowledged the effort with a nod. Then he smiled. 'Now tell me what were you on when you said yes to Zara?'

17

The week that went by was like Valentine's Day. There were flowers and dinner and hours spent talking. They were officially out as a couple. Sitara called up her parents and sister and let them know. Her mother wanted to know what time she was waking up at.

'Eleven. With difficulty,' Sitara said, past the lump in her throat.

'Good,' was all she had to say on the subject.

One night Nasser called her home to dinner 'to show off what I learnt in Italy'. Along with the tiramisu, he even rustled up some poetry. 'Family tradition,' Nasser grinned, at her disbelieving expression. 'I got it from Abba. It's the Khan way of driving women crazy.'

'Alongside betting on them and breaking engagements,' she retorted. It was only when she heard the words that she realized how she must have sounded.

'It's okay, Sitara. And you are righter than you know. Abba had a broken engagement in his background too.'

She bit her lip and said nothing.

'You aren't going to ask me, are you?' He leaned back against his chair. 'Abba told me the magic lies in opening up. So in another family tradition – Richa developed a drug problem.'

Sitara nodded.

'You knew?'

'One of my colleagues told me.'

'Oh okay. Mukul would know. Not too many people did.'

'But she's off them right?'

'Yes.' He marshalled his thoughts. 'I introduced her to the crowd that does them.' He looked at her to see how she had taken it.

'Hard not to, I hear. Loads of people doing it,' Sitara said.

'You're not going to let me wear my hair shirt, are you? Fine, I won't beat myself up over it. To cut a long ugly story short, I used to do drugs, too. Socially. Who knows – I might have become an addict if Richa hadn't gone over first. But she did. By the time we tried to interfere and get her off them it was too late.'

'Who's we?'

'Her parents, her manager, we tried everything. Stopped her cash, tried to stop her access, stuff like that. But you can't stop a junkie till they want to. She found a way around it.'

Sitara didn't need him to add that it was by sleeping around. 'Your relationship?'

'We didn't have one. She hated me, and she was my burden. I couldn't abandon her. In a way I hated her too.'

'Did your parents know?'

'Shiv did, so I guess Abba and Amma must have too. But I couldn't write her off. And I didn't feel up to talking about it. I think verbalizing it would have made the hell all too real.'

'So you slept around,' Sitara said neutrally.

'Yes.'

'Good.'

He hadn't been expecting that. 'I cheated on her,' he said, trying to make her understand.

'We'll have to have a long discussion about the "her" in the picture. We could argue that the Richa you knew wasn't around. But basically, we all do what we have to do to get through shit. You can stop the self-flagellation. And anyway you helped her get into rehab.'

He shook his head. 'I didn't. She had to decide. And ironically, she did it because of her nose. All that snorting finished it off. She was more worried about the face that had made her famous. That's why she went into rehab. And she's stayed off so far.'

'And you got engaged when she came out?'

'Before she went in. We set a date for the wedding so she'd have something to work towards.'

'So why did you break up?'

Nasser had known the entire conversation was leading up to this moment, and he still didn't know how to answer it. 'Because I met her one day and I just couldn't stand her. I was physically repulsed.'

'I know exactly what you mean,' Sitara said. 'There was this guy I dated a couple of times. Every time we met he would trot out one more Neanderthal view. One day I literally couldn't bear to look at him.'

Nasser gave a baffled laugh. 'You're always surprising me. I thought...'

'You thought I'd be put off?'

He paused, wrestling with himself. 'She went from doing drugs to a cosmetic surgery binge. She came back from a shoot one day with a new job – her chin, I think. And I...snapped, I guess. I couldn't bear her anymore. And I couldn't hide it. She called it off.'

'Do you really find me attractive?' Sitara asked.

'What?'

'Because if you do, you can stop torturing yourself about being a superficial slut. If you really like somebody, you like the way they look. That's what's been bothering you, right? We can argue about that, but you'll get to it one day. Now, can I thank you for this lovely dinner?' she said pulling his face down to hers. 'I might need some practice though.'

'I suppose I could sacrifice myself,' Nasser said.

Sitara heaved a sigh of relief when the last award was announced and Anil handed out the phallic-looking statuette. It really was the most obscene-looking award; and made worse by the light that gave it an almost flesh tone.

Debashish and Anil, riding high on their brilliant turn out, hadn't caught on to the fact and had both absently caressed it on stage, sending the audience into nervous titters of laughter. They had presented the first two awards, and after that it had been almost funny to see presenters unburdening themselves off the statuette as fast as they could. The poor awardees had no such luck. Nasser had held his gingerly, and flung it under his chair as soon as he could.

This awards evening hadn't been as unbearable as her first, but that wasn't saying much. She'd spent much of it thinking about her relationship with Nasser. One week of being wooed had been immensely pleasure. The second week was tipping over to frustrating.

Not that she hadn't enjoyed the time they spent together. They'd been together every day after work or before shooting. He'd taken her out, he'd come home, she'd gone over to his place and had a family brunch. Shiv had been there too. He'd told her all about the latest people to suffer at the hands of the hotel prankster. Debashish and his paramour. His underage paramour. Who just happened to be the publisher's darling daughter. Oh baby, Sitara could barely control her glee. She was so looking forward to that confrontation.

There was no problem on the 'being together' front. It was just that Nasser refused to make a move toward her. He hadn't told her he loved her again, and physically he was staying platonic. He responded if she made a move, but refused to take things beyond first base. It was like being back in school. She had a pretty fair idea why he was holding back, and she planned to do something about it. Tonight.

But first there was an after-party to go to.

She was walking up to it with Nasser. She linked her arm into his. 'Our second after-party,' she said. 'The first one was quite fun.'

'Because you weren't the one to get puked on,' Nasser told her austerely. 'Or the one whose colleagues were being told to take care of their face.'

'Admit it, you had fun.'

'You let me know when I throw up on you. And tell your colleagues what I think of them. And their awards.' He looked distastefully at the one he was carrying.

'Don't you like yours? I think it's full of character.'

'It'd be perfect if your magazine was called *Playboy*. I think I'll give it to Anjali to keep.'

'I forbid you.' Sitara exclaimed. 'It's got to occupy pride of place at home.'

'Certainly. It can occupy pride of place in yours.'

'Oh I meant...' ours. The word was at the tip of her tongue when she stopped herself.

Nasser pulled her away from the lift doors, planted her in a corner and leaned in front of her. He looked at her intently. 'You meant what?'

Sitara gathered up the nerve to complete the sentence, when a hand fell on Nasser's shoulder.

'Hello! Just like old times,' Anurag said. 'Are you drunk already?' he asked Sitara. 'Because you have to be. This is your arena.'

'Hello Nasser,' Richa said from behind them, looking like a goddess, and flashing a monster of a diamond ring. She saw Sitara looking at it. 'You can be the first to congratulate us,' she glittered at Nasser.

So this was what Richa had been after, Nasser mused as he congratulated the couple. The entire set up with the cola had been a ploy to get her noticed by Anurag. Well, good luck with that. He had checked up on Anurag after Lokesh's party and from what he had heard it seemed like a match made in heaven.

'Shall we go into the party together?' Richa said after the flurry of congratulations had subsided. 'It would be a pity to waste the photo op.'

'What a great idea.' Anurag had them turned around and into the lift before they could protest and moments later they were sending the shutterbugs into frenzy with their cosy foursome.

There was no chance of a private moment after that. At some point Sitara realized that somehow she had drunk four glasses of wine and was consequently a little buzzed. And she'd lost Nasser somewhere.

'Hello Sitara. Are you making the most of the free wine?'

Sitara smiled widely at Debashish and raised her glass in acknowledgement. 'Absolutely. It's rather good. I can see you have too.'

Debashish ignored the hit. 'So you and Nasser are a couple? Congratulations.'

Sitara inclined her head in acknowledgement.

'I hope you have better luck than Richa. I hear he wasn't very faithful to her.'

'I'm sure I will,' Sitara said cheerfully. 'And may I wish you the same. Anil must be very happy about you and his daughter.' She watched the blood drain from his face. 'How old is she?' she mused. 'Somebody said eighteen. A little young to be getting caught in hotel bedrooms.'

'Who told you?' Debashish demanded. 'I'll sue the hotel. And you can't prove it,' he blustered. 'So don't try and say anything to Anil.'

'Proof,' Sitara scoffed. 'Suspicion should be enough, don't you think. But I'm not going to say anything to Anil. I like my job, and just want to be left in peace to do it. Do you think we could manage that?'

He'd lost Sitara somewhere, Nasser realized. As he made his way around the crowds to find her, he found himself face to face with Richa. There was no way to walk on without talking to her.

'Oh hello. All alone? Where's Anurag?'

'Gone to get me a drink.'

Both their eyes drifted toward the bar, where they picked out Anurag having an animated conversation with some woman.

'So, congratulations,' Richa said. 'When's the wedding?'

'Isn't that my line?' Nasser said.

'I asked first,' Richa smiled.

Nasser smiled. His eyes fell on Anurag talking to another woman. Openly flirting in front of his new fiancée? Anurag really did have Richa on a string. That boozy, affable exterior was just that, a way to mask the very hard, calculating man underneath. Did Richa know she had been played? Did it matter? If there was one person who could take care of herself, it was Richa. 'Did you enjoy the awards?'

He found Richa watching Anurag too. She turned her attention back to him and replied mischievously, 'Tonight, it was better to give than to receive.'

Nasser laughed and Richa joined in. It was probably their first pleasant interlude since...he couldn't remember. Nasser felt an old stirring of protectiveness. 'Do you know what you're doing?'

Richa's gaze rested briefly on Anurag. 'Oh yes. We have a good pre-nup, an excellent settlement. I turn a blind eye to his affairs, and he turns a blind eye to mine. I get his family off his back, and he likes being married, and I want it right now.' She looked at him. 'Same old Nasser. Don't look so worried. I've got long-term plans.'

'Same old Richa,' Nasser mocked. 'Your long-term plans – who should I be warning about them?'

Richa laughed, and they shared a moment of perfect understanding. 'Go on, your girlfriend's returning.'

'You look like the cat that ate the cream,' Nasser commented.

'Let's say I put Shiv's information to good use,' Sitara replied. 'Bless him. And the secrets one knows as a hotelier.'

'Fucked Debashish's happiness?'

'Totally,' Sitara replied happily. 'I think we should celebrate with some champagne.' She picked two glasses off a passing tray and handed one over to Nasser.

'To getting your own back.' Sitara touched her glass to Nasser's and swigged back the contents before Nasser had taken a sip.

He put his glass down. 'Are you preparing for a repeat of last time?'

'You're really traumatized, aren't you?' Sitara cupped his face and kissed him. 'Don't worry sweetie, I've other plans for you. Ready to blow this joint?'

'Anything to know these plans,' Nasser said.

'Then c'mon.'

Sitara led him to the lifts.

'You've pressed the button to go up,' Nasser said.

'Oh no, have I? We'll have to get out now, won't we?' She pushed him out two floors up and walked him down to the end of the corridor, at which point she brought out a swipe card and opened the door.

'Welcome to my chamber.'

Nasser strolled in lazily, his eyes alert taking in the candlelight, the roses strewn on the bed, the soft music playing in the background. 'Are you planning to entrap me in your web?'

'You're already entrapped,' Sitara said, 'I'm just planning on making it formal.'

Nasser raised an eyebrow.

Sitara danced hers in response, while she fished about in her pocket. She finally found what she was looking for, and fell to one knee. 'Nasser Khan, I love you. And I love that you wooed me. But I think it's time for a little fast forward. Will you marry me?' She waved a thin steel band at Nasser.

Nasser rocked back on his heels. 'You love me? You're sure it's the real thing?'

'Yes,' Sitara said impatiently, looking up at him. It was a long way up. Sitara realized she was still sitting on the floor and stood up. 'I've been sure ever since the dinner Anjali set up. I was hoping to prove it to you.'

'And you think the last two weeks have done that?' Nasser asked.

'You're just making me suffer for earlier, aren't you?' Sitara exclaimed. 'It won't work. I have secret weapons.'

'Yes? Like what?'

In response, Sitara pulled down the zip of her dress, parted it from her shoulders and stepped out of it.

Nasser absorbed the impact of the flirty little camisole and underwear from under hooded eyes.

Sitara held out the ring again. 'And again, I love you. Will you marry me? If you say yes quickly, we can move on to our bonk fest.' Her tone was light, but her eyes were dead serious.

Nasser laughed. 'How could I refuse such a proposal?'

'Is that a yes?'

'Yes.'

'Uh uh. I want the whole caboodle.'

'Sitara with the multi-syllabled surname, I love you and I will marry you.' Nasser held out his hand and watched as she slipped the ring on. She took a step forward, her intent written large on her face.

'Uh uh.' Nasser stayed her with a gesture. 'You aren't the only one who wanted fast-forward.' He slipped a hand in his pocket and took out a box. He flipped the lid to reveal a gleaming emerald ring. 'Your turn now. Sitara Gopalasundaram, I love you. Will you marry me?'

'I don't know if I want to marry a man who doesn't get me diamonds,' Sitara teased.

'Diamonds, black, too common, too colourless for you. Now be a good girl and answer quickly. There's only so much temptation a man can handle,' Nasser said.

'When you put it like that, yes,' Sitara smiled, the happiness lighting up her eyes. Nasser slid the ring on her finger and kissed her.

'Now what was that about the bonk fest?'

Acknowledgements

I'd like to thank my parents Anis and Farida Hussain for putting up with me, and putting me up, as I wrote the book, and asking ever so gently only every six months when it was likely to be done. Azfar and Sabiha Hussain for all the advance publicity, begun even before I signed the contract. Sheetal Vyas, Kalyani Prasher, Vandana Malhotra and Deepa Menon for reading rough and rougher drafts. Aishwarya Subramanyam for catching a bunch of mistakes and even asking how the book ended. A hairball called Dubuk for giving me company through the rewrites.

Big thank you to my editors at Hachette: Nandita Aggarwal for signing me on and waiting through the deadlines, and Amish Raj Mulmi for taking a fine toothcomb through the text.

And, thank you Sudha Mehta, for being my sounding board and cheerleader, problem solver and asskicker since the moment I put pen to paper. This book would not have happened without you.